The Family Izquierdo

ALSO BY RUBÉN DEGOLLADO

Throw: A Novel

THE FAMILY
Izquierdo

A Novel

RUBÉN
DEGOLLADO

W. W. NORTON & COMPANY
Independent Publishers Since 1923

Stories from *The Family Izquierdo* have appeared in slightly different form in the following publications: "Turroco" in *Hayden's Ferry Review;* "La Milagrosa Selena" in *Dreaming: A Tribute to Selena Quintanilla-Pérez;* "It All Starts with This" as "This" in *Beloit Fiction Journal;* "Maggie Magic Fingers" in *Relief Journal;* "A Map of Where I've Been" in *Juventud: Growing Up on the Border* and *Throw: A Novel* (Slant Books); "Host" in *Image Journal;* "Our Story Frays" in *Fantasmas;* "Padre Nuestro" in *Image Journal;* "Family Unit" in *Nepantla Familias.*

For information about permission to reproduce selections from this book, write to Permissions, W. W. Norton & Company, Inc., 500 Fifth Avenue, New York, NY 10110

For information about special discounts for bulk purchases, please contact W. W. Norton Special Sales at specialsales@wwnorton.com or 800-233-4830

Manufacturing by Lakeside Book Company
Book design by Daniel Lagin
Production manager: Lauren Abbate

ISBN 978-0-393-86682-7

W. W. Norton & Company, Inc.
500 Fifth Avenue, New York, N.Y. 10110
www.wwnorton.com

W. W. Norton & Company Ltd.
15 Carlisle Street, London W1D 3BS

1 2 3 4 5 6 7 8 9 0

For Evaristo and Guadalupe
Roberto and Juanita
Felipe Nerí and Elvia, who brought them together
With love and gratitude

Contents

Part 4

Part 5

Part 6

Epilogue

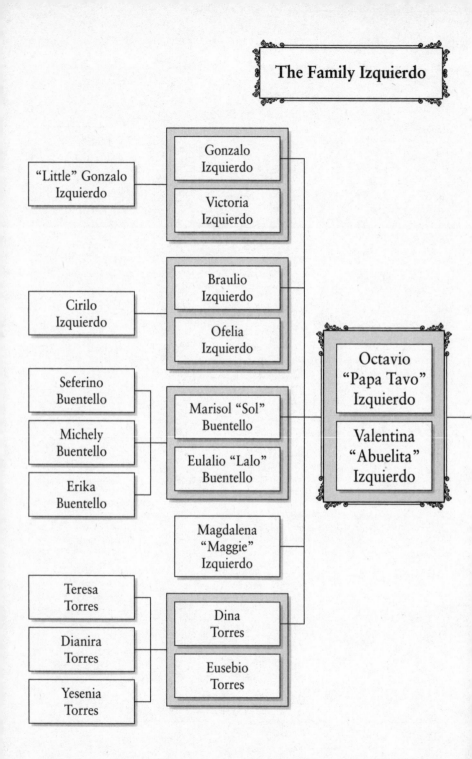

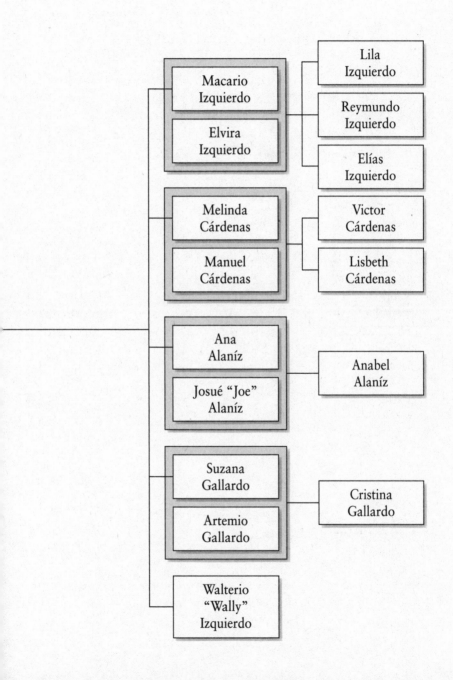

Part 1

La Tierra

1952

Octavio and Valentina Izquierdo rode up and down the streets of barrio la Zavala in his work truck, looking for a lot that was on a higher part of the street, a place where water would not pool and flood, a piece of land here in Tejas where they could build a casita for their son Gonzalo and the children who would, con el favor de Dios, follow him. As Octavio considered the effects of flooding on a home, the river came to mind, how generations ago his family had lived on both sides of it. They used to come and go, crossing freely, still in their own country regardless of which side of the river they found themselves on. Though the Río Bravo was called the Río Grande on this side, and the imaginary line separating the two countries now ran along its path, the dirt beneath them, the huisaches, cacti, and mesquite trees were unchanged. Now, having brought his family across the river, Octavio was reclaiming a piece of the north for the past Izquierdos who had their homes taken away, for his family now, and the generations to come. This made him turn to his little family—his wife and son—and smile.

Gonzalo stood on the bench seat between them, looking out of the back window while Valentina held her hand across his back, steadying him anytime they lurched to a stop or turned down a different street. Every minute or so, Gonzalo would look to his mother and reach for her trenza as he always did when she held him, wrapping his small dimpled fingers around her thick and lustrous braided hair to give himself comfort when he was unsure of the people or the world around him.

"McAllen is the place to be," Octavio said in Spanish, pronouncing it Macalen, as everyone did. "This is where all of the jobs are now. Everything is going north, always north. I will always have jobs." Octavio, having learned how to tape and float, and paint, while working on houses for his boss, Jimmy Guerrero, the mayor of Primero, had started his own business, Izquierdo's Painting and Drywall. As the Río Grande Valley grew and McAllen became the wealthiest city, so did opportunity in building new homes and businesses.

"Gracias a Dios," Valentina said, even though she had been happy in their first home with her macetitas in the front, her chile pequín tree, her sábila, her agave. She had also been content when they lived in their pueblito of Montemorelos, Nuevo León, where she and Octavio first met and were married. This had been Octavio's dream, his plan for them to cross over the Río Bravo and start a family en el otro lado, but for Valentina family was home, and if she was with family, it did not matter on which side of the river they lived.

"And you, chiquito, when you're big enough, you're going to help me paint and hang drywall. Right, chiquito? So I don't have to turn down all these jobs."

Gonzalo was too little to understand, but he nodded, which

was what he did whenever his father asked him a question. The boy smiled and grabbed at Octavio's felt western hat.

On the corner of Aurora and an unpaved road, Octavio stopped. There was a lot on a slight hill, not like the *cerros* he remembered from his younger days in Mexico, but a place where water would not pool and their home would not flood.

"Here," he said. "This is it."

The lot was staked off, and was not big, but was just enough for them. In his mind, he saw it. The house in the center with maybe two bedrooms, a yard in the back where Valentina could grow her *tulipanes, teresitas, madreselvas,* and other flowers that would grow and bloom and bring color, a carport where he could park his pickup, and a little room he could build separate from the house where he could lock up his tools, buckets, and brushes.

"*Amor,* bring Gonzalo. I want you all to see what I see." Valentina brought Gonzalo's little hands together and clapped them gently. "*Vamonos, chiquito.* Let's go see what your father the dreamer wants to show us."

As she held her son, Valentina took turns shielding hers and Gonzalo's eyes from the sun that was setting.

"Here will be the yard," Octavio said, and marked a line in the dirt with his boot. "You can plant whatever you want because it will be ours."

Octavio saw generations ahead, to the children he did not know, to the painting and drywall business he would pass on to Gonzalo and his brothers and rename Izquierdo and Sons Painting and Drywall. Valentina was the one who saw the steps and the work it would take to get them there. So she said, "One thing at a time, Tavo. We have to see if we can buy it first."

"Ay, Amor, mi Capitana, always navigating ahead."

Valentina playfully slapped his shoulder and said, "Don't call me that." Octavio sometimes called her Capitana because even though they crossed over where the water was shallow enough to walk across, the only way she would do it was if Octavio made her a little boat so she would not get wet. Octavio had waded across, pulling the boat with a rope, making up a song about his beautiful Capitana, his strong Capitana, his wise Capitana who could read the waves and know in which direction they should go, singing it until he carried her past the river shore and onto dry land.

"Well, then, my Valentina, over here along the fence you can plant whatever you want. There's even room for a lemon tree if we want it." He looked up and down the street and there were small, sturdy wooden houses, nothing like the jacales from their youth. He would start here, building a house similar to the others on the street, but bigger and built in such a way that he could easily add rooms as the family grew.

Valentina said, "What if we bought one of them instead of trying to build a house? Building will take too long and cost too much."

"Ay, Amor, one of the many reasons why I love you. Because that is too much like what we came from," he said, pointing at all of the humble casitas. "And this is where we are heading. For him, and his brother or sister you carry now, and all of the ones to come, con el favor de Dios. This will be the house where the children of our children will come see us, and when we grow older and smaller, our nietos will call us Abuelito and Abuelita."

"Yes, con el favor de Dios. Me, yes, they'll call me that because I am small in size. But I do not think you will ever let *them call you Little Grandfather. For you, Tavo, we'll have to give you a different name. How about Papa Tavo?"*

"That," he said as he reached to caress her smooth cheek and then ran his hand down her long braid. "That, exactly."

Valentina set Gonzalo down because he was squirming, wanting to play on the ground. He knelt down, grabbed a handful of dirt, and flung it into the air. Then he grabbed another and put the dirt into his front pocket. The boy looked up at Octavio and Valentina to see if he had permission to do this.

Octavio said, "Of course, mijo, this little piece of earth will be ours, for the Izquierdos before and those to come. No matter how far they move away, how old they get, it will always be home to them."

Turroco

Mama shook me awake, then led me into the pickup, and I was staggering, half-lucid, wanting to be picked up, but knowing I was too old for that now. I sat between them, Mama and Apá. Every minute or so, a car would face off with us, light up my parents' faces, then pass and leave us in the darkness of those hours before the sun comes up, what we called La Madrugada. All I knew was that we were going to my grandparents' house in the Zavala, but neither of my parents said why.

"Are you sure about this?" Mama asked.

"Pues tenemos que hacer algo," Apá said.

"Yeah, Gonzalo, but we aren't doing right," she said, her face lit up by an incoming car.

"Mi mamá lo conoce." Apá's face again faded into shadow.

"Yeah, Viejo, your mother knows him, but that doesn't mean anything."

"Es un hombre de Dios."

"But is he even a priest?"

"Tú sabes bien que no, Victoria. ¿Y por qué me preguntas otra vez?"

"I'm asking because I want to remind you that he isn't."

This was the way they spoke when they were in front of me, Apá in Spanish when he didn't want me to fully understand what he was saying, and Mama responding in English, translating what he had just said because she wanted to make sure I kept our heritage. Language was very important to Mama, both Spanish and the tongue of angels.

Apá clicked his tongue against his teeth like he always did when Mama said something like that, which was often. Even though my mother was younger than my father, she was never afraid to translate what he said to me or call him out when she believed my father was wrong.

They did not speak again until we got to Papa Tavo and Abuelita's house on the south side of McAllen in the Zavala neighborhood where Apá grew up, just seven miles north of the border. As we walked through the gate, I thought of my grandfather. Sleep had always been difficult for him, but a few months ago he had begun sleepwalking and suffering insomnia in which he would walk around the house, agitated, looking for things he could not explain. One night, he had discovered a rotting goat hoof and a rooster foot buried in the front yard. My grandfather believed these things were a curse meant to ensure that the devil would either keep him from sleeping or walk through his dreams whenever he did. Soon after, our Papa Tavo had been sent to Charter Palms for evaluation. When this became too hard on the family, and Papa Tavo still wasn't better, he bounced around from nursing home to nursing home all over the Río Grande Valley, because when he got bad, none of the orderlies could control him or calm him down. Only my father was able to ease his nerves. On this night of our visit, Papa Tavo was staying with my uncle Braulio. My father had decided to take advantage of his absence, hiring a curandero to help my grandfather by doing a limpia of the yard, a clearing of any curses against us.

Not everyone in the family agreed on what had caused Papa Tavo's troubling condition. Some blamed it on the stress of having to provide for our tíos and tías when they were little and said that it had finally gotten to him. Others said that the nervios were just a part of who we were as Izquierdos, that we all suffered from anxiety and susto in varying degrees. But according to Papa Tavo and most of our family, what transpired was because of curses buried in the yard in secret by Emiliano Contreras, a jealous brujo who lived down the block. They suspected that the Brujo Contreras had been so jealous of our Papa Tavo, his many children, my tíos and tías, and our family's success, that it drove him to make hechizos and maldiciones against us. My father believed Papa Tavo's condition was a combination of Contreras's brujería and Papa Tavo's built-up stress and anxiety from the years when he had labored hard to provide for the family. He said our grandfather had been strong enough to resist the evil until Papa Tavo's first nervous breakdown back when my father was a teenager. And in Apá's opinion, after that first one, Papa Tavo had only gotten weaker over the years and he was due for another unless they intervened.

Abuelita and Apá had lit candles at the feet of San Juditas, the patron saint of lost causes, asking him to intercede for us. They had also prayed at the feet of the Blessed Virgencita and Jesus Himself. Mama had stood in Papa Tavo's place at our church, Living Waters, a ring of brothers and sisters praying for his healing in a language I only understood sometimes. Even with all this praying, Catholic and Charismatic, my grandfather had not gotten better and the family knew it was a matter of time before the next nervous breakdown.

When we got to Papa Tavo and Abuelita's house, Abuelita and a man were at the table talking. I could see Abuelita through the burglar bars and the window screen, sitting there staring into a cup, listening to the man, but not saying much in return. Abuelita got up quickly when she heard us get closer to the door, as if she were relieved for the interruption.

"¿Cómo está, mi Gansito?" she said, grabbing my face with her small hands and kissing it. She was the only one who called me Gansito, her little goose, while everyone else in the family called me Little Gonzalo, as I bore my father's name. My grandmother smelled like hand lotion. I was always surprised by how soft her hands were even though she was so old, because in my young mind, they were supposed to feel like leather.

"Salúdalos, mijo." My father always reminded me to greet my elders. A wave was not enough; I had to hug and kiss my grandmothers and aunts. It was the lowest form of disrespect to not give your elderwoman an abrazo y un beso when saying hello or goodbye, especially your grandmother. For the men, you *had* to shake their hands. In his thinking, a pattern of giving anything less merited a nalgada, and since my father's hands were like sandpaper, I always gave my saludos.

So I shook this stranger's hand. "Mucho gusto," he said to everyone shyly. The curandero's matted hair looked much like Papa Tavo's hair after he had been wearing his Stetson all day. I noticed that his brown eyes became lighter toward the edge of the irises until there was only a yellow ring separating them from the whiteness.

Apá and Mama sat as my grandmother served them her coffee, which always smelled delicious. Although I wasn't allowed to drink any, my mother often let me sneak a drink while the elders were talking. Abuelita always made the coffee with lots of sugar and milk, but her secret was in the canela. She put weedy cinnamon sticks into the brewer, which gave it a taste my mother was never able to copy.

Apá was saying that the Brujo Contreras down the block was the reason for the evil that had befallen the family. He attributed the violence, miscarriages, breakdowns, accidents, anxieties, and sadness in our family to this man. My older cousin Cirilo had almost been shot in a drive-by, and had lost one of his friends instead. My uncle Wally had been a school bus mechanic in the district where all those kids died in a bus accident, and though he was cleared of any negligence, he always blamed himself for not servicing the brakes better, which was apparently one of the contributing factors in the tragedy. Since then, tío Wally often found himself in days-long depressions where he wouldn't answer the phone or show up to work, and he was now on so many different medications just like Papa Tavo. Because my mother was a nurse, my tías Ofelia and Melinda had called her when there was trouble with their pregnancies, and so I knew that they had both lost babies. By burying the goat hoof and rooster foot, semblances of the devil's feet, in Papa Tavo's front yard, the man's evil had gone too far. It was time to do what was necessary.

"Evil spirits like these only understand greater power," the man said in pure Spanish. Pure, meaning real Mexican-from-

Mexico Spanish, not like our pocho mix-and-match Spanish we used on our side of the river.

"I have helped your mother light the candles at the altar."

He meant the altar in my tía Suzana's old room. When Tía, the last one to leave the house, had moved out after marrying this Mexican national named Artemio, they had turned her room into a shrine.

So now Suzana's room was a place to pray for Papa Tavo, with the framed picture of the Virgin looking over it. The Queen of the Universe wore a baby-blue cape covered with stars. At her feet was the upturned crescent moon. I never understood what any of this meant other than maybe the Virgin liked the night.

It was at this altar that we then said the Rosary on our knees, all except for my mother, who was sitting on the bed, praying silently to herself. I had to keep shifting my weight from knee to knee because my grandmother's floor was hard, with no carpet. Abuelita led the prayer, most of which I did not understand, and my father and the stranger repeated. Of course, Mama did not share their prayers. A few years earlier, Mama had started going to a full gospel church. But even before that, she had never knelt in front of the Virgin or any of the saints, not even at Christmas.

After Abuelita had gotten through all of the beads of the Rosary, which seemed to take forever, the man asked Apá if he was ready.

"Brujos bury objects in the yard that stay with the family and curse them without them knowing it. These entierros are sometimes possessions of the family. We must find the entierro and burn it to cleanse the house. But, I must warn you, evil will be unleashed when we burn this. The demons will be leaving, but looking for somewhere to rest." The curandero held his own rosary, thumbing the beads.

"¿Está listo?"

"Sí," my father answered, while looking at us, telling us he was ready to do what he needed to for the family.

Abuelita and the curandero walked out first. As my father got up to go, my mother held his arm and looked into his eyes. Mama's small oval face was beautiful. In formal portraits, there was always anger in the darkness of her eyes that were so dark brown they looked black. It was dancing there now. "You're wrong about this, Viejo."

"Tenemos que hacer algo, Victoria."

"I been praying in tongues at the church."

"¡Ya! I don't want to hear it. A man-made church will fall, Victoria. Tú sabes. This man is a good católico, faithful to the Virgin. Those people at your church hate the Virgin, and God will punish them for hating His mother."

"I don't want to talk about that, Viejo. I am only telling you that this man is just as bad as Contreras."

"Sí, lo que tú digas. Whatever, Victoria." This was how their conversations about religion usually ended, even though my father was not a big believer like my Abuelita or my mother, and never even went to either of their churches.

With that, he walked out and left us in tía Suzana's room, which was lit only by the religious candles scattered around. Like the ones lit in Abuelita's room, they had pictures of angels and saints on them, including the one with the Archangel Michael stepping on a bug-eyed Satan's neck. That one was my favorite, Michael with his sword held high and his shiny breastplate, even if my father said he looked too feminine and too gringo.

I could hear the curandero and my father walking around the yard, praying the Our Father. Abuelita stayed in Suzana's room praying, while Mama and I moved to Abuelita's room so we could see. I sat on the bed, trying to watch them through the lace curtains, wanting to hear what they were saying. Mama held me, praying in tongues like she used to when my father was at work or out with my tíos. I didn't mind it, because it was always in a singsong way. At times I even understood some of the words, even though it was not in a language I had ever heard. One word I always understood was *turroco*, which meant *holy*. I did not like it at her church with all of them running up to the front, yelling at the top of their lungs, trying to outdo each other. Even though Mama said I was her little interpreter for the language of God, I always hid under a chair during altar call.

Through the lace curtains, I could see my father following the curandero. The man walked a circle, holding a small medallion of San Cristóbal. The healer held it out in front of him like some kind of divining rod. The medallion was still, but began swaying when he reached a spot directly under Suzana's open window, near my grandmother's mesquite tree.

"Here," he said.

My mother came up behind me and watched what they were doing, praying under her breath, the heat from it feeling good on the top of my head.

"We have to cleanse the area before we dig out the entierro. Your mother has prepared the tools. You must get them from her."

I did not like the way this man ordered my father around, and thought Apá was going to tell the curandero to get the tools himself, but he came back with a shovel and a galvanized metal bucket. He set them down and looked at the healer for instructions. I had never seen my father act this way. At barbecues and parties and whenever he was working on Abuelita's house, Apá, being the oldest son, was always the one to lead his brothers, assigning the jobs, giving the orders.

The curandero said, "Give me the knives and the alcohol."

He placed the kitchen knives on the ground in the form of an inverted cross.

My mother gasped and said, "God protect you, Viejo."

The curandero then poured alcohol over the knives and told my father to kneel with him. The curandero lit the ground with matches, starting a weak blue fire. He then began the Apostle's Creed, with Apá joining in. As they recited their beliefs, I realized that from where they were, the cross looked right.

The fire died down, and the curandero said, "It's ours now. You must dig around the entierro without disturbing it."

My father got up and kicked the shovel, cutting a circle into the earth. Once he finished, the soil inside the circle collapsed, as if the ground had long been ready to unburden itself. The man sifted through the earth and rocks, then found the entierro. My father moved away as the curandero stood and cleared dirt from something in his hands.

"What is it?" Apá asked.

The curandero held out something square and black, wrapped in plastic. "It is the picture of a man and a boy, probably you and your father." With this, Apá snatched it from the curandero. Later, my father would explain that it had indeed been a photograph of him and Papa Tavo. Brujo Contreras had punched two nails through the picture, piercing an X through the torsos of Papa Tavo and my father, the oldest patriarchs, crossing out our entire Izquierdo bloodline.

"We must burn it," the healer said.

"I wouldn't doubt if the curandero put them there himself," Mama said, and turned to me. "Mijo, promise you'll never get into it, curanderismo and brujería. Promise me." I looked into the pitch of her eyes, now mingled with something like sorrow, and it became blood to me.

I said, "Yes, Mama."

"You have to promise to Jesús, mijo," she said, and squeezed my hands in hers.

"I promise, Mama. I promise to Jesus."

Her grip relaxed and she said, "Good, mijo. Everything's going to be good for you now."

The curandero explained that my father would have to burn it himself, since he was the oldest son and closest to being the head of the household.

Apá laid the portrait in the metal bucket. He poured alcohol over the entierro, lit a match, and dropped it in. It sputtered out. My father lit another, then another, his anger growing with every failure.

The obscenity began slowly, under his breath, as if my father were a child saying the words for the first time.

The maldiciones became more specific, directed at the Brujo Contreras down the block. In Spanish, Apá damned all of the brujo's family to hell, where they would watch their father be eaten alive forever. The only time I had ever heard my father curse was the few times when he drank liquor, which seemed to have a different effect on him than beer. Where beer mostly put him in a relaxed mood, hard liquor made him defensive and suspicious of everyone.

Mama covered my ears and spoke in tongues even louder,

trying to drown out his cursing. Although I did not know all of the words he was saying, I could still hear him. And I understood what he meant. Apá was yelling now, the veins in his neck throbbing and thick. His head was thrown back and I could see spit catching the light, which filtered through the thorny mesquite branches.

And then I saw my father's eyes. Even in the darkness, I could tell that they were bulging. There was too much white in them. His eyes didn't look right. They looked wild, and I'd never seen him look this way, even at his angriest. Even though it frightened me to hear those things, see him this way, I could not turn away.

The fire started—much like Apá's cursing—slow at first, and then engulfing the entierro. As my father cursed the Brujo Contreras, fire lighting up his face, dogs in the neighborhood began to bark. At first it was just dogs in the houses nearby, but soon all of the Zavala's dogs were howling like they do when they hear a police siren. Some of the barking was desperate but vicious, like that of little dogs who had been cornered. Through the chain-link fence of the house next door, I saw Teddy Ramírez's half-breed Doberman, teeth bared, the fur on its back standing up. It barked like it wanted to get at Apá. Then it threw itself nose-first into the fence, circled around, and did it again. In my head, I thanked my mother for covering my ears, because the fence was jangling so close it sounded like it was crashing against the wall. I clung to her, but I could still hear, and the dogs would not stop.

Under the howling, the curandero said, "They are barking because they sense the evil spirits leaving your family."

"Gracias," Apá said. "Gracias a Dios." He was calmer now. My mother put my head on her lap and stroked my hair.

"Ssh, mijito, it's okay," she said, because I was shaking and crying now. Mama began singing in tongues, and this was the first and only time I ever understood *all* of what she said, not just a few words here and there. It was this, over and over: "Coming, not leaving. Coming, not leaving," in her sad singsong way.

Part 2

Cruzando

1989

Now that both Abuelita and Papa Tavo had their papers, they loved crossing over into Reynosa on Saturdays with the family. All of their children were grown, but sometimes their eldest daughter Marisol and her children crossed over with them, and sometimes they brought Cirilo so he wouldn't be home alone getting into trouble with his friends. Papa Tavo would drive them in Marisol's van because then they could all go together.

On this Saturday, Papa Tavo had driven with Abuelita, Marisol, and their grandchildren for haircuts for the boys, a day of shopping at the Mercado Zaragoza, and to buy medicines at the pharmacy. Now Abuelita pointed to an open parking spot along Calle Guerrero. It was along this stretch of street, when Papa Tavo had lived in the city for a few months with his tío Roberto and tía Juanita, that he had shined shoes for the soldiers and the boots of the rancheros who crossed over for the day. The entrance of the Mercado Zaragoza was only a few hundred feet away, so it would be okay for Abuelita, who did not like to walk far.

Papa Tavo turned his head to the back of the van. "Tie your shoes, babies. It is walking time." He made eye contact with Cirilo and winked because at ten he was no baby, and was the oldest grandson. He was there to help with Seferino, to make sure he didn't run off on his own inside the market.

Papa Tavo got out of the van, put his bone-colored Stetson hat on, and as soon as he did, a self-appointed parking attendant came over and started wiping the headlights.

"Joven," Papa Tavo said, despite the man being perhaps only ten years younger than he. Papa Tavo held out his cupped hand to the attendant for a handshake and the man took the American bills and slipped them into his front pants pocket. "Unas dos horas," Papa Tavo said in a way that was both a question and a directive. The attendant turned the corners of his mouth down and nodded, and they both agreed. He would watch the van and make sure no one got near it for two hours.

Marisol said, "Apá, I am going to the boticas," and pointed her chin over to the row of pharmacies across the street. She had been off the diet pills, but was on them again and he worried for her. Marisol was beautiful the way she was, and those pills were not good for her. Papa Tavo thought to tell her not to go buy them, but he had been trying to let his children make their own decisions without his consejos now that they had their own families and he would not always be with them. And besides, Papa Tavo always felt like a hypocrite telling her about the pills because his own doctor had prescribed pastillas for him and his anxiety, which he had not so secretly been taking for years just to calm himself enough to sleep and go to work.

"I'm taking the girls with me," Marisol said.

Abuelita looked at him and with her eyes told him that she would go with the girls as well, that it was better this way.

Papa Tavo nodded at Abuelita, then looked over at Marisol and made sure she was looking at him as well. With his right hand, he formed an O with his thumb and forefinger, held up his fingers, making the okay sign. He kept it there for a few seconds like he had always done when she was little and had suffered some small disappointment or a scraped knee while playing. Está bien, mijita, he would say without words, and he would wait for her to make the sign back to him, which she did now. This gesture, this way of communicating, was for Marisol, Papa Tavo's little sea and sun, the first daughter to come into his life. After his first two boys, Gonzalo and Braulio, who sought only Abuelita for comfort, Marisol had been the one to teach Papa Tavo fatherly compassion, as she sought it only from him. So he created this gesture between them, a flash of the okay sign for small hurts. For the larger disappointments, the fears of life and sad tomorrows that might happen, he would hold up the okay sign longer, then bring his hand to his heart, and look into her eyes so she would know that it would be all right and wait for her to smile or make the sign herself.

Now, as they stood there on the street in Reynosa, there passed a melancholy between father and daughter. So Papa Tavo held the gesture because he wanted her to know that it was not just about her going to the boticas to buy diet pills, but about today and every day after. He believed in his soul at that moment that Marisol's life would be blessed and bright and that one day she would see herself as God saw her and no longer feel she needed those pastillas, beautiful as Marisol was. Though he had often told her this with words, he said it now with his eyes and his hands: Está bien, mijita. Mi Sol. *She made the okay sign and smiled, and when Papa Tavo was sure she believed it, he dropped his hand and watched her walk away.*

When Marisol and Abuelita and the girls made their way across the street to the boticas, Papa Tavo said to the boys: "Look at my machos!" He patted Seferino's belly. "What do you all want? Your abuelito is buying you each something today."

"¿Camote?"

"Of course, but that is not what I am talking about. You can get candies anytime. Do you want a wrestling mask? A wrestling ring?"

Seferino pumped his fist into the air.

To Cirilo, he said, "And you, little man, what do you want?"

"I'll know it when I see it."

"Eso."

They entered the Mercado Zaragoza from the main entrance on the corner, and their eyes took time to adjust. There was the smell of leather, fresh and candied fruit, and the faint smell of Mexican beef coming from the carnicería part of the market in the interior. Dresses, guayaberas, and piñatas hung from the ceiling of one shop and Seferino ran there, where he saw a brightly colored toy wooden wrestling ring with a package of luchadores wrapped in a plastic bag.

"Abuelito, can I get this one? Can I?"

Papa Tavo laughed and said, "Look, papito, you never go with the first one you see. Here at the entrance everything is more expensive because they have higher rent to pay. If we go farther in, we will get a better deal. If we do not see a better one, then we will get this one right here, but I am telling you, you will see the same thing farther in. Right, Cirilo? I told you *this before."* When Cirilo did not answer, Papa Tavo went to where he was looking into a glass case full of flasks with ornate designs, leather wallets with Aztec pyramids embossed in them, and assorted knives. The boy was transfixed on one in particular.

"What are you looking at in this case, Cirilo?"

"You said you would get us whatever we wanted, right?"

"Well, it was a figure of speech, but almost anything. I mean, if you want a pair of alligator boots, then we are going to have to figure something out." Cirilo did not laugh at the joke.

"I want that one there," Cirilo said, and pointed at a knife on the top glass shelf.

"I do not know, Cirilo. That one looks pretty big. I do not even know if we can cross something like that over."

"It's a butterfly knife. I haven't seen one like that at the pulgas on the other side or even the Bargain Bazaar."

"It is a what?"

"That is the kind of knife it is. And it even looks like a mariposa," Cirilo said.

Papa Tavo understood now, and the boy was right. With its flecks of green and the bluing on the handle, it glittered like the wings of a mariposa in the sunlight.

His parents Braulio and Ofelia would not be happy about it, and with the way these new parents were, they would probably never let him or Abuelita bring them over to Reynosa again. But Cirilo was almost a man, and he needed to start making his own decisions.

Seferino's nose was against the glass case, and Papa Tavo gently swatted him on the back of the head. "Get out of there. It is dirty, papito. Get your nose off of there."

He turned his attention back to Cirilo and said, "Listen,

mijito, I am going to buy it for you, but I am going to keep it until you are at least fifteen. When you come over to my house, you can always go to my drawer and look at it. It will be in a special place just for you."

"Really?"

"Yes, really, Cirilo. It will always be there ready for when you are old enough. A man should always have a knife with him." He patted his front pocket, where his own wooden-and-brass-handled Buck knife clinked against the coins there.

"A knife is a tool, but it is also there to protect you and the ones that you love. A knife is a part of a man, but you have to be a man to know when to use it."

By now the shop clerk had made her way over and was listening to the conversation. She got out a key and began to open the glass doors on her side of the counter.

"Which one do you want to look at?" she said.

When Cirilo did not say anything, Papa Tavo said, "Part of being a man is also speaking up and saying what you want in life. So tell her, mijo. Tell her what it is you want."

Mariposa

That Fourth of July, when Papa Tavo and Abuelita were visiting their cousins in Reynosa, the family celebrated at our house on the north side of McAllen. Apá had built the house with my tíos Braulio and Macario off of Dove and Twenty-Ninth in the newer part of McAllen, which was closer to the Mac High stadium. It had a better view of the fireworks show than my grandparents' house on the south side.

When my tíos ran out of beer, and someone suggested going to the H-E-B supermarket to buy more chelas, my cousin Cirilo offered to drive anyone to the store in his green '69 Impala. Any of my tíos could have gone with Cirilo to buy beer, but they were having too good a time. They were sitting around the ice chest laughing and listening to their rancheras, eating the shrimp cocktail Apá made each Fourth of July. He made it with his special blend of avocados, cilantro, spicy cocktail sauce, and the fat shrimp he bought from the truck on North Tenth Street. Also, none of them offered to drive to the store because they had all been drinking and they knew the penalties for DWI in Texas. My

uncles didn't want to lose their licenses forever, or have a Breatha-
lyzer installed in their pickups just so they could drive to work.
Apá himself would not drive anywhere if he had been drinking, a
choice that was part responsibility, part fear because of the time
his camarada had been caught drinking and driving when he went
out for menudo. Somehow, the friend got the DWI bumped down
to public intoxication. How he managed that was a mystery; if
there had been an exchange of money, Gonzalo knew he didn't
have that kind of cash for a mordida if he himself got arrested.

"Victoria," Apá called. "Go buy us some birongas."

"What, Gonzalo? I didn't hear you." Though Mama was
inside, she had heard him just fine because the windows were
open. Apá had said all the kids running in and out were costing
him too much in electricity and so he had turned off the air-con
and opened the windows, even with how hot it was. Since Apá
had turned over the family business to my tíos, and started working as a commercial and residential roofer for a living, energy-
saving had become a priority for him.

"Please go to H-E-B to buy some birongas. *Esta vieja.*"
The last was whispered so only the men and I could hear it. He
winked at me, as if I were one of the men, which at nine years
old made me puff out my chest and feel proud. Apá had been
in a good mood all day, buying me sparklers, bottle rockets,
jumping jacks, and Black Cats. We had gone through the cuetes
quickly out by the canal behind our house. Apá showed me how
if we timed it just right, the firecrackers could explode under the
murky water, making a muffled pop. My favorite part was how
the smoke bubbled up in a cloud. I was waiting for my cousin
Seferino to come over because he always had the most fireworks
during New Year's and the Fourth of July. His dad, my tío Lalo,

always spent at least a hundred dollars at the stands and Sef had fireworks year-round.

Mama came out to the back patio and said, "Mijo, come on, we're going to the store and I'll buy you some beef jerky." This was something only my father did. Whenever Apá went to buy beer at the Tex Mart, he'd let me use the tongs to pick whatever long teriyaki stick or peppery jerky patty I wanted out of the clear plastic cases.

"No, Mama, I don't want to. I'm going to miss the fireworks."

"Va ser de volada," she said, then snapped her fingers and whistled through her lower teeth like she did whenever she was rushing me out the door. "It'll take us fifteen minutes, mijo, we'll be back in time for the fireworks."

I knew I would miss the show no matter what she promised.

Then she looked at Cirilo, who was standing near my tío Braulio, and said, "You going to drive us in that bomba? I'm not driving."

Since Apá had been in a good mood all day, drinking beer and not the harder stuff, and Cirilo was her nephew, no one raised an eyebrow when she said this. They all knew that whenever Apá drank liquor he became jealous, suspicious, and seemed to be looking for a reason to fight. But Apá had refused tío Artemio's offers of brandy and soda, and so Mama's question to Cirilo didn't put anyone on edge.

Apá even said, "That's a good idea. You been drinking a little too. Mi lightweight." He held up his hand with the thumb and pinkie extended, and tipped an imaginary bottle back, his gesture for drinking. Apá handed her his thick, falling-apart wallet.

We took the long way there, Cirilo showing us where he cruised with the car clubs on Tenth Street, the places where they would park and raise the hoods to show off their engines with the braided hoses and chrome-plated valve covers. He and Mama were laughing as he told her stories about the vatos and the rucas and the lengths they would go to impress the others. With the way my mother was laughing easily, how her breath smelled sickly sweet from wine coolers, I could tell that she was buzzed. Mama knew her limits and would stop drinking at a certain point because she always said if she had any alcohol after that, then she would start backsliding. She was close to that edge now, I could tell.

At the store, Cirilo stayed in the car with me while Mama went inside. He put his arm on the bench seat, turned around, and started asking me how school was the previous year and what grade I would be in next year. These were the only questions the older cousins and grown-ups ever thought to ask. Even now that I was going into fifth grade, I still got these questions. Despite how boring this was, Cirilo was still my favorite cousin. He was so cool at Sharyland High School with his tricked-out classic car, his lean, muscled body, and the flock of girls that were always calling him, giving him compliments on his colored eyes with their green and brown mixed together. Sometimes my other cousins made fun of me for going to the crazy church with Mama and for wanting to read books instead of playing outside, but not Cirilo. Any time my cousins started in on me, calling me *nerd*, *schoolboy*, *hallelujah*, or *professor*, Cirilo defended me by giving the cousins wrist-burns or nacas, a thing he did where he got them in a headlock and used his middle knuckle to pound them on the tops of their heads, but not too hard, just enough to make a point. Cirilo would then take me to throw around the football, even though he could never manage to teach me the spiral and my throws just wobbled. Seferino, Reymundo, and Elías would stand by and watch us playing, not sure if Cirilo was still mad at them. Cirilo would say, *You fools going to sit there and pick your butts or are you going to play?* They would join in and play five-hundred or two-hand touch and everyone would ignore that Cirilo made a point to throw the football softly to me.

I said, "Do you have La Mariposa?"

Cirilo looked around to see if anyone was near the car and then reached into his pocket. "Here," he said, holding out his butterfly knife. With a nod of my chin, I told him to open the knife. With turns of his wrist like some indefinable gesture I had not yet learned to read, Cirilo made his hands dance with the blade, the steel flashing in the lights of the parking lot, the blues and greens of the handles glinting.

"Lend it?" I said.

Cirilo closed it with the same dance, handed it to me, and said, "Be careful, La Mariposa is sharp. Remember, vato, knives are a man's tool and you should always respect them." I spread the steel handles without my cousin's skill, latched them together, and ran my thumb across the blade. It was always sharper than I expected and I loved how it rubbed harsh over the grooves of my fingertips. The handles, blued with flecks of green, resembled the wings of a real butterfly.

"You like it, LG?" Cirilo knew I did. I liked it when he called me that instead of Little Gonzalo. It always made me feel important and tough, like I was cool enough to go cruising with him anytime I wanted. One time when Aaron, one of Cirilo's friends, had come with him to Abuelita's house, he had said, "LG, Little Gangster, huh," in a rhythm, as if he were rapping. Cirilo just looked at Aaron and didn't need to tell him never to say that again. With his silence and his stare, he communicated that I would never be a gangster, that there was something better for me.

"You can have it when you're old enough," he said to me now. "Give it to me, though, because your mother will kick my nalgas if she catches you looking at it."

I held it out to him, said, "Psyche," and pulled it back.

"No, for reals, hand it back before your mom comes back."

I played the trick again.

"'Ta bueno, just put it under the seat when you're done. Don't open it while I'm driving because it could stab one of us if we get into an accident. Just keep it closed. You don't ever drive with an open knife because you could kill someone. You hear me, vato?" He gave me his look, and I nodded yes.

Mama stood outside the entrance of H-E-B. Cirilo started the Impala, which had a throat louder than any car I had ever been in. As he drove to pick her up, his eyes never left her. I saw what he saw, how beautiful my mother was. She wore shorts and rubber flip-flop chanclas and a spaghetti-strap halter that showed her thin brown shoulders. Her black hair, straight and long, was down like it was on her days off, when Amistad Home Health did not have her on call. Cirilo got out, took the bag of beer from her, and opened her door. As she buckled herself in, I could smell her, all sweet perfume, shampoo, wine, and the night air in her skin.

Mama had forgotten the beef jerky, which was okay because it would have been the packaged kind, not the kind Apá let me choose from the plastic bins at Tex Mart.

We must have been gone longer than we should have because there was a silence as the three of us came from the canal behind our house where Cirilo had parked. We passed through the circle of tíos who were still sitting in the backyard, and when my mother pulled out a beer and handed it to Apá, he refused and held up the same kind of red cup Artemio had been drinking out of.

"¿A dónde andabas?" Apá asked.

"Dimos la vuelta," Mama answered. Though it should not have been the wrong answer, I knew it was, because going for a ride was something Apá, Mama, and I did together. Apá didn't say anything, just took another drink from his red cup. Cirilo kept quiet and went inside to talk to our tías.

Mama said, "Well, anyways, I brought you a present," and put the case of beer into the ice chest, a beer at a time, burrowing them into the ice so they would stay colder. She leaned forward to kiss him and touched his nose all flirty. I thought maybe everything would be okay, and I'm sure my tíos did too.

Apá asked me if I had fun on my ride and if Mama had bought me beef jerky.

"Yes," I said, "but I ate it in the car." I looked to my mother to make sure she had heard the lie, but her back was to me as she walked inside. I felt the weight of the butterfly knife in my front pocket, and turned so Apá wouldn't see the outline of it against my leg.

"Good, mijo, I know you like it." He patted my stomach and asked me to get beers for my tíos. I loved doing this, sticking my arm deep into the ice chest, waiting to see how long it took before my arm went numb, trying to break my record. By then I was up to seventy-two seconds, which was longer than Seferino or any of my other cousins could endure.

As I walked up to the back patio I could see through the sliding glass door where Mama was inside, sitting at the kitchen table with Cirilo and my tías. They were playing Spoons, a card game they all loved. My tías were all smiles and sweaty faces from the heat of cooking rice and beans and the AC being off. A few of them were drinking coolers and beer, and in spite of how hot it was, some were drinking Mama's weak coffee. I didn't understand the rules to Spoons, but enjoyed watching it because of how animated it was. They passed cards and jumped over each other trying to get the spoons on the table, and these were just ordinary spoons no one got to keep afterward.

I sat down next to Mama, and Cirilo was on the other side of her. He was winning the game now because he was the quickest. His thin, muscular arms moved in before my tías, and he grabbed the spoons at exactly the right time while they laughed and tried to keep up with him.

"Ay," tía Marisol said, "I just don't know about this stupid game." She kept playing anyway, even though the tías were laughing and joking about how slow she was, calling her pachorra. Every now and then Mama and the others would hit Cirilo on the arm playfully whenever he beat them.

What happened next with Cirilo and Mama was not what my father would later say he saw through the sliding glass door. I know because I was sitting right next to them. Mama brushed Cirilo's face with the back of her hand, saying that a mosquito was about to sting him. It was just a brush, and not a linger of the eye or a flirtation; it was nothing like what Apá must have seen through his liquor-drunk eyes, or what he would accuse my mother of. Even the tías who were sitting at the table thought nothing of it, as they themselves would have done the same thing.

Everyone went home at about eleven except Macario and Braulio, who were outside talking about the Demócratas and the Republicanos and who really stood for Chicanos. When my uncles got going about that, they went around and around in circles for hours while Apá sat by the radio and listened to Radio Estereo Mar or strummed his guitar softly. Tío Mac's wife Elvira had gone home when my tío told her he would be home later, that he wanted to spend time with his brothers. Tío Braulio, who didn't even drink anymore, could pretty much do whatever he wanted to now that he and tía Ofelia were separated again.

Apá went into the kitchen, where Mama was cleaning up. When he passed by, I saw that he held an empty bottle of Bacardí at the neck as if he had been drinking straight from it. I heard him open the refrigerator, probably to look through the crisper, where he always kept a few backup beers. I was in the living room on the couch, pretending to sleep. Each time a bottle clanked I blinked my eyes hard like I did when a firecracker went off.

My parents thought I could sleep through anything, but the truth was, I could fake sleeping through anything. I did it often at dances and parties, and heard things I was never supposed to, which was why I did it, to enter the world of the adults.

I heard Apá say, "Why did you touch his face?" Whenever Apá drank liquor, his voice was never slurred. It was always too steady, too controlled, too monotone even as he swore more freely, and said things he would never say otherwise.

"Gonzalo, calm down, he had a mosquito on his face," Mama said.

"No, vieja, I saw. You touched him. Mosquito ni qué mosquito."

"Gonzalo, please. Andas pedo, and you don't even know what you're saying. And what were you doing drinking brandy and Bacardí? You said you wouldn't."

"I know what I saw. I saw you touching him."

"Okay, Viejo, you're right, whatever you say."

"Victoria, you can't treat me that way. What do you think? That I'm some pendejo you can talk to like that?"

"I'm going to bed," Mama said. "I don't even need to listen to all this."

"You're going to stay here until we talk about this. Tell me all about your sancho."

"I'm not going to talk to you when you're like this, todo pedo, and you don't even know what you're saying. I mean, Cirilo my sancho? Really?" Mama walked out of the kitchen and into the living room, going past me without stopping to wake me up and tell me to go to my room. There was fear on her face, her small chin quivering like it did when she was upset. She went into the hall to their bedroom. Apá didn't stumble or sway as he followed her. Whenever he drank, he could do the figure-four and walk a straight line and pass the other field sobriety tests, except for the light-in-the-eyes test, which was the test he would fail if he ever got pulled over for DWI. Once when he and my tíos had been drinking out of a bottle of Oso Negro vodka, they had challenged him to do the tests, and he had passed them all with ease. The only thing liquor seemed to affect were his perceptions. He misunderstood everything anyone told him and somehow thought he was being attacked. He always dredged up offenses from the past, either real or perceived.

My tíos would say, No, hermano, that's not what I meant. You heard me wrong. They had learned not to bring liquor around him. He was mostly a gentle, generous drunk when he only drank beer. But tío Artemio, having recently married

Suzana, was new to the family and did not know the unspoken rules. But somehow, since my father had been in a good mood that day, they didn't say anything when Apá accepted tío Artemio's offer of a drink. I figured that my uncles always hoped that, despite his history, somehow Apá could change. I would regret this later: as soon as I saw how he was acting with Mama, I should have gone outside to where my tíos were talking and told them what was happening. In that moment, however, my only thought was to run to my room once Apá was down the hall.

I made my way to my bedroom without being seen by either of them. I quietly shut my door most of the way, but left it cracked open so I could see what was happening. I put my hand in my pocket and stroked the handle of La Mariposa.

From their bedroom at the opposite end of the hall, I heard Apá say, "Vieja mentirosa. I know there's something going on with you and Cirilo." I could only see their open doorway and their shadows.

"I'm not lying to you, Viejo. Ask your sisters tomorrow. They were there."

"And where did you all go when you went for your ride?"

"What do you mean?"

"No te hagas, you know what I'm talking about. 'Ay, Cirilo, let's go in your bomba.' I saw how you acted when you got to go somewhere with him, acting like nothing but a huila in front of everybody."

"That's it. Vete, ya. Now!" I saw Apá step back into view as if my mother had tried to push him out of the room.

Apá said, "You don't talk to me that way." He was yelling now, calling her names. His eerily calm, measured drunken voice was gone.

Mama was crying now. "No, Gonzalo, there's nothing going on, I promise."

Tío Macario and tío Braulio rushed in, as if they had felt something like this was going to happen. I'll never know if Apá would have gone further in violence against my mother, as he had no history of laying a hand on her, but in that moment we all believed it was possible.

My uncles said nothing, but pulled Apá away from Mama, out of the room. Whatever they had seen, it must have been enough for them to react this way. As he started to struggle, turning his anger toward them, they pinned him down in the hallway, his stomach to the floor. The sound of their struggle was unremarkable, nothing like the sound effects from the fights I saw on TV shows or from the Mexican action movies my father liked to rent where there always seemed to be a glass table around to fall through. I flinched anyway, and then thumbed the latch of the knife open. I tried to make my legs move forward into the hall, tried to make my hands pull out Mariposa, but I could not move. I could only watch.

They had him on the carpet, and Mama was quiet now, still in her room. Apá, though he was shorter than both of my tíos, had always been the strongest. Tío Braulio or tío Mac alone could never have held him down, because they were barely doing it now together. Tío Braulio put his weight on Apá's legs so that he could not wriggle free, but he kicked and busted through the Sheetrock wall behind them. Tío Mac had one of my father's arms bent behind him. Apá's other arm was reaching back, trying to claw at them. Now that it was just him and his brothers, and my mother was out of sight, the physical violence he had held back earlier surfaced, aimed at my tíos.

"Cabrones," he said. "¡Déjenme, cabrones!" As his voice broke, I realized that this was the closest to crying I had ever heard from my father.

"Sosiégate, güey. Tranquilo, tranquilo," tío Mac said.

Braulio's mouth was moving, a steady but silent murmur of words flowing from him. Beneath their bodies and twisted arms, Apá's head was thrown back, his legs caked in white powder from the Sheetrock. His eyes were red-rimmed and bulging, worse than I'd seen them when he was cursing out the brujo while trying to cleanse Papa Tavo's and Abuelita's property. I didn't recognize anything of Apá in them.

What seemed like forever later, Mama stepped out of the bedroom and over Apá. She had changed clothes and was carrying an overnight bag. I went to my bed and pretended to sleep, as if I had not seen the whole thing. She pulled me out of bed, not saying a word, and as we passed Apá and my tíos, my father said nothing, would not even look at us. Tío Braulio tried to look calm and hopeful as he waved us away, telling us it was okay now. Tío Mac smiled weakly and wiped sweat away from his forehead.

In the car, Mama was crying and saying that he was under the influence of the devil, that you could see it in his eyes, how they were demonic and bloodshot and there was nothing of him left because he did not have the Spirit of God to protect him.

"Solamente el diablo," she said, "You saw, right?"

I knew she wanted me to say, *Only the devil, yes, Mama, I saw*, simultaneously translating what she had said and agreeing with her.

I stayed silent, and again she said, "Right?"

She kept looking at me, alternating her eyes between the

road and my face, my face and the road. In one of those moments when she had her eyes forward, I pulled La Mariposa out of my pocket.

After a moment, I relented from my silence and said what she wanted me to say. This was how we spoke to each other. Whenever we were alone, right before bed when she came in for bedtime prayers or when we were riding in the car, she would pray in tongues or in Spanish and I would speak when the meaning came to me.

She tried to smile at my translation, tell me by nodding in agreement that I was a good little prophet of God. Then I turned to her and lifted my chin and kept it there, the corners of my mouth pulled down like a chingón, like how Cirilo taught me to do when some vato was throwing a challenge and you wanted to show them you were not afraid. Mama reached out to touch my cheek, then turned her head to look at me. She stopped, drew her hand back, and her eyes widened. Mama looked into my face, saw the boy was now gone, and envisioned the man I would be someday. The only prophecy sure and true: I would always make sure my father or anyone never hurt her or threatened to hurt her. She patted my hand and did not notice me unlatching Mariposa with the other, swinging the handles open to reveal the blade inside, practicing for a day when I would be transformed, a man who would find the courage I'd lacked there in our hallway, unable to move.

What You Bury, What You Burn

Since you were nineteen, Gonzalo—after that summer when you saved the family from hunger and from losing the home on Aurora—it has always been you the family turned to. During those months when the Río Grande Valley grew and the burden to provide for the family was too much for Papa Tavo, he withdrew into himself and stopped showing up to jobs. So you stepped up to lead your brothers, sisters, and your mother. You hustled hard to get painting and drywall contracts, drove your brothers Braulio and Macario to the job sites, and picked up the day laborers on Bicentennial when there was too much work for the three of you. Even if you had not been the oldest son, and it had been Braulio, Macario, or even Wally to be born first, it still would have been you, the strongest Izquierdo, el mero mero. You were the one to make sure there was enough milk, enough rice, beans, flour, oil, and even meat, which not everyone in the barrio had. You did that for the family, and they will never forget it.

Although Abuelita had other grown sons and daughters she could have called the night Papa Tavo had his worst and final breakdown, it was you and only you that Abuelita called on this full moon night. Papa Tavo's behavior was no longer manageable and you tried to make him better by being there for him at his worst, but when you knew your presence alone would never be enough, you had to make the hard decision to have him committed.

After your mother pleaded for you to come across town to your childhood home in the barrio Zavala, you got off the phone and lay in the darkness of your bedroom with Victoria, looking at the white religious candle that was now more liquid than solid. This was the house in North McAllen you built with your brothers using your own hands and everything Papa Tavo had taught you. This was the house Victoria had left you in by yourself those months after you got drunk, put your face in hers, and called her all of those awful things, the house she came back to when your brother Braulio spoke up for you and you promised to be better, to never drink liquor again.

Victoria looked to the circle of candlelight hovering on the ceiling and then turned on her side to face you, trying to find your eyes. Now she draped her long, thick hair like a rebozo over your chest and said, "What can I do, Viejo? How can I help your mother?" You heard the word *Viejo* and knew it to be true, you being forty-three and she being thirty-four, but wiser and stronger and more perceptive than any woman you had ever known, either lover or sister.

Though you kept your gaze fixed on the dwindling candle and wondered when it would go out altogether, you could feel those brown-black eyes of hers boring into you, those beautifully curved eyebrows raised in expectation of an answer. Each time you heard her call you *Viejo*, how she said it softer than other

words she spoke, you knew it was out of love you didn't deserve.
To hear her call you her old man was a reminder of your difference in years, yes, but it always brought the question of what she
saw in you, or why she stayed with you now that she fully knew
you. Why had she come back after that horrible night on the
Fourth of July, what you foolishly accused her of, how you had
frightened her? Instead of focusing on that night, you tried to
think of the day you first met her, back when you were installing
drywall at the condos off of Nolana. It was on your lunch break
at the Mill, where she was working as a waitress while she finished nursing school, when you first walked into her life. You in
your work clothes, drywall dust on your jeans, paint splattered
on your Red Wing boots, were nothing much to look at, yet Victoria made sure she bypassed the hostess and had you sit in her
section. And though your mind tried to cling to that happy day,
you wondered about how she still called you *Viejo* with love in
her voice, even after all the hurts, all the things you had said and
done. Why had she ever forgiven you? Why did she come back to
you after she had taken Little Gonzalo, living in her own place
for months, proving that she didn't need you and never did? Her
leaving for the shameful things you'd said out of your jealousy,
rage over Cirilo, your teenage nephew who was closer to her in
temperament, was understandable. *You touched his face*, you
had said in your drunken jealousy, and called her things you are
ashamed of. You hadn't put your hands on her, but you'd seen
fear in her face while you said these disgusting words, which you
could not bring yourself to repeat. You had frightened her, and
to you, it was unforgivable. Yet she had forgiven you and come
back, which was a mystery.

When you got more serious with her, when dates were

expected, but you still wanted to impress her, you took her to the Santa Fe Steakhouse. It was then that Victoria looked across the table, and she told you she didn't have time for marriage, that you weren't in her plans. *Let's hammer this out right now*, she said, even though you had never even mentioned marrying her.

Victoria put her hand on yours and said, *After I'm done with school, I'm going to be a nurse and I'll never be a former waitress who became a mantenida who thought she won the lottery, happy to have some man take care of her. Just so you know, Viejo.* It was the first time she or anyone called you this and it became your name and it was dear to you, knowing you were Victoria's old man.

So all of this, she said, waving her arm around the restaurant, *is nice, but don't ever think I have daddy issues. When I do marry, it will be out of love, and not out of need or some unresolved stuff I'm pushing down. You got that, Viejo?* And later in the conversation, she jokingly asked you if you had any daddy issues. You had never told anyone about the summer when you were still a teenager and you took care of the family and kept them from estampillas or begging for handouts. You surprised yourself by telling her all about your own buried emotional issues, how you had been a father before you were a father, the weight on your young shoulders. You found it easy to say these things to Victoria, and after you said them, you felt like something heavy and burdensome had been unearthed from your chest.

All of this, the desperation in your mother's voice on the phone, those first days with Victoria, and the later days in your marriage you fought to forget, played out in that failing candle and the circle of light on the ceiling it created as your eyes alternated between them. Then you turned on your side and brushed

Victoria's rebozo of hair away from your chest, from her small face. You rubbed your finger over the shallow cleft in her chin.

Even though it was the most frightened you had ever heard your mother sound, and you knew Victoria could help, you said, "It's all good, Amor. It's all good. The best thing you can do is stay here with Little Gonzalo."

"Are you sure? I can call one of your sisters and they can come take care of Little Gonzalo, or we can all go together and be strong as a family for Papa Tavo. I'm here for the family, Viejo." And even though you knew she was right, that either option was better than going alone, that she had proven herself by coming with you the night you hired a curandero to undo the curses against your family, you took it upon yourself to do this deed alone because it was always you who dealt with the unpleasant, hard-to-do things you wanted to spare your family from.

"No, Amor," you said.

"It's not a problem," Victoria said. "I want to be there to help if you need it, even if it's to calm down mi suegra. I can at least help with your mother. It's what a daughter-in-law is supposed to do, right?"

You repeated, "No," and your voice was too loud for the room, louder than you promised yourself you would ever speak to Victoria again, just like you promised you would never drink hard liquor or lash out in anger. And now, instead of apologizing for your tone, which would have been the right thing to do, you walked out of the room, hoping to leave your volume and the shameful memory, even though it was always before you and not behind you.

When she followed you to the front door where you sat on the bench putting on your boots, you focused on Victoria's hands wrapping her robe over her body, her thin but strong fingers tying the knot at her waist. You knew if you looked into her eyes you would see wisdom there, and she would convince you she should come along. You knew what you were about to walk into at the house on Aurora, and you would witness a vision of Papa Tavo that only you and your mother shared. You wanted to spare her the catatonic glaze of Papa Tavo's eyes on the nights when he was sleepwalking and Abuelita was afraid waking him would forever trap him in this somnambulistic state of limbo. If she awoke Papa Tavo, she thought he would remain in the dream world for the rest of his life, forever searching for food to feed the children who were all grown now, but were small and hungry in his dreams. These children, your brothers and sisters, were never hungry or afraid that summer you took care of them. You made sure they had *everything* they needed. Despite being a child yourself, you knew that food was not enough and they also needed spirit, so you gave your brothers and sisters your blessing, such as it was, each night in Papa Tavo's place, making the sign of the cross on their foreheads. You did this because all of them—Wally, Suzana, Ana, Dina, Macario, Melinda, Maggie, Marisol, and even Braulio, who was just a year younger than you—needed it, and not for your belief in blessings or your ability to impart them.

Once your boots were on, Victoria kept her eyes on you like she did when she wanted you to see her way, or when she knew you had something to tell her. If your eyes met hers, she would draw out the reason you could not bear the thought of her seeing Papa Tavo: some small part of her would see you in him and she would believe that you would meet the same end. If you stayed any longer in that entryway, Victoria would uncover the reason why you worked on people's roofs and had sold your part of the

Izquierdo business to your brothers. She would discover that you feared becoming weak and inútil with the stress of running the business, that you feared everyone's doubt in their own mental fortitude if you, the strongest of them, had your own nervous breakdown. So you had to get out of the house, beyond her knowing gaze, and were almost thankful that your mother and father needed you, the strongest son, the only one who could do the ugly things that everyone else was too fragile to do.

Even though the entryway was dark, lit only by the light over the stove in the kitchen, you looked down at your boots like you were inspecting them for a shine, and said, "Está bien, mi amor. If everything goes okay, I'll hopefully be back before it's light out. I just need to get him settled. Si no, it might be time for—" And you meant to say Charter Palms, evaluation, stronger medication, a long-term care facility, but you did not know what was best. You knew the family could not continue this way, but you also knew speaking these words out loud would hasten your father's departure from home. And because it was beyond possibility, you could not say that all you wanted was your father back to how he used to be: strong, lifting fifty-pound bags of cement like they were bags of cereal, lighthearted in how he would joke with the workers and motivate them to work harder through the afternoons, and kind, always kind, buying you and your brothers and sisters paletas on those better days when the Hygeia truck came through the neighborhood.

When you got to Papa Tavo and Abuelita's in your red F-350, you knew all was not well when you saw the outer burglar-bar door wide open, all of the lights on in the house, as if your mother believed she could expel any mal espíritu if only she could pour enough light on them. She came to you, grabbed your face, and pleaded with you, body shaking, the beads from the rosary in her hands trembling. You kissed her forehead like she was a child and rocked with her as she wept into your chest. The thing in life that was hardest for you to bear—even harder than Papa Tavo's manias—was this, the sorrowful sound of your mother's anguish. Still, you held her tight, swaying back and forth to calm her like you learned how to do with your brothers and sisters when they were little, like she had done for you when you your- self were little and afraid, like you still did from time to time even when you stood alone and no one was in your arms. You swayed and swayed until she found enough of her strength to tell you where Papa Tavo was.

Even though none of this was good and she had every reason to be tormented, you said, "Está bien, Amá. No te mortifiques." You scanned the kitchen and the small living room beyond. It was then that you noticed the wreckage around you. Lalo's black boom box stereo was on the kitchen floor, the cover to the bat- tery compartment broken and the batteries laid out like drunken men. All of the kitchen drawers were hanging open, their items scattered and rifled through, as if a thief had broken into the house, looking for something of value. When you saw the black toaster in the sink, you carefully unplugged it and set it back on the small counter. You took stock of everything, and found a pat- tern in the disarray, in all of the items strewn across the room. They were black in color.

From the sala in the back of the house—where Papa Tavo liked to watch his programs when the grandchildren rested in the air-conditioning—you could hear your father straining with something, the sound of furniture being moved around and scraped against the old wooden floor.

As you moved up the step to the original part of the house, Abuelita covered her face with her hands and collapsed onto a dining room chair, relieved that you were going to deal with it. You noticed more disorder in the sala, all black objects thrown and broken on the floor: remote controls, the small TV, speakers, Abuelita's leather sandals, and even a comb. You then found Papa Tavo in a state you had not wanted Victoria or any of the rest of the family to see. Again, because they would see what he had become and see what might be coming for you.

Papa Tavo turned to you and said, "Ayúdame," and he was very much awake, not sleepwalking; his voice sounded calm enough that you almost convinced yourself that everything was okay. He seemed just slightly manic, as if he were in a rush, trying to rearrange the furniture in preparation for guests who would soon be arriving, guests who would want another place to sit. This illusory calm disappeared as you looked into Papa Tavo's face and you saw the skin drawn back, eyes too wide open, all of his teeth showing as if he were in pain. "Ayúdame," he said again, and it was now that you heard distress in his hoarse voice.

Papa Tavo tried to lift his favorite chair, a copper-brown corduroy recliner he had bought at a yard sale. This was his trono, the special chair where the family came to give their saludos, gave him gifts on his birthday or Christmas, presented their new babies to him, where they asked for his consejos back when he was able to give them. This was where Papa Tavo relaxed on Saturdays, where he watched *The Lawrence Welk Show*, hoping to see an appearance of Anacani the Mexican singer, where he was lulled into sleep by the happy sounds of his grandchildren playing outside or the sounds of cereal and milk, of spoons clinking against bowls while his nietos ate breakfast and watched cartoons.

Papa Tavo held his arms out wide like he did when he was asking you and your brothers to get back to work, to stop slap-boxing each other during your lunch breaks. He was motioning for you to help him turn it over.

Even though this made no sense, you went to him and easily flipped the chair over on its back. Papa Tavo went to his knees and ripped the white gauze-like fabric from the bottom, pulling it completely away from its staples. You saw it at the same time he did: a black cross formed out of the recliner's frame, structured not like a crucifix as the boards intersected in the middle, but a cross nevertheless. You caught your breath at the revelation of this omen, which had always been there, hidden underneath Papa Tavo's trono as he entertained or educated his family. While you only gasped, Papa Tavo howled when he saw it, and it was loud enough to make your ears ring. With this single note of anguish, the one only you and Abuelita were burdened to hear, Papa Tavo fell to the floor as if all of the strength in his body were finally taken from him.

"The evil I have suffered," Papa Tavo said. "There it was all this time."

"But it's a cross, Apá," you said. "A cross is good, right?"

Papa Tavo ignored you then like he did when you were younger asking obvious questions just to have something to say, just so that he would talk to you when he was within himself.

"The darkness is all around us now and it is taking over. All of these things wanting to swallow up the light. All of these years, that Brujo Contreras wanting to fill my whole world with darkness." The years he spoke of started the summer when he was enfeebled by low-level manic episodes and could not work anymore.

Because you didn't know what else to do, you said, "Apá, we need to burn this. I will help you." From your years of leading work crews you knew that if you sounded confident enough in a decision, those around you would believe it was the right course of action, even if it wasn't. Even if you didn't fully believe it yourself.

As happens between parents and their children, Papa Tavo communicated to you without words, using only his eyes and a tilt of his head. *You would do that for me, son?*

You patted Papa Tavo's bony shoulder, and helped him up off of the floor, surprised at how light he was. This was the heavy-hearted moment you and Papa Tavo had been building up to, the reckoning when a son realizes he is stronger than his father. Still, you wanted to slow it down, meditate on these last moments when Papa Tavo was a semblance of the man he had been. You pulled him up and breathed him in, how he always smelled like he had just come in from outside, his older workingman's smell, the sweat on him for you and the family. His essence was dear to you, his Pinaud Clubman aftershave to cover the cigarette smoke clinging to his guayaberas, his favorite Clorets gum to hide his coffee breath. This was the last time you would remember him this way before the smell of a dying man permeated Papa Tavo and your memory of him.

⁂

WHEN PAPA TAVO AND ABUELITA were sitting side by side on the bench seat of your pickup, the can of gasoline and recliner loaded, you saw a car pull up, and despite how you knew you could handle this alone, you were relieved to see it was Victoria's Mustang.

You leaned onto the roof of her car, and you looked in the back where Little Gonzalo was asleep in the cramped backseat.

Even before Victoria had rolled her window down all the way, you said, "What are you doing here, Amor? It was better to stay at home. It's bad. I didn't want you to see this. I didn't want you and mijo to be out this late." You immediately regretted saying this because Victoria was there for you and she was defending the family that was hers as much as yours. She was loyal and chingona and fearless, and you should have given her more respect.

"Can't you see, Viejo? I'm here for all of it. Do you think your mother over there has the privilege of looking away? If she is to see it, I should too. Till death do us part, güey." The way she said this like a chola, she meant to lighten the heaviness she saw bearing down on your shoulders. It did make you smile, but also made you remember that you did not deserve her now, and never did.

"Anyways, Viejo. Where two or three are gathered, you know," and even though you never applied her biblical speeches to your life, you could not deny the inviolable wisdom of her words and knew that any argument would be useless.

"Órale, pues," you said, "Follow me. We are going out to the fields south of us."

You caravanned out of the city and into the darkness, toward the acres south of the Balboa barrio on South Twenty-third to that uninhabited land, the international trade zone between McAllen and Hidalgo, just a few miles from Mexico. Just past the last levee and the bridge where the streetlights ended and darkness blanketed all things, you turned off a dirt road that ran parallel to a canal and then took the lower branch to the field below. Papa Tavo never spoke the whole time, his eyes fixed before him, no recognition of the task at hand. Abuelita prayed in whispers, some petitions remembered and some resulting from this moment.

You came to a stop, but kept your lights on and the engine running.

"Amá, please stay in the pickup with Apá," you said.

You heard Victoria's door open at the same time you were opening yours. You moved to the bed of the truck and started moving the recliner yourself, but Victoria helped you lower it. Together, you carried it to a patch of bare dirt in the field, recently tilled land that was free from any dry grass. You were not surprised by her strength, knowing that a big part of her work in home health involved lifting the viejitos in and out of their beds and chairs, and doing so with gentleness.

You turned over the recliner to reveal the black cross underneath, and looked to Victoria to see her reaction. She tucked her long mexica hair behind her ears, pursed her lips, and gave a quick nod in agreement, confirming what had to be done. You wondered why she supported this, how this burning was okay, but hiring a curandero to burn curses had not been and never would be in her mind.

As you cleared away any grass or leaves that might make the fire spread across the entire field, you felt Victoria's palm on your shoulder as she placed the can of gas into your hand. With her touch, this gesture, the way her eyes were soft when she looked at you, she was telling you, *We are doing this together, Viejo,* and then you understood her approval. Because it felt right, and this moment required some kind of ritual to give it meaning, you walked a full circle around the chair, dousing it from every side. You heard the door to your pickup open, and your mother came to stand next to you just as you were about to light it.

As the flames rose, the heat came against you and Victoria and your mother. You looked over to Papa Tavo where he sat in the middle of the bench seat. His eyes seemed to be looking past the flames to the south, where the twinkling city lights of Reynosa on the other side of the border were the only other illumination to be seen. Maybe he was thinking about when he and your mother had moved there from Montemorelos, Nuevo León, and the months they had lived there when they were first married, before they crossed over and had you. Or maybe his eyes saw nothing at all.

The fire soon did its work of disintegrating wood and cloth, exposing springs and frame. The foam popped as it melted away. Then there were the words, the unintelligible, guttural whispers that could be heard coming from the air, from a space between the flames and smoke. Though you could not understand the message exactly, you knew the intent, how these susurrations foretold the demise of the Izquierdo family only after a long period of suffering. Victoria was always the one to interpret spiritual things, but this much you knew.

Victoria and your mother heard them as well, and so they too began to speak, proclaiming love for their husbands, the children who had gone on to heaven and the ones still on earth, the children to come, and for all of the brothers, sisters, cuñadas, cuñados, comadres, and compadres. And as the whispers continued to come from the flames, the women's words grew in strength, became supplications and commands, both recitative and glossolalic, pleading for deliverance, a hedge of protection around the Izquierdos, and demanding an expulsion of any curses or evil spirits from your lives.

You chose not to speak because you wanted to bear witness instead.

As you stood with Victoria watching the fire blaze in the night, the whispers were soon silenced as they surrendered to the two most important women in your life. Your mother walked back to the pickup to check on your father, and you reached out your hand to Victoria. She clasped it tight to tell you it was only you and her now. After the fire began to smolder and the smoke became nearly invisible in the night sky, you tried to pull away, but she kept you there and did not release you. This was how Victoria had held hands with you that night at the Santa Fe Steakhouse & Cantina when you had finished your story about the summer when you were nineteen, and the tears that you had never allowed yourself finally came. Victoria had held you then like she held you now because—despite how everyone in the family would always see you as the one who had saved them—she saw you as the one that needed saving. If only you would let her.

La Milagrosa Selena

Even though I know La Milagrosa Selena Quintanilla-Pérez, the Queen of Tejano Music, was a Jehovah's Witness, and was not baptized into the Catholic faith, I still believe she is a saint. My name is Lourdes Montelongo Sepúlveda, and for the sake of my comadre Marisol "Sol" Buentello, whom she healed from her eating disorder, I would like to explain why. I hope you are open to what I have to share.

But before I go any further, you have to know that I am more Catholic than a mantilla, more Catholic than the smell of incense, more Catholic than making the sign of the cross when you drive by the smallest Catholic church. I even cross myself when I see a sign pointing to a church. So you have to know where I am coming from.

I know one of the things someone has to do to become a saint is perform at least two miracles. Selena has performed two on my comadre Marisol, and I bet if I or anyone else looked we would find she's done a lot more.

The first miracle Selena performed on my comadre Marisol

happened a little more than a year before Selena was murdered by that desgraciada Yolanda Saldívar. Selena y Los Dinos were playing at La Villa Real in McAllen, recording a show for *Puro Tejano*, and Eulalio "Lalo" Buentello, my comadre's husband, bought them tickets at the Boot Jack just because. It wasn't my comadre's birthday or their anniversary. Lalo was always in love with her like that.

Comadre Marisol believed she had a connection with Selena. She felt like Selena was family. Before that night, my comadre had only seen Selena on *Puro Tejano* and *The Johnny Canales Show*. Watching Selena on the TV, trying to ignore *Puro Tejano*'s host Rock-n-Roll James as he interrupted her performances with his bad dancing and man-chongo, was not like seeing Selena for real, up close and in all of her regal Tejana glory. It was at her last show at the Villa Real that my comadre Marisol experienced the miracle of La Milagrosa Selena.

At the Villa Real that night there were lots of people dancing and waving their hands. Comadre Marisol stood with Lalo and watched as all those fans, the men in their silk shirts and gambler hats, the women with their tight jeans and high hair-sprayed hair, danced with pure happiness. Comadre Marisol saw how all of them mouthed the words to the songs. Onstage, Selena shimmered in her green one-piece outfit that showed her flat stomach, and she was twirling, making those washing machine moves like she knew how to do. The men couldn't take their eyes off her. The women couldn't stop looking at her either. Selena was that kind of person.

At the beginning of the show, Comadre Marisol's favorite song "Amor Prohibido" came on and Lalo took them up front. He threw his shoulders into the crowd and they had to move for him. Eulalio "Lalo" Buentello is a big, wide man, about six feet tall with a thick beard, like a Mexican Grizzly Adams. Comadre Marisol just followed behind her husband. They finally got up there, and that was when it happened. I've known Comadre Marisol for many years and there have been a few life-changing moments in her life. This was one of them. The other big moments were when her children, Seferino, Michely, and Erika, were born, and when her father Papa Tavo got really sick and needed twenty-four-hour care. And when I really think about it, even though she has always struggled with her weight since we were in high school together, losing and gaining, losing and gaining, it wasn't until her father got sick enough to go into the nursing home that it got really bad and she became obsessed about it, to the point of hurting herself. But I'll tell you more about that later.

Comadre Marisol got up to the front, and just for a second Selena looked at my comadre. No big deal, right? Well, let me tell you, it was. Selena didn't just look at her like she looked at all her fans.

Selena looked down from the stage into Comadre Marisol's face. She looked at her like someone does when they think they know you, but they're not sure. Comadre Marisol smiled. Even though she was older than Selena by about ten years, had three children, and had lived life more, she felt like a chiquilla again. Comadre Marisol felt like an angel was smiling at her.

Then Selena performed the miracle. She held out her hand to Comadre Marisol and made the okay sign with her fingers. She mouthed the words, *Everything's going to be okay*, just as Comadre Marisol was thinking them in her mind. Selena must have had a don espiritual to see inside my comadre's heart and into her past. You see, Comadre Marisol always says this to herself when she's scared or sad, because her father used to make the okay sign and tell her this, and she believed it every time. My comadre Marisol looks into the mirror, makes the sign with her hands, and says, "Everything's going to be okay," just like her father used to do before his cirrhosis and nervous anxiety made him too weak to lead the family. Since you are a man of the cloth, and you are sworn to never tell anyone and you are supposed to be free from the sin of chisme, I'll tell you this, my comadre once told me that her father always feared not making enough money to feed all ten of his children, that the construction jobs would stop coming and they would lose everything. It was so bad that he would have nightmares about seeing his children starving.

But that's not important to this story. What is important and astonishing is that as all those thousands of fans were saying the words to Selena's songs, Selena was singing the words to the song of Comadre Marisol's life. You can't get more amazing than that.

Now, about a year after Selena left us, when Comadre Marisol needed her most, she performed another miracle for her, and I was physically present for it. This is what caused me to petition you to recognize the miracles Selena has performed. This is what got me to write to you.

Selena healed my comadre Marisol of her sickness. Like I said, my comadre didn't have cancer or anything serious like that. She had susto, which we all have to some degree, I suppose. I know you don't teach this in the Church, but susto is in all of us where we can never forget the bad that has happened to us, and we wait for it to happen to us again or something worse. Some people are crippled by this irrational fear. They stay depressed or can't sleep or, in cases like my comadre Marisol's, they have

these eating disorders. I worried about susto taking control of
her life, but I also worried about her physical health. It's real,
Your Excellence Padre Peña, believe it.

Almost every night for about a month, when Lalo and the
kids were sleeping, Comadre Marisol would get out of bed and
go to the refrigerator. She would sleepwalk and eat cookies, pan
dulce, leftovers (Molina's barbacoa, El Pato, La Casa Del Taco,
China Palace, Red Barn barbecue, Casa Don Eusebio botana
platter), peanut butter and jelly, cereal, etc. She ate so many
things while she was asleep, I can't even imagine. My comadre
never remembers getting up, and she couldn't stop herself. The
difference between her and a bulimic was, one, she was sleepwalking when she did it, and two, she didn't throw up. She kept
it all inside of her, and then went back to bed that way, with a
big full panza. She gained almost sixty pounds. Like I said, she is
beautiful. I think so and Lalo thinks so. But I was really afraid for
her health. She didn't want to explain to Lalo how the food was
disappearing. The thing was, she didn't want him to think she
was turning out like her father, that her problems with food, her
image of herself, were a manifestation of her being his daughter.
She couldn't hide what was happening, though. One morning,
after a night of having binged like that, she called me up and said
she needed me to come over.

When I went over to her house, she said, "Ay, comadre, I just
don't want to live this way." What could I tell her that I hadn't
already said? Regardless, I had to be there. You see, Your Excellence Padre Peña, my comadre has always been there for me.
Once, when I was working as a server at Applebee's, I carded
this loser who I'd served before. Of course, he didn't have his ID
and I refused to serve him. Well, this chillón went to the man-

ager, and because I'd served him before, I got fired. Long story short, I lost my apartment and Comadre Marisol was the only one to take me in. She didn't give me problems when one week turned into a month, and she wasn't a metiche asking me about my comings and goings or what my job prospects were like. She's that kind of person. She helps without wanting anything back. So even though I didn't know what I would tell her that I hadn't already said, I knew I had to be there for her no matter what. That's what comadres do. Marisol taught me that suffering and being there for someone's suffering is its own sacrament and you don't always have to be the one to baptize someone's kid to be a comadre for life.

My comadre and I were not alone. Another woman was with her, Comadre Marisol's sister-in-law, Victoria. She was wearing nursing clothes. I had seen her once or twice at Comadre Marisol's mother's house. Automatically, I guessed why she was there. I had heard that Victoria prayed for people and they supposedly got better. I sucked my teeth when I saw her and couldn't help wrinkling my nose and making my face all pinched. Sadly, Comadre Marisol must not have thought I was enough to help her, that my prayers and consejos were not enough. I mean, Comadre Marisol could have called any one of her five sisters. Maggie, Dina, or even one of her baby sisters could have been there to support her, and of course I would have been fine with it, but I just couldn't understand why it was her cuñada Victoria who was there. Victoria, who is so flaca and not even Catholic and couldn't even begin to understand what was happening to my comadre.

Victoria was listening to Comadre Marisol go on about how she hated herself for the things she was doing, living the lie that everything was okay with her. If Victoria hadn't been there, I might have told my comadre Marisol that maybe the reason she was eating like this at night was to show her father in the dream world that she had enough food in her refrigerator, to show him that she would never be hungry, that she had married a good provider in Lalo, that she could even provide for herself, that Papa Tavo had taught her to work. But as it was, I didn't know Victoria that well, and my consejos were for my comadre Marisol, and her only.

"Ay, I just don't know about this terrible life." She looked so old and sad, Padre, like all the good things in her life had never happened. Victoria just sat there in her scrubs like she was some kind of medical authority, but didn't know what to say because I don't think she'd ever dealt with something like this. Victoria looked like one of those actresses from the skits on *Sábado Gigante*, a model who had everything she wanted. Like I said, I didn't understand why she had invited her. She couldn't even come close to understanding Comadre Marisol's situation.

Then, because it was obvious Victoria had no answer for this, I broke in and said, "You have so much, a husband who loves you, works for you, and three kids who don't get into too much trouble. Your girls are beautiful just like you, and Seferino's a good boy. You will always have enough of everything in your life."

My comadre Marisol nodded and said, "Pues sí, pues sí, you're right about that."

Victoria started talking then, saying that if Comadre really wanted to be healed she had to have faith and the Spirit of God living inside of her.

Comadre Marisol said, "Whatever it takes."

Then they prayed what Victoria called the sinner's prayer, where she and Comadre Marisol asked God to forgive her sins, that Jesus was the lord of her life, and to baptize her with the Holy Spirit (even though we both know that was done during baptism and she was baptized with the Holy Spirit upon Confirmation). Victoria got out a little vial of oil.

Comadre Marisol's whole body was shaking from crying as Victoria laid her hands on her head and anointed her, saying, "She has confessed You, heal her Father, heal her, sánela, sánela, en el nombre de Jesús we rebuke this sickness, we speak against it."

When they were done and Comadre Marisol calmed down, I just sat there watching, wondering why Comadre Marisol had even invited me if all I was going to do was watch them pray and hug and cry. I'm not proud about it, but I was a little frustrated with her.

Then, like Selena had given me a message from heaven, I knew exactly what to do, and knew exactly why I was there.

I got up and went to her stereo and turned on the CD.

Of course Selena was in there, so I put on "Techno Cumbia." It took Comadre Marisol a little while, but soon, after I asked her to get off of the couch and join me, we were swinging our hips, doing the Selena twist like we know how.

Victoria just sat on the couch not sure what to do, but then she got up and was on the carpet with us, all of us swiveling and twisting Comadre Marisol's sadness away. I saw those tears dry on Comadre Marisol's face, and I knew Selena was healing her from the grave. I knew that Selena was communicating to her that everything was okay, that Comadre Marisol was and had always been beautiful, that she didn't need to prove anymore to Papa Tavo in her dreams that she had enough food to fill her stomach. Selena was telling her that whatever had given her problems with food and her weight all these years was leaving her body like an evil night air burning away with the sun. The mal viento that had passed over her life was gone.

I bought Comadre Marisol a CD Walkman so she could listen to the music of Selena, because sometimes healing happens quickly and sometimes it happens over time. Every night, Comadre Marisol puts on her headphones. Selena's music comes to her as she falls asleep as if through the cosmos all the way from heaven, and she never gets up in the middle of the night to eat all that food. She doesn't need to do that because La Milagrosa Selena's music fills the emptiness inside of her. Selena visits Comadre Marisol in that magic place between sleeping and being awake and sings, "Everything's going to be okay." Selena does this and Comadre Marisol knows that all her problems are so small compared to Selena's love, to the everlasting reach of Selena's songs. And I'm so proud of her because she even puts that CD Walkman in a fanny pack and takes her children on afternoon walks to the San Juan Shrine Stations of the Cross walking trail. She passes by those life-sized bronze statues of Jesus on the Via Dolorosa, and "Bidi Bidi Bom Bom" puts the bounce in her step as she meditates on what the stations mean.

My comadre Marisol is even more beautiful now that she's lost a little weight. It's not the weight, really. It's what she thinks about herself that is changing her whole face, making her even prettier than she was when she was a teenager. Lalo is the only one who doesn't seem to notice how much prettier she has become. To him she is the same gorgeous woman she always was.

So, you see, Your Excellence Padre Bishop Raymundo Peña

of the Diocese of Brownsville, La Milagrosa Selena (yes, that will be her new name) performed a miracle on my comadre Marisol and continues to do so every night. She took a woman trapped in sadness and freed her. I know that my comadre Marisol still goes up and down with her weight, that she is always trying some kind of new diet, but it's not like it was. She's not having the dreams, and I know she's not buying diet pills from Reynosa anymore. I know it is a miracle, since La Milagrosa Selena spoke to both Comadre Marisol and me. And I myself saw my comadre healed. I hope you believe in the Miracles of Selena, and do everything you can to make sure La Milagrosa Selena becomes a saint.

If you do not believe me or think Selena is outside of grace because she was a Testigo de Jehová, don't worry, because God will forgive your blindness to the truth of what Comadre Marisol, Victoria, and I witnessed. He is good that way, to forgive us no matter what. If you do believe, but do not help me in my efforts to make La Milagrosa Selena an official saint because you are afraid of what people will think, I will not hold it against you. You're a new bishop and maybe you don't want to make waves, so I get it. Do what you have to do. However, un aviso, I tell you this. When people hear of these miracles, and you don't recognize them as miracles, they will still believe. For miles and miles, they will hear this story and La Milagrosa Selena and her music will heal them too. At yerberías and grocery stores all over the Valley, and wherever there are Mexicans, Selena's candles will be next to Jesus and Mary's, the All-Powerful Hand, and El Niño Fidencio Constantino's. All you will be able to do is ignore what is happening.

Whatever you decide to do, gracias for listening. God bless.

Part 3

Vecinos

1972

A ny time *Josefina Ramírez tried to take her son Teodoro to get a haircut, it always ended in frustration because he would not sit still, and would even scream out loud, his high-pitched squeal drawing exclamations of "¿Ah, ching', quién es este niño?" from the barbers. Little Teddy was four years old, still wore Pampers, and could not speak full sentences to express himself. Yet Josefina kept hoping past hope that he would be able to do this everyday thing: get a haircut. Josefina had tried every barbershop in South McAllen and every barber with his white smock had turned her away.*

On this Saturday morning, Josefina stood by the fence, her fingers peeking through the chain links, and told all of this to Abuelita as she watered her plantitas and maneuvered past the black needles of her agave plant.

Abuelita pinched the hose, stopped her watering, and said, "So, you are saying he has not had his first haircut?"

"Pues, no, vecina, I take him out and everyone asks me if he has a promesa. I'm tired of telling them it is just that he reacts

like we are killing him as soon as the clippers or scissors touch his head. I have to defend and protect him all the time, and it just makes me tired." The promesa was the tradition of keeping a child's hair long, cutting it only when a prayer had been answered. Sometimes the promise was made in hopes of a sick relative getting better, or, if the child's birth was the answer to a prayer, the hair was cut at a predetermined age. Abuelita kept it to herself, but she had assumed this too, that Teddy was a child of promesa, and thus had never asked about his hair.

"They all judge me. Like I am a bad mother who does not discipline her child. I cannot do it anymore. It is like they do not understand that he is different. He is still one of God's children no matter what they say. He just does not like the way some things feel on his skin and he does not see the world like we do. And he will talk when he decides to."

Abuelita smiled and reached for Josefina's fingers through the fence.

"I know what we can do. Bring him over. We will help you."

⁂

JOSEFINA HELD TEDDY'S HAND *as she walked up to Abuelita and Papa Tavo's open front door.*

"Pásele, vecina," Abuelita said. She knelt down low and caressed Teddy's chin. "Little man, you are so handsome and strong and smart. Today is a special day. You get to eat all of the cookies in this house, as many as you want." Abuelita pointed at the boxes of Gamesa cookies on top of her refrigerator.

"Vecina, you cannot—"

"Ssh, vecina, this is my house and anyone who comes here

is welcome to anything we have. My house, my way. Especially since you are my neighbor."

She turned her head to the living room and said, *"Viejo, our visitor is here. Come and see him."*

Papa Tavo, Marisol, Maggie, Dina, and Macario came from the living room, where Papa Tavo had been looking through his collection of maps while the children watched cartoons. Gonzalo and Braulio had ridden their bikes downtown and were on Seventeenth Street and around the bars on Bicentennial, shining shoes to make their money.

It was then that Josefina focused her eyes on the towel draped over the chair, clothespins, the spray bottle, and the scissors on the clear plastic cover of the kitchen table.

Papa Tavo also knelt down, put his hands on Teddy's head, and whispered something none of them could hear.

Then he spoke to Teddy, but was also speaking to them all, letting them in on the plan. *"Do you want cookies? Do you like cookies? Did my señora mention you could eat as many cookies as you wanted?"*

Teddy nodded that he understood, but said nothing.

"Eso," Papa Tavo said. *"A real man only speaks when he has something important to say. A fool lets the words spill out of his mouth like chorro."*

Abuelita lightly cuffed his arm, correcting him for his coarse talk.

He faked wincing at the blow, said, *"Protect me, papito, protect me,"* and this made Teddy smile.

"Okay, Teddy, you are going to sit in this chair, and I am going to give you a haircut. I am an expert at cutting hair. I cut all

my boys' hair, and guess what, they get all the girls with the hair-cuts I give them. And you are much more handsome than them."

Teddy held on to Josefina's leg.

Papa Tavo said, "No, no, Teddy, you have to be a brave little man if you want the good things in life. Right now, it is cookies. Later, it will be other good things." Papa Tavo motioned his chin to the top of the refrigerator and Abuelita followed his cue, and brought down the boxes of cookies.

"Sit here, papito, and it will be over before you know it. And guess what? The girls are going to show you all of the funny faces they have been practicing while they were watching the cartoons."

Dina and Marisol got in front of Teddy, opened their eyes wide, and stuck out their tongues. Despite himself, Teddy smiled a little at the attention he was getting. Macario got bored and went outside, while Maggie pulled up a chair for Teddy and another in front where she planned to sit during the haircut.

Papa Tavo led Teddy into the chair, and when he protested, he said, "Ssh, ssh, papito. It is going to be good. Remember, I am an expert. Think about my boys and how much you will look better than them and steal all the girls away." Papa Tavo knew that Teddy always watched the boys play through the fence, and how sometimes Josefina would even let him come over. Even though she always wanted to protect him from get-ting hurt or made fun of, and the Izquierdo boys were mischie-vous traviesos always in the streets, she also knew they were bien educados, taught to never stare when Teddy got excited and flapped his hands, and to include him in their games. And so she trusted them.

Once Teddy was in the chair, Papa Tavo said, "My barber's

assistant Maggie will now put the towel around you, if that's okay, papito, so you don't get any hair on that nice shirt."

Maggie took pride in being the barber's assistant, gently draping the towel around Teddy, placing the clothespins to keep it in place, and stroking the hair that was over his eyes and ears.

Josefina looked at Abuelita and nodded in appreciation at Maggie's skill and confidence that was beyond her years.

As Maggie did this, Papa Tavo said, "Oh yes, papito. You're going to be even more handsome. I mean, you are a man of the ladies right now, but just wait. Right, Maggie?"

"Yes, Papá, when he starts school, all of the girls at Thigpen will be all over him like flies at a party. Right, sisters?" When they didn't respond, she said again, "Right, sisters?" and raised her eyebrows for them to move. Marisol and Dina then took the cue and flapped their arms and made buzzing sounds.

Teddy laughed at that and the girls laughed too.

Papa Tavo showed Teddy the spray bottle and the scissors. "See, papito, they are not going to hurt you. They aren't even going to touch you, only your hair. This is only water to make it easier to cut your hair, and these scissors have cut the hair of all my children and a lot of kids in the neighborhood."

He handed the spray bottle to Maggie, who then covered Teddy's eyes with one hand while she spritzed the crown of his head, then the sides, and wiped away the excess water on his ears and nose.

"There," Maggie said. "Your client is all ready for you, Papá."

Teddy winced the whole time and even cried, but Maggie sat in front of him and put her hand on his hand to reassure him and kept it there during the entire haircut like she did for Macario when he was little. The sisters did their part and laughed and made faces and pretended to be flies, and he laughed through his tears. He did not have his usual full-body tantrum and he did not make his piercing scream. Papa Tavo had to gently shush him a few times, straighten his head, and remind him of the cookies, but after about fifteen minutes, his hair was on the floor and Papa Tavo was done, brushing off loose hair from his neck and ears. Even though Teddy's hair was still longer than the buzz cuts the Izquierdo boys had, it was shorter than it had been and you could see more of his handsome round face.

Josefina was now sitting at the table and under her breath kept saying, "Qué milagro, qué milagro." Abuelita patted her hand and said, "Con el favor de Dios, con el favor de Dios," each time Josefina called it a miracle.

Papa Tavo stepped back and said, "¡Mira, qué guapo! Don't you all think? Listo pa'l baile."

As she got the broom that was next to the refrigerator and began to sweep up the hair, Maggie said, "¡Guapísimo! I'd go to any dance with him!" The sisters clapped.

Josefina again said, "Qué milagro, Diosito. Qué milagro," and made a tight fist in front of her face, as if trying to hold the emotion inside of her.

Abuelita said, "Teddy is the miracle, mi vecina. Right, Teddy? You're the miracle."

Teddy pointed to the boxes of cookies on top of the counter and said, "Galletas," the first intelligible word any of them had ever heard him speak.

It All Starts with This

"They don't call me Maggie Magic Fingers for nothing."

That's what I tell my sister-in-law Victoria after church when we're sitting up front watching all those people on the carpet being prayed for and she asks me how my job at Short Cuts is going. Sometimes, when my brother Gonzalo is at home asleep all crudo from the night before, she has time to talk because he's not awake waiting to take her to lunch.

"Let me tell you one thing."

My cuñada smiles because she knows it's coming.

"I work my magic every time the guys come in. I know what you're thinking, but listen. The other girls, Sandra, Eunice, and Andrea, they always whine, 'Why don't these chafones tip?'

"I tell them it's *all* in the fingers.

"When you shampoo their hair, you got to work it. Me, this is what I do. First, I ask them if they want the tea tree shampoo. Like this guy Al I'm going to tell you about.

"They go, 'What's that?' And I explain it, pero bien sexy. Because us llenitas, we got to work it. So they don't say, *Ay, but she has such a pretty face,* and then not even mention our bodies as if they don't exist." Victoria smiles like she understands, but she's so pretty and skinny she doesn't know anything about that.

"I go, 'Oh, it's something cool that makes your head tingle and feel like a massage.'

"Some guys, they hate it and they're all like, 'You're not using that tea stuff, are you?'

" 'No, I wouldn't do that. Unless you asked me.' They all like it when I say that.

"I go, 'Is the water too hot?'

"And they go, 'No, it's fine.'

"So I run the water through their hair like I want to make sure every strand feels special. As I do it, I run my hands strong across their head about five or six times back and forth. The girls think you got to be all gentle, but they don't know that the guys like you to be a little tosca with them.

"I go, 'How you doing?'

"I rub the shampoo in my hands in circles and I let them see me do this. We talk about their wives, or their jobs, or they ask me how their hair would look with a different style. Most of the time, they only like *me* to talk, because I talk all soft to them about nice things, and they're all tired from work. Sometimes I tell them stories about the family or my father and how we used to cut hair for the kids in the neighborhood for free. I tell them this is when I learned I had a gift for cutting hair, when Maggie Magic Fingers was born. Or other times, I tell them about something fun I did on the weekend, like going to Padre Island or to the movies. And if I didn't do anything, I make it up. They don't care anyways, because it's my voice, not the words, that almost makes them fall asleep in the chair. All safe and sleepy like a little baby, qué no?

"When I put the shampoo in their hair, I don't just put it on like I'm a kid putting glue on construction paper. I work it into the scalp. You got to rub *real* hard, massage it in. I even scratch their scalp a little bit with my nails, but with this, you got to be careful you don't scratch too hard. I do that for a couple of minutes. You got to massage the temples too. Ay, they *like* that. Then you turn on the water and do the same dance like before." Victoria wants to roll her eyes because she's heard all this before, but I keep going anyways.

"Here is where most of the girls stop. They towel them off and get the guys out of the shampoo seat like they're little boys and make them go back to their chairs. But what they don't get is that sometimes when I got a man in my chair I can feel all their pain and loneliness under my fingertips. Some of these men sitting there, this is all the love they get, a woman they don't know playing with their hairs. It's like their highlight of the month, when they can forget about not having joy in their lives. Qué triste, right, but I'm happy to help them in my little way. Or maybe I'm just projecting and I'm the one that's lonely."

Anyways, I lighten the mood because I can see I'm losing Victoria, and I say, "Me, I could do guys' hair all day."

Victoria looks at me like, *I bet you could.*

"Entonces, the man is sitting there thinking too bad it's already over. That's when I put some more tea tree in my palms and work it in even better than before. Because this is what they remember when they get out their wallets to pay.

"I go, 'Does it tingle?'

"They go, 'Yes,' and I know they like it."

Victoria wants me to get to the point already.

So I get to the point.

"*Anyways*, sister, like I was telling you. There's this guy Al whose hair I been cutting for a couple of months. Bien cute y todo perfumado. Every time he walks in he's dressed all kicker. You know. Tiene Ropers y Wranglers. But *real* tight in the butt."

And I stop describing him that way because Victoria's looking at me like, *Okay, sister, that's enough; we're in church*. Like my cuñada is a santita, right? I know how she is, and she's not one to be judging.

"One day after a couple of visits Al tells me, 'You got hands like my wife.' I don't know if she's magic fingers too or if she's got chubby thumbs like me, big round ones with wide nails. But he says that they're always warm and strong, and I'm sitting there wondering why he's flirting with me."

Victoria laughs like she's thinking, *I wonder why*.

I look at her like, *Por favor, sister*.

"Anyways, he always comes in and gets this fade-cut where I use the number three clipper at the top, number two in the middle, and number one on the bottom until it fades to zero. Tú sabes, blended como un fade? But, before I do that, he always asks for a shampoo first and says it's because it's hot and he's been sweating all day. But, you know." Victoria definitely knows.

"In the sink, he's all like, 'You got good hands. You should be a masseuse.'

"And then I go, 'I been thinking about a change of careers.'

"So then we talk about that, about how much they get paid and how good the hours are, being a massage therapist I mean. I like this guy Al because he actually talks to me and *really* listens to me. You can tell because he looks for my eyes in the mirror and isn't looking down at all the hair on the floor like he's barely listening."

Victoria's giving me the eyes.

"No, sister, let me tell you. Sandra, you know the one I told you about who gets all the tips because she's so flaca like a toothpick and wears the white stirrup leggings where you can see the lines of her calzones, she tells me that she would sometimes see him at Powerhouse working out with his gringa wife. Of course, she rubs it in about how skinny his wife is in a leotard. You *know* how the flacas stick together." I'm thinking I should not have said the last part because Victoria's one of those flacas I'm talking about, bien pretty with a skinny waist and nice legs. Diosito forgive me, because now I'm judging her.

"I tell Sandra I haven't seen him in a while. I tell Sandra to ask around, because it wasn't like my highlight of the week when Al came, but I kind of liked it.

"So she comes back the next day and she says to me, Sandra says, 'I talked to Bobby my trainer at Powerhouse who kind of knows him. Ay, Maggie, you're not going to believe it.'

"But I believe it, Victoria, even before she says it. Because, you know, I get like a word of knowledge about things." Victoria nods in understanding, because even though she doesn't have my prophetic giftings, she can bust out in tongues without even trying.

"Sandra goes, 'Deja tú, Al's got to take care of their kid all by himself now that his wife is gone.'

"I ask, 'What'd she die of?' even though I know it don't matter because we all got to go anyways.

"She says Bobby didn't know when she talked to him."

Victoria had been getting bored, but now she got *all* interested all of a sudden.

"A couple more weeks pass and no Al. So I'm thinking, he's *got* to get his hair cut sometime, right?"

Victoria nods.

"Then he comes in one day. He still looks good, dressed all kicker, but his hair is all over the ears, casi todo Erik Estrada style, circa the *CHiPs* days. Anyways, I can tell the girls are trying not to stare and see how his face looks, but he's not looking at any of us.

"I skip the five other clients and their greñudo kids that are waiting. The mamas look at me like, *What's up with that?*

"I lie and say, 'He called in ahead of you.' Diosito forgive me, right?

"I sit him down and start the water.

"I say, 'Hi,' because I don't want to ask how he's doing. I mean, what do you say?

"He says, 'Hey,' back.

"So I talk to him about my weekend, thinking maybe it'll get his mind off things. But he's got this look on his face that I haven't seen on him before. And you *know* faces when you cut hair. You got to study them to know if they're liking their cut or not. Because most of them won't say anything until *after* you've cut their hair, and then what can you do, right? And if they don't say anything, they just give you a fake smile and no tip and don't come back.

"So, I rub the shampoo into his temples in circles."

Victoria's got this look on her face like she's thinking I should've witnessed to him about Jesus, like I should have laid out the blood-of-Jesus talk right there and then.

"Ya, ya, Victoria, I'm getting to that. By this time, I start telling him about Living Waters. About the nice people here. Then he's got that face again with the wrinkled forehead like he wants me to stop talking for some reason.

"I go quiet and massage his forehead and wash his hair twice like always. Except this time I'm not working it for a fat tip and I really want to give him something nice. We don't say anything at all the whole time I cut his hair. No más clip, clip, y clip and brush the hairs off so they don't pica under the shirt. And put the talco on his neck afterwards.

"Then, Victoria, I get this word of knowledge about why he don't want me to say anything and why he's got his eyes closed the whole time.

"Get this.

"I'm thinking, because my hands are like hers, he's spending time with his wife in his head, or he's saying goodbye or something like that, and he just needs me to be quiet. As I see a tear rolling down the side of his face, I know he just needs me to rub his temples and be quiet and I try to make love shoot through my fingers into his brain and into his heart." I feel like telling her more about this, but I can see she's not going for it. Victoria looks all disappointed, like she wants me to say that he accepted Jesus in his heart right there in the chair or that me and him ended all happy ever after, that I won't be the only unmarried Izquierdo daughter anymore. Like she wants the *Guideposts* version.

Or something.

Victoria says, "That's great," with a fuchi face, looking like a disgusted client whose cut is three inches shorter than she'd wanted, like I gave her bangs without asking or something.

I don't say anything, and touch her hand with all the shiny

silver rings that's resting on her Bible. I want to tell Victoria how my father taught me that sometimes a haircut is more than a haircut, that it can give someone hope and dignity. I want her to know about how it all starts with this, love coming from our heart and shooting through our fingertips just like my father taught me, but I can see she's just not ready to hear it.

Maggie Magic Fingers

When I see this man come into my salon, I know something is off about him, like he's not so típico. Forgive me, Diosito, but it's like he's a little *different* in the head, maybe a little atormentado with the way he's looking around the salon. He walks into Short Cuts and signs his name in big broad letters: TEDDY. I think, *Válgame wow, those are big letters, Teddy, like you took up two spaces just to write your name.* He sits down and his eyes go big at the two men drinking a free beer and the sign that says: FREE BEER AND SOFT DRINKS. The other clients, they pull their kids in closer as if he is the Cucuy coming for them. I'm thinking, *Whatever, ladies, right, get over it, por favor. Why would the boogeyman want your feote kids?* And then it hits me, this is Teddy Ramírez from the old neighborhood, the kid whose hair my father and I used to cut on Saturdays. I think to tell him who I am, that I was his neighbor and my father's barber assistant, see if he remembers me, but I can see it's tough for him just being here. If I ask if he remembers me, it will be too much for him and he'll run away. Maybe it's a true word of knowledge, or just knowing what I know about him, but I get a sense in my spirit that Teddy needs to be here in the present right now and I just need to be his stylist. Besides, it's tough for me too, just thinking about my father and all he's gone through over the years.

I have two other people in front of him, who've been waiting there for a while. And like I've done before in special situations, I let Teddy go before them. These ladies look at me all ugly, but when they get a better look at Teddy, when they hear his flip-flops smacking across the floor, they understand. I look at them like, *Ni modo, ladies, what can I do?* Poor ladies like these, they only see the outside; they don't got the spiritual vision to go deeper. But me, sometimes I can see *inside* a person. Like as soon as Teddy came in, I knew something was up with him, even if I didn't recognize him right away. Es como un prophetic word of knowledge like the pastor is always talking about, saying we got the power of life and death in our tongues. I don't know about that. Thunders never came from my mouth and killed anybody or brought anybody back to life. But, nobody really knows, right? All I know is right now that sign promising cold beer in the mini-fridge is like a little dwarf demon to him. What he really wants to do is open that refrigerator and drink *all* the beer. Diosito forgive me for encouraging an alcoholic, because the free beer and sodas was my idea to bring in more clientes.

I go, "Teddy?"

He looks at me relieved, like he's being delivered from the drink.

I go, "Teddy, are you ready for your haircut now?"

When he's in my chair, I run my fingers through his greña.

I feel something else coming off Teddy, though, not just the everyday loneliness I get from some clients. I feel like some terrible thing had happened or is about to happen in his life. I know his mother Josefina (que con Dios descanse) passed away, and maybe that's it, or maybe not. These spiritual perceptions, sometimes they're not too specific.

Now that he's in my chair, I smell him. Teddy smells like newspaper ink and sweat and tiredness, you know, that smell that workingmen get. A man odor, not like a baby at all. The reason I'm thinking of Teddy as man-baby is because of how I saw him move and talk and look at everyone when he walked in. Pobre hombre looked afraid of the world, like kids do, those ones who've been hit and yelled at their whole lives. He was looking sideways at everything as if he saw things none of us could see, like those scary shadows you see on the corners of your vision when you're small, like La Llorona or La Mano Peluda coming to take you away because you disobeyed your parents.

None of us are perfect.

Por ejemplo, take me. I know I'm a little chubby, that people look at me and think, *How did you let yourself get like that?* When they do this, I send them thought messages, my eyes open wide, all Walter Mercado–style, as if I had psychic mind powers or something. I tell them we're all under this big, ugly, stinky blanket of not being perfect and none of us can get out to the place of beauty until Jesús comes to pull us out. I look over at all those single men drinking their free Miller Lite, the mothers and their kids waiting for haircuts, and I tell them with my mind that God's power is made perfect through our weakness, through me being llenita and Teddy being filled with fear. So there. I never say anything out loud. Because, really, in this world, we got enough problems. ¿Qué no? Besides, I'm a little shy sometimes when it comes to the things of God.

"So how can I help you today?" I ask Teddy.

"I would like a haircut," he says in this deep voice that sounds all practiced, and he just doesn't get it. Po'recito.

I go, "I can do that," and decide not to worry about the specifics.

So I take some big-time liberties with his hair. I shorten up the ears and straighten the bangs, which look all crooked as if he's done them himself. It's like when my sister's kid, Michely, chopped off all her hair because she thought it would make her look like Mariah Carey. Pobre huerquita, she looked like one of those orphans they put on TV, those ones they show to give you this big old guilt trip so you'll "adopt" a child and give them money, which I always do. My fridge looks like a missing-kid bulletin board from the post office. Mis babies.

When I'm done, I ask him to take a look. Teddy holds the handheld mirror, but he's not quite sure how to hold it to see the back of his head. He keeps turning his head in all these crazy ways.

"Let me help you," I say, *bien* gentle, like a lady, and take it from him. "*There*, now you can see."

He smiles at me, and a little of that kid he was back in the day comes through his expression. Teddy's turned out to be a nice-looking man, especially with one of my fresh fades. He has a kind round face with a nice mustache that he takes care of.

We get up to go pay.

Teddy hands me his money, and I give him his change. He takes all the money and stuffs it back into his wallet all wrinkled. I don't think he knows about a tip. He doesn't look me in the eyes when he says, "Thank you." Sometimes, in special cases like

Teddy's, a thank-you is enough, and I don't need a tip, especially since we grew up next to each other.

As he's walking away, I see him looking at the dudes sipping their beers. Then, like a whisper, I get another word about Teddy. All of a sudden, I know what he's going to do as soon as he walks out of here. He's going across the street to the Economy to buy a twelve-pack of cheves, except my spiritual perceptions tell me he doesn't want to.

I call him, I go, "Hey, Teddy."

He turns around and he's like, "Yes?"

I go, "I almost forgot to give you your shampoo," thinking, what a coincidence; I forgot for real.

"Oh," Teddy says, and I can't tell if he's relieved or what.

I get his head in the bowl and his eyes are closed. I do my thing, running my fingers through the water, making sure it's exactly the comfortable temperature. Teddy's eyes are shut so tight it looks like he's about to go in his pants or something. Po'recito.

"It's okay, Teddy, I'll try real hard not to get any in your eyes."

He loosens up just a little.

I go, "How's that? Is that okay?"

He gives me this short little nod as if he's afraid that by moving his head any, he'll get water in his brain through his nose. Since he's so afraid of the water, I forget about the tea tree shampoo, the one that makes your head tingle. Because, really, what's Teddy going to think if he walks out of here and his head's still cool and tingly? He'll think the air's going into his skin and he'll get sick or something. That's the last thing he needs.

Instead, I use the apricot shampoo. I rub it in my palms,

doing the sexy dance with my hands even though he can't see it. I mean, you got to do your art, right? People can't call me Maggie Magic Fingers and then see me slacking off on the job. I got a reputation. Any real cosmetologist will tell you what we do is art.

Anyways, I rub it in real good like I do when I'm working it for a tip. Sometimes when I'm doing a wash, I see a man's forehead flatten out from losing all his worries. For the few minutes they're under my hands, these men become like little babies, falling asleep or making happy sounds in their throats. Teddy's no different.

I do the shampoo twice like always, and then run the water through his thick, wavy hair and cover his eyes with my hand, just like I did when I was a kid and would help my father cut Teddy's hair on Saturdays. As I'm doing this, my mouth fills with exactly the right words, words I would never say in normal situations.

"Estás perdonado, estás limpio, en el nombre del Padre, del Hijo, y del Espíritu Santo," I say, blessing him, sounding like some woman I've never been.

The water washes away down the drain, and I'm not kidding, the water's black. If it's from the newspaper ink he smells like, or some things he's let go of, I can't say. Either way, it's bad news being washed down the drain, away from him forever. He opens his eyes as I begin to towel him off, massaging his temples.

When Teddy gets up, he tells me thank you again, and he walks away with that same way of walking, as if he's going to step on broken glass if he doesn't watch it. But when I look at his face in the mirrors on the left and right, I see his smile multiplied so many times I can't even count. I know that when he walks out into the sunlight, Teddy is going to get in his car and go somewhere besides the place that would've taken him back to the darkness where he didn't want to go. Teddy has come out from under that blanket of ugliness, out to that place of beauty and perfection I found a long time ago.

Part 4

Padres, Hijas

1990

As Papa Tavo and Abuelita's fortieth wedding anniversary approached, they were clear with the family that neither of them wanted the expense, fanfare, and extravagance of an anniversary party. Their children's arguments for a party were simple: Papa Tavo and Abuelita had worked hard to start the painting and drywall business, the children, all of whom were grown and married, would pay for it themselves as a thank-you, and it was time for Papa Tavo and Abuelita's sacrifices to finally start being recognized. God had been good to them.

When their eldest sons had presented the idea of renting a salón with a full Mexican dinner catered by Casa Don Eusebio, Papa Tavo had made his position known, saying, "Somos sencillos," a simple family that did not partake in such extravagances as a dance hall.

So instead of renting at any of the event centers across the Valley, the family decided to celebrate Papa Tavo and Abuelita's anniversary at the house. They also decided to provide the food

*themselves as a family, turning down the offer from Eusebio,
Dina's husband, to cater from his restaurant.*

*On the day of the party, cars, vans, and pickups lined Aurora
Street all the way down to Twenty-Third and some were even in
the parking lot at St. Joseph the Worker Church.*

*There was a bottleneck to greet Papa Tavo and Abuelita,
who were sitting under the carport in front of the door to the
extra casita they had built to first house all of Papa Tavo's
painting and drywall supplies, then to accommodate the children when they were growing up. They sat under multicolored
banners of papel picado in wrought-iron rockers that Lalo had
welded and painted white for the occasion. Papa Tavo was in his
best cream-colored guayabera, a new Stetson on his head, which
he'd received as an anniversary present. Abuelita wore a matching colored huipil Marisol had bought for her with tiny embroidered flowers sewn into the open collar and sleeves, which were
gathered on her arms in the traditional way.*

*The greeting line was long as the daughters and sons, grand-
children, cousins, friends, neighbors, and even the cousins from
Arteaga, Coahuila, came to pay their respects.*

*Papa Tavo and Abuelita took their time talking to each fam-
ily member and friend, first asking about the babies, then asking about their trip over, and directing them inside or to the
barbecue pit for a plate of food. True to their word, the children
had pitched in to complete the cena. Gonzalo and his brothers
bought the meat: fajitas and costillas, even mollejas for Lalo
and Wally, who loved these the best. For the children, there were
hot dogs and hamburgers. Marisol and her sisters had cooked
large pans of steaming rice and pots of charro beans, and Victoria brought her handmade tortillas. Suzana and Artemio had*

brought the cake from De Alba's Bakery and Maggie had provided the drinks, Topo Chicos and bottles of Joya sodas. Everyone brought beer, of course.

All day, as Papa Tavo and Abuelita greeted their guests and were served platos of food and cold drinks, and the music played from the standing speakers that Artemio had set up, they wondered when Dina and Eusebio and their three girls would arrive. When their son-in-law Eusebio had heard that they'd turned down his offer to cater the event, along with false rumors that Papa Tavo had mocked him for giving himself such a highminded title as Don, he had taken offense, and since then had refused to bring Dina and the girls to any Izquierdo function. What Papa Tavo did not say with his words but instead communicated with his nervous patting of Abuelita's hand between their rocking chairs was the hope that his yerno Eusebio would get over his pride just this once and bring Dina and his nietas to see them.

Abuelita leaned over and whispered into his ear, "They will come, they will come, do not worry." And understanding passed between them. The truth was, it did not matter how many had come and from how far, for if just one family member was not present, they were incomplete, diminished as a family.

As the sun went down late that summer day, the chicharras started their songs in the mesquite trees, and everyone settled in. Papa Tavo and Abuelita accepted that this would be the way of it; the girls were not coming. Just as they started to enjoy the party for what it was, they sensed a commotion out by the street. Something in Papa Tavo's heart moved as he hoped it would be Dina and the girls. For the first time in his life, he was disappointed to see mariachis. They stepped out of a van *in front of the gate, adjusted their maroon charro suits, shifted their trumpets, guitars, and violins. Papa Tavo saw that they had even brought a harp. If his children were going to this length for them, Papa Tavo was glad at least that Gonzalo had hired Voces de Saltillo, the best and most experienced group in McAllen. However, he didn't even want to think about the expense.*

And as he watched them, Papa Tavo felt Abuelita's hand on his arm.

"Tavo," she said. "Look."

Behind the mariachis, he saw Eusebio, and then Dina, Teresa, Dianira, and Yesenia hugging their cousins and tías and tíos.

"Mis hijas," Papa Tavo said, and sprang out of the rocking chair. Abuelita leaned forward to make sure he was okay, while Marisol and Maggie, who had been standing nearby, also reached out to steady him.

"Mis hijas," he said again, because no other words would come from his mouth. Dina and the girls came to him. Dina held her arms out wide, tilting and lowering her head in apology.

"Do not worry, mis hijas. What matters is that you came. Late or early, you are here, and that is the only thing that matters to me." He gathered them into his embrace. One arm he put around his daughter and the other around his granddaughters Teresa, Yesenia, and Dianira, chiquitas that they were.

Ascensión

On the night of his daughter Teresa's quinceañera, follow-ing the traditional order of events and the dinner, Eusebio Torres made the rounds among the tables of family and friends, checking in with them just like he did with guests at his restau-rants on a busy Friday night. As he moved among them, he felt his familiar confidence and displayed the singular hospitality he was renowned for at Casas Don Eusebio, #1 and #2. Except here at the Villa Real Special Events Center, he was paying for the cena, the soft drink setups, the bottles of Bacardí, Presi-dente, Crown Royal, and even the disposable FunSaver cam-eras that were at each table. All of this for the three hundred invited guests, uninvited guests of guests, and a handful of men-digos that had shown up to the wrong event center, the wrong quinceañera entirely.

He paused at his sisters-in-law Maggie and Victoria's table, and noted that despite his cuñadas being hallelujah holy rollers, they had managed to polish off a quarter of their bottle of Crown Royal, and opened more than a few of their cans of Coke.

He leaned forward, gave them a knowing look, and said, "Are you enjoying yourselves, ladies?"

Maggie held up her red cup and replied in an affected high-society voice, "You throw the finest soirees, cuñado. And nice haircut too. Believe me, I'm a professional."

Victoria nodded at him, approving of the party. Then she motioned her hand like a game show hostess in obvious apprecia-tion of his fancy tuxedo and shiny patent-leather shoes. "Iralo, you clean up nice, Eusebio. And thank you for giving my Gon-zalo the honor of being the MC. I know he appreciated the ges-ture, cuñado." Eusebio brought a hand to his cummerbund in a show of magnanimous humility, all the while knowing that the cumulative effect of his haircut, Halston Z-14 cologne, open bar with setups, chicken cordon bleu dinner catered by Casa Don Eusebio #1, the decorations and centerpieces, and full quincea-ñera court of fourteen pairs of damas and chambelanes exuded the relative wealth he possessed. Because he loved his daughter, he wanted to give Teresa the quinceañera to remember, one that would elevate her status among her friends and cousins. And it wouldn't hurt that the Izquierdos would finally recognize and appreciate everything he did for his wife Dina and their three girls, Teresa, Dianira, and Yesenia. Despite the Izquierdos' dis-regard for him (evidenced by how they never frequented his res-taurants) and his brother-in-law Braulio's sangre pesada, they would finally have to admit what kind of man he was.

As he continued circulating among his guests, doing his best to balance his time between the Torreses and the Izquierdos—not staying too long at any one table so he would not have to answer any questions about where his wife Dina was—he made his way closer to his brother-in-law Braulio's table. Everything in Eusebio recoiled at the thought of having to pay respects to him, but he knew it had to be done because they would call him sangrón if he bypassed even just one table, especially Braulio's. Since the borlote where Braulio and Eusebio had quit talking to each other for a time, he knew they were paying close attention to any exchange between them.

"Buenas," Eusebio said to Braulio, "I'm glad you could make it."

Braulio's handshake was firm, which Eusebio regretted not remembering in time, as matching his cuñado's grip now would seem like a feeble attempt at proving himself.

"Glad to be here to celebrate Teresa and your beautiful daughters. You're a blessed man, compadre." And the way Braulio threw this word *compadre* at him, it made Eusebio want to remind him and all of the Izquierdos that there had been no padrinos or madrinas. No one else besides Eusebio had paid for the dress, photos, cake, the corona, the regalos, DJ, live band, or cena. None of them had even offered to help him with the cost of renting out the Villa Real, the largest event center in McAllen. Therefore, they had not earned the right to call themselves padrinos or madrinas, and certainly not the right to call him compadre, if they were using the word in its most literal sense.

As they shook hands—and just as Eusebio thought Braulio should have withdrawn—Braulio squeezed his palm tighter, and put his other hand on Eusebio's shoulder. He opened his mouth as if he were about to speak, and Eusebio wondered if he meant to bring up the bronca between them, as if this were the time or the place to drag up the past.

When Eusebio had proposed to Dina, he thought he knew what would be involved when he married into the Izquierdo family. He knew how proud they were of their family construction business, but also their superstitious ways. However, he had no way of knowing that their pride and superstition would converge to create an unstoppable grudge between Eusebio, Braulio, and the rest of the family. Years before, just as he had expanded to the mid-Valley by opening Casa Don Eusebio #3 in Weslaco and was starting to turn a profit, a sign had been erected across the street from his restaurant: COMING SOON JALAPEÑO JUAN'S. And as the rival restaurant started to go up, and it was time to finish the interior, he saw one of the Izquierdo and Sons vans parked in front. When Eusebio saw Braulio in the parking lot, he found himself leaving the restaurant in the middle of the lunch rush to run across five lanes of traffic to confront him. He asked Braulio just what it was he thought he was doing, and his response had been, "Lo siento, cuñado. It's a big commercial contract I couldn't turn down. You know how business is. The family needs this right now." It was how Braulio had said it, dismissing the outrage, not even stopping to face Eusebio directly or address him properly as a man. Instead, Braulio kept going about his business, walking to the back of the van to help his workers unload panels of drywall. He only said sorry one more time and then went inside the building, leaving Eusebio standing alone in the parking lot, like some vagrant asking for pocket change whom Braulio had turned away.

Eusebio should not have been surprised by how Braulio dismissed him that day, as Braulio had always shown this kind of disregard for him. And when Eusebio did have to eventually close down Casa Don Eusebio #3 because of pinche Jalapeño Juan stealing his business, Braulio's failure to acknowledge his part in it or apologize fully confirmed what kind of man he was. Compounding the ill will between Eusebio and Braulio, and the Izquierdos by extension, was Dina's self-imposed seclusion. Eusebio believed they blamed this on him, when it was the Izquierdo superstitions that had caused his wife to hide herself away.

Braulio said, "Compadre, there's something I've been wanting to tell you—" but was interrupted as Gonzalo walked up to the stage to make an announcement. Both men ended their saludo and the conversation Braulio was about to start with a mutual, brusque pat on the shoulder.

Begrudgingly, but out of respect for the formality of Gonzalo's announcement, Eusebio sat down next to Braulio. They watched Gonzalo as he led Teresa up the steps to the stage while she held her dress so she would not trip on it.

"Tu hijita, compadre," Braulio said, and Eusebio nodded and smiled, taking pride in her radiance. Teresa was hermosa, as hermosa as Dina had been on their wedding day. She had the clear skin and lustrous auburn hair of the Torres women and the fullness of body that the Izquierdo women were known for. Her curly hair was piled high, and the makeup she wore made her look glamorous, older than her fifteen years, a visage of how she would look on her own wedding day.

As Gonzalo and Teresa got into place side by side on the stage, he said, "Damas y caballeros, ladies and gentlemen, the birthday girl, our querida quinceañera Teresa, would like to say a few words. So, please, let's have everyone listen to what she has to say." Eusebio thought it was a typical Izquierdo move, the way Gonzalo made his voice deep to put all of the attention on him. However, he had to admit his cuñado was pretty good. The dance hall was silent and they were all focused on him.

Teresa leaned forward to speak into the microphone and

Gonzalo adjusted it to her height. She looked tiny up there with him and all of the band equipment.

"Okay," she said, her voice tremulous. Eusebio thought, *Breathe, mija, breathe.* "Okay, first off, I want to thank my beautiful sisters Dianira and Yesenia, who are damas here and in life. And to all my damas and chambelanes for supporting me tonight. But most especially, I really, really would like to thank my father for throwing me such a wonderful quince. None of this would have been possible without his hard work." She looked for Eusebio in the audience. Everyone clapped and whistled, and craned their necks to find Eusebio. Braulio raised his hand and pointed down at Eusebio so everyone could see where he was. Eusebio did a half stand and waved his hand to them all.

When their applause died down, a little sooner than Eusebio wanted, she spoke again. "I wish my mother could be here, but she's at home tonight." A quiet fell over the room. Eusebio felt his forehead go cold. Why did Teresa have to mention her mother?

Dina was at home, which she had refused to leave in recent months—absent from the most important event of their daughter's young life—because of a nightmare, which she had called prophetic. In Dina's pesadilla, she had seen her former neighbor, Emiliano Contreras, partnered with the devil himself to dispatch grackle birds from all over the Valley to give her the evil eye and sing curses against her and the Izquierdos. Eusebio didn't believe in brujería and thought his wife's fears of leaving the house were irrational and typical of an Izquierdo and their foolish superstitions. Maybe Contreras was jealous because he had stayed a pobre while Octavio Izquierdo had become a moderately successful businessman, but the idea of him having the power to use the black birds against her was ridiculous. The terrible thing was that Dina was dragging their daughters down with her. She told them stories about the saints and spurred them on to pursue their own religious experiences when they should have been allowed to just be kids. As far as Eusebio was concerned, Dina had become a nun, but without the habit and the orthopedic shoes, secluding herself away in the big house Eusebio had given her. She was not the example he wanted them to follow. Eusebio only wanted them to live like normal teen girls, going out to bailes and parties and La Plaza Mall on Saturdays, spending the money he gladly earned for them. Eusebio had thought a fancy quinceañera would be a good way to jump-start a normal teenage life for his girls, that once word got out about the lavish party, his daughters would be elevated in the social circles of their respective schools and they would focus on being popular rather than on their mother's stories about saints and visions, curses and brujos.

Teresa was still going on about her mother. She said, "Mama sends her saludos and she says she's okay, that she spends her days praying for you all and reading the Psalms. She says if you all could pray for her too. She's just going through some things right now. Anyways, the reason I'm up here is because I have an announcement to say." Eusebio heard himself swallow.

"What I would like to say is that I was thinking about this dress I'm wearing and how pretty it is and how it looks like a wedding dress. Today, my fifteenth birthday, marks me becoming a young woman.

"But this dress and my quince are also important in another way. This party here tonight is like a marriage feast. Tonight, my family, I make a proclamation of faith. I am the bride of Jesus. I am up here, and I would like to say that I will always be His bride, and I don't know what the future holds, but I do know that. That's all. I just wanted to say that." She said this last part unapologetically looking straight into Eusebio's eyes, and everyone knew it. There was only a smattering of applause, because, like him, the family wasn't quite sure what she actually meant. Was she seeking the life of a nun? Vowing to never marry and become an old maid for Jesus? What was clear to Eusebio, however, was that whether she would be a nun or a solterona, she was following in her mother's footsteps, adopting the religious ways of the Izquierdos.

Eusebio sensed their gazes flitting between him and Teresa, gauging his reaction to her pronouncement. Now that they were full-on staring at his pinched smile, presumably thinking what a poor, dumb pendejo he was because he had lost his wife and now his daughter to religion, Eusebio tried to smile more naturally, but found his face would not move, as if his cheeks were made of lead. It was an unfamiliar feeling for him. Even on his worst days when he was simultaneously mingling with customers at his restaurants and thinking about Dina and the tragic turn their lives had taken, he had always managed to smile naturally and radiate an aura of confidence.

His limbs had gone cold and numb. Eusebio managed to bring his hands up to rub his fingertips across the stubble of his cheeks, but neither his fingers nor his face had any feeling in them. His legs were heavy too, and he felt his feet swell in the shiny rented shoes. And without welcoming the thought, it occurred to him that perhaps he was sangre pesada too, weighed down by his prideful heavy blood like Braulio.

He mustered enough strength to stand up, but because his legs and arms felt so heavy, he knocked over the metal fold-ing chair he was sitting in. This would have been enough of an embarrassment, but there was more to come. It seemed like there was always more. He walked sideways toward the stage, squeezing between the chairs, pushing himself forward. Eusebio did not know what he would say if he ever made it up to the stage, but he knew he had to say something, do something. Just as he was about to step onto the dance floor, his foot got caught on a chair leg and he went down hard, his glasses skittering across the floor. All their eyes were on him, so no one noticed at first that Teresa was slowly rising into the air, almost imperceptibly, but rising higher nevertheless.

It was then that Braulio reached down to help him. Eusebio shook him away because he was convinced he had intentionally put the chair in his path, trying to tear him down like a crab in the bucket, the same way he had by supporting his competitor's restaurant. Eusebio was going to stand on his own as always and he didn't need Braulio to help him, just as he hadn't needed padrinos for the quinceañera. One limb at a time, he managed to pick himself up. He then looked around the room, and though everyone appeared to be underwater, all blurred together in one mass, and he could not see one face distinctly, he felt their eyes on him.

Then, in the completely silent dance hall, he heard Maggie say, "¡Mira! Look at Teresa! Válgame, wow!"

They all turned their eyes toward the stage and Teresa.

Eusebio, because he was afraid of what he would see, refused to look at Teresa right away. He picked up his glasses and put them on and instead looked to see the reactions of the family and friends. Eusebio saw his suegra, Valentina, their beloved Abuelita, crossing herself at what she witnessed, with the others around her doing the same, their hands a flurry of movement, bracelets and watches glinting with gold. Teresa's quinceañera court, the damas in their powder-blue dresses and the chambelanes in their matching tuxedos who had been waiting on the edge of the dance floor to start dancing again, now moved as one across the floor toward her and the stage. The family's children followed behind the court and pointed at Teresa, all of them with openmouthed disbelief. Other than Victoria, who remained seated, her eyes upturned toward the ceiling, her mouth moving in prayer, the Izquierdos and Torreses got out of their chairs to move closer to the stage, still not able to believe what they were seeing, hoping to confirm by getting closer to her. Small flashes from the FunSavers went off, and Eusebio heard their clicking plastic wheels quickly turning as everyone tried to get as many pictures of her as they could.

Gonzalo stepped aside for all of them to see and to get a better vantage for himself. Por fin, the celebrants were no longer looking at Eusebio, either in respect or in ridicule. They stood blinking with awe at what was transpiring before them. When at last Eusebio mustered the courage to look up at Teresa too, he could see that her dress was no longer touching the floor; it levitated a few inches off of the stage. Teresa continued her slow rise, and the high heels she had received in the ceremony signifying her transition into womanhood dropped away. Teresa's eyes were fixed on a space above their heads, her expression not one of surprise or fear, but of a girl who has recognized her beloved across a crowded room.

In the days to come, the family would forget the lengths Eusebio had gone to, to make this a beautiful quinceañera, and would only remember his daughter's rise, but this didn't matter now. He shared in their collective wonder, and the pressure to impress, the burden of convincing them of his worth, and his embarrassment at falling in front of them, were all meaningless in the presence of this miracle. There was only Teresa now, his wondrous glittering Teresa.

Braulio placed a hand on Eusebio's shoulder and quietly said, "Tu hijita, compadre." He flinched and leaned away as the past tried to reassert itself, but Braulio kept his hand there. Absent in his touch was any implicit challenge, the proving of one man against another. There was only a conciliation of wrongs that needed mending brought on by Teresa before them, and the foolishness of their grudge was now laid bare. They clasped each other's shoulders and, not clearing his throat or trying to hide the quiver in his voice, Eusebio said, "Ay, pues sí, pues sí, compadre." Though this was no sacrament they were sharing in, Braulio was a padrino of this observance of grace, and Eusebio felt right calling him compadre at last. They stood there among the Izquierdos and Torreses, the guests of guests, and mendigos, beholding Teresa's floating beauty and the lengthening space between her feet and the stage. Together, they tracked her rise, measuring the ingravidez of her body against the weight of their own.

The Virgin Dianira

With the way they didn't linger at stop signs and looked around to see if they saw anyone they knew, Dianira knew the boys in the front seat of the Impala were embarrassed to be seen with her. It was not because she was that much younger than her cousin Cirilo or his friend Aaron. They were seventeen and she was thirteen, but she knew she looked much older than she was. It was not because she was ugly. Dianira had skin with no blemishes at all, just like her sisters Teresa and Yesenia. She was proud of that, the fact that she had a smooth, clear face. It was not that she had messy hair either. Dianira kept her brown-auburn hair long even though it was curly, especially because it was curly. If she left it alone, it would frizz, and then forget it. Not that curly was bad, but with hair at her current length, it would look like she was wearing a helmet. If she was going to have it curly, she liked it long so everyone would say she looked like a queen. When she took care of her hair, the compliments on its fullness and how it sometimes looked like it glowed when the sun hit it a certain way never stopped.

No, the boys up front were embarrassed because they had a life-sized version of the Virgin Mary in the backseat; Dianira was dressed in the costume of the Queen of the Universe. Because it was Christmas Eve, Dianira thought being dressed like this was appropriate. Besides, Cirilo drove a lowrider and dressed cholo-style, and so many of their shirts, necklaces, trunks, and hoods had her image on them, the brown Virgen María, her palms open, the moon beneath her airbrushed feet. Cirilo and Aaron should have been proud even though Dianira was not *really* the Virgin Mary or the Virgin of Guadalupe or any other manifestation of Santa María. She was just a virgin of the normal kind who played the role of La Virgen year after year when Christmastime came around and her mom's side of the family had the Posada plays in the Zavala.

Dianira was wearing the costume she and her mother Dina had made. They had gone to the fabric store in downtown Pharr and out of two colors, baby blue and white, they had made a dress and robe that would have made the real Virgen proud. Dianira had sewn wavy gold trim onto the robe, and dropped gold glitter to make the stars. This was before her mother had become too afraid of life, too afraid of the zanate birds who she believed could give her ojo, could utter curses against her on behalf of Papa Tavo and Abuelita's jealous brujo neighbor.

At the next stoplight, Cirilo and Aaron swiveled their heads around again, hoping and hoping they would not see anyone they knew.

Dianira said, "I thought you were real Mexicans. Y'all are acting like you're expecting a drive-by."

Both of them turned around and said, "*What?*" As soon as she said it, she regretted it because of what had happened to Cirilo, the shooting he had been involved in before. That was the most stupid thing to say, because as the words sank in, she saw Cirilo's face in the rearview mirror, thinking about the friend he had lost, the whole crowd he no longer ran with from his previous school.

She went on anyway, but took a different approach, a challenging one she knew her cousin Cirilo would appreciate. "If you were real Mexicans you'd be proud to have a life-sized version of the Virgin Mary in the car with you. I mean, come on, it's like a dream come true. Especially you, Cirilo. You're like an OG driving around in this bomba."

Aaron turned his head to look at Dianira and said, "Whatever," but did not turn back to face the front. Though she kept her eyes on his, he looked at the length of her, not caring that she knew. He was stupid to be looking at her like that with Cirilo right next to him. Aaron was looking because Dianira had outgrown the white dress, and the baby-blue robe with the glitter-drop stars did not close like it was supposed to, like it had when she began wearing it in sixth grade. Dianira was showing a little leg too. She did not mind that he was looking at her, for two reasons. One, because Aaron was one of those pretty morenos who knew it, a senior with deep brown skin and white teeth and the blackest hair. The other one was that he had secretly been writing letters to her. She had first met Aaron months before, on a ride like this one when he was up front with Cirilo. He found her number by looking in the phone book, but never called her after the first time.

The first time he had called, Dianira's mother had answered. In that high-pitched voice of hers she had said, "Hijo del Diablo, you have no business calling us here." She hung up on him. Dianira had called *him*, though, thankful for star 69. With the way Cirilo was so protective, staring down any older malcriado who even looked at her, Dianira would never have asked Cirilo for Aaron's number. She called him, gave him her address, and said it was better this way. She liked the idea of getting letters in the mail, like some of her friends who got letters from boys who were in juvie. Besides, her mother never went outside anymore, and Dianira was the one to get the mail, so she was all good there.

So, this was when the letters began. Aaron wrote in pretty script, and he said wonderful things. He said how he knew there was something special about Dianira, that he had never met someone like her. He called her Santa Dianira, a girl too pure and beautiful for this world. He also drew on the envelopes and letters. He made thorny roses and in one picture he drew two laughing gangster-looking theater masks, instead of one laughing and the other crying like usual. At the bottom it said, *Always Laugh.* In another picture, he drew a bleeding heart wrapped in a purple ribbon. The ribbon stopped the flow of blood, and on it Dianira's name was written in Old English script. Below the picture was this: *You are the only girl who can heal my hurt.* He had written six letters to her, each one more perfect than the last, revealing more and more of his love and his need for them to be together. Each time, Dianira wrote back that they had to keep everything a secret because her mother and father were very protective, and something bad might happen because of their growing love. If her mother found out, forget it. She would lose it altogether.

She memorized each word of Aaron's letters like she had memorized the prayers of the Rosary, the Magnificat, and the songs of the Posadas, the stories of the Holy Family's search for shelter. She was Abuelita's only grandchild who could do this, memorize all the adult prayers, even before she could read. When she *did* learn to read, Dianira read the accounts of the Christmas story in the gospel of San Lucas in English and Spanish. Her hungry mind was not satisfied by these few verses so short in details. To find out more about the Virgin, she researched what she could at the McAllen Public Library. It was there she learned the Virgin's other names: her original Hebrew name, Miryam, Our Lady of Lourdes, Our Lady of Fatima, the Virgin of Guadalupe, and even the syncretic names of Coatlaxopeuh and Tonantzin. She knew the story about when La Virgen came to visit San Juan Diego and miraculously appeared on his cloak. Dianira knew this story best, but she knew the other stories too. She could rattle off dates, names of European towns where Mary's icons had wept, the life stories of children who had received visions of Mary and how their lives had changed afterward. She read their stories and was often jealous because La Virgen de Guadalupe had not appeared to *her* or changed *her* life at all, even though she had been faithful to her for all these years.

What Dianira wanted most out of life, but had only told her sisters and her mother, was for the Virgin Mary to manifest herself, give her some visible sign of her love. Even with all the beautiful things Aaron wrote and how much she was falling in love with him, this was always first in her mind. Dianira could take or leave his love, but if the Virgen never showed herself to her, she did not know what she would do, and this fear grew each passing year, especially now that this would probably be her last time playing La Virgen in the neighborhood Posada play.

Cirilo turned his head toward Aaron, and this was enough for him. Aaron turned his eyes away from Dianira and faced the road again. He wasn't *that* stupid, after all. Cirilo was her cousin, her protector, and the blood of her blood. Because she was his baby cousin and too young for Aaron in his mind, he would throw down on Aaron if he ever found out. For good or bad, he would always be there, strong and caring. He would not fail her like everyone else had. Her mother Dina and his father Braulio were brother and sister, but thank God, Cirilo had not inherited any of the Izquierdo nervios or their blood that was prone to anxiety, depression, or other mental maladies. Cirilo was strong emotionally, but he also knew how to box, so he was also strong physically. One time, when they had gone to the dollar movies at El Centro Mall, some loco had called her a nalgona. Cirilo didn't say anything, didn't give the vato any sign he was going to throw down on him. He just walked over and popped him in the nose and the loco went down like a montón of candy falling out of a piñata, and that was it. None of the loco's friends were around to pick him up or to fight with. In other words, Cirilo was a chingón.

Dianira leaned forward and touched the top of Cirilo's head now, and said, "La Virgen de Guadalupe blesses you."

"Gracias, Reina, put in a good word with God for me."

She rubbed her fingers together, and they were greasy with Tres Flores Brilliantine. She loved the smell. To her, it was the smell of the Mexican man, strong, proud, and suavecito.

They pulled up to Abuelita's house and none of the cars that would fill up the street were there yet. On Noche Buena, even Papa Tavo's cousins from Arteaga and Reynosa would show up. But it was early and the sun was barely going down.

When they walked in, Abuelita gave her saludos to her two grandchildren, and a polite, pleasant saludo to Aaron, whom she had only seen a few times. She hugged them, and even though

Cirilo was a man with his own car and a job and had seen the things he had seen, he blushed like a child when Abuelita pinched his cheeks and in Spanish said, "Look, my Cirilo is here."

Abuelita looked up and down at Dianira and her eyes got big. And even though she had seen Dianira every week in the past year, her eyes seemed to say, *A year has changed you.* Abuelita tried to pull the robe around Dianira more, but there was no give, not enough fabric for too much young woman. Dianira knew she was kidding herself thinking she was a full-grown woman, but she had to admit it felt kind of good to see what her body did to people.

"¿Y tus hermanas?" Abuelita said.

In Spanish, Dianira said, "They spent the day with tía Marisol in Reynosa, and they'll be here soon." Abuelita didn't ask about her mother Dina. Instead, she looked down and whispered a prayer that their mother would come back to the family again.

"¿Estás lista?" Abuelita said, a little unsure. It was the same way she sounded when she had found out that Dianira was spending so much time at the library with her sisters reading all those books about saints and the Virgin instead of being on the phone with boys or outside playing. "¿Está bien?" Abuelita had asked Eusebio, meaning, *Is she turning out like her mother?* Everyone said it was good that Dianira and her sisters were so interested in religion, but secretly, or not so secretly (because Dianira knew some of the things her family said about her), they were all afraid they would end up like Dina or Papa Tavo, especially after what had happened at Teresa's quinceañera. She could have a breakdown too if she didn't watch it, because the brujo's curse was on them all.

Dianira's mother Dina had suffered from the maldiciones in

her own way. She was agoraphobic (a word Dianira had learned at the library), hiding away inside the house from el Mal Ojo, which she claimed could be *anyone* or any*thing's* eye. No one outside of her sisters and her father had seen her mother since she started being afraid of the Evil Eye. Dianira knew what they all said: her mother only left the house to go to the weekly six a.m. Mass and to light candles at San Judas Church at midnight, and that she had lost at least a hundred pounds because she only ate the hostia. Truth was, her mother didn't even leave the house for religious purposes. Nothing could get her out, cloistered as she was, and though she had lost weight, they were exaggerating.

Dianira did not even want to think about this now. It was Christmas.

When Teresa and Yesenia got there with tío Lalo, tía Marisol, and the kids, she was glad they were finally going to start the play. Her cousin Seferino, with his big belly like tío Lalo's and his unhappy face, was a laughable Joseph.

Tía Marisol tried to straighten his costume, and he said, "Ay, Mother, please leave my shepherd hat alone."

Teresa and Yesenia, who babysat the kids together, or helped keep an eye on them whenever they accompanied the Buentellos to Reynosa, also tried to help.

He slapped at their hands and said, "Por favor, cousins, leave me alone." Seferino could be so exagerado sometimes. He looked like he wanted to say more, but tío Lalo gave him the eye, and he kept his thoughts to himself.

The shepherd's robe was high-water on him, brinca-charco-style, so Dianira had to say, "Sef, I think this is your last year as Joseph. Next year Little Gonzalo's going to have to do it."

He smiled at this, at the thought of Little Gonzalo wearing

the itchy sheet and carrying around the statue of the Baby Jesus instead of him.

They were walking down Aurora Street now. Last year, Dianira had to be careful not to step on the dress. But this year her chanclas with the leather straps did not catch on anything. It was hard to keep pace with Sef because he was so short, at least four inches shorter than her, and he went slower than all of the Posada players.

They made their pilgrims' way as they sang the Posada song "Santa María del Camino." It was dark and the luminarias were beautiful. They were just candles standing inside paper bags, but they lined the sidewalks and made Abuelita's neighborhood look better than it was, with all those rusty fences and over-grown lawns and patches of dry, ugly earth. Some of the younger families had chosen the store-bought "luminaries" that had light bulbs instead of candles and plastic covers instead of paper bags, and even these were beautiful to Dianira. The neighborhood kids and their parents all walked together in one group, and Dianira wished Cirilo had come, but he thought this part of Christmas was for little kids so he stayed behind at the house.

They got to the first house, where an old man and child blinked at them, acting surprised, playing the parts of innkeepers who would turn away the Holy Family.

The lines of the play, *Cantos Para Pedir Posada*, typed on blurry photocopied handouts that were copies of copies of copies, were simple. Everyone, whether outside with the Holy Travelers or inside with the heathens who would turn them away, got to sing them. Dianira did not need the handouts. Joseph, speaking through the singers, asked the old man and his son for lodging, saying that his pregnant wife could no longer walk. Seferino's lips were moving all wrong with no sound coming out, and Dianira was glad the play was all about group participation. It would be embarrassing otherwise. Abuelita was standing behind her singing with joy, but out of tune like she always did in church. It was funny how a woman who could pray so musically could sing so badly. She sang from her heart, though, and this was what mattered. Dianira's voice carried them all, and she had to wonder: If this was her last year as the Virgin, who would play her next year? Her sister Teresa had played the Virgin before her and was now fifteen, even older than Dianira. Her little sister Yesenia was too shy, and would sink into herself anytime the attention was on her. Her cousin Michely? She was too little and too much of a Selena wannabe, twirling and wiggling her skinny butt and those hips she did not even have yet. Her cousin Lila? She was too muy muy, always in her books, always talking about the trips she was going to take when she was older, the grunge band she was going to be in when she moved to Seattle. Next year, Dianira would probably be just another person in the chorus, telling the story of what had happened two thousand years ago, listening to another cousin sing out of tune in the Virgin's dress that she had made with her mother.

They made their way in a circle, up and down the street, back to Papa Tavo and Abuelita's house. They went to the door, and her cousins and aunts and uncles opened up and pretended not to know her.

Dianira and the others sang their story about how cold it was and how Mary was the Queen of the Universe, and she was carrying the Divine Word inside of her.

Dianira's family sang, "*Is that you, José? Your wife is María? Enter, pilgrims. I did not know you.*"

The travelers sang, "*May God repay your kindness, good sirs, and heaven shower you with felicity.*"

After the play was over, they went inside, where tía Marisol was pulling the skin from the surface of a big pot of Mexican hot chocolate she'd made. Sef leaned over the pot, making these asco faces at the milk skin dangling from the spoon.

Lila and Michely stood by her too, and the cousins moved closer to see what was happening.

Tía Marisol held out the spoon in front of their faces. "Here, mis hijas, you all can have this if you're so hungry. You too, Lila."

Lila and Michely went "Ee-*yoo!*"

Marisol said, "No que no, you all were hungry," and laughed. She then tore open the Popular brand package, broke off two more squares of chocolate, and dropped them in. She dipped the molinillo into the pot and spun its handle in her hands, the mace-like tip breaking up the squares, frothing the milk, and keeping it from congealing on the surface.

But they *were* hungry, having done all that traveling. It was quiet as they drank their chocolate and chewed on their buñuelos, those plate-sized flour tortillas deep-fried and sprinkled with cinnamon sugar. The buñuelos reminded Dianira of the elephant ears her father liked to buy her when they used to go to the carnivals in the fall. What was he doing now?

The Izquierdo family had outgrown Abuelita's house, and now with these neighbors inside, the family from el otro lado, it was even more full. It made Abuelita happy, which was important because now that Papa Tavo was not at home everyone wanted her spirits up. Dianira saw this in the way she walked around the room, touching each of her grandchildren, blessing them, thanking God for them.

After the neighbors finished their hot chocolate and buñuelos and went home to their own Christmas celebrations, the Izquierdos gathered around the Nativity scene Abuelita had arranged in the carport. Year after year, it was there with subtle differences. The base was made out of two wooden boxes painted white, the bottom one bigger than the top. Tío Gonzalo had made the miniature wooden stable, and had even varnished it.

The way it was decorated this year was how Dianira would forever remember it. It was about five feet tall from the concrete floor to the tip of the star. Spanish moss, which tío Braulio collected fresh each year from the trees in Anzalduas Park, covered the floor of the stable. On the lower tier were plastic chickens, mules, zebras, and some green army men that Little Gonzalo or Seferino or one of her other many cousins had left while playing there when no one was looking. On the upper tier an assortment of mismatched figurines: a lamb bigger than a bull, a horse smaller than both, the Wise Men taller than the rest, a gilded doll chair, faithful saints from a thousand years in the future kneeling in front of the empty manger, and even a stray luchador standing guard, frozen in the wrestling stance ready to defend the infant upon his arrival. The statue of the Baby Jesus would not be there until after they finished saying the Rosary. Shiny gold garland, intertwined with multi-colored Christmas lights, framed the scene. A five-pointed star fashioned from green wire, a white string of lights wrapped through it, was on top. A bluebird and a cardinal sat inside. Dianira thought it was just a little tacky, but she knew how important it was to everyone, especially Abuelita.

They stood in front of it, and everyone got quiet. The rosary hung from Abuelita's fingers and everyone knew it was time to stop talking, to move in closer to the prayer.

Dianira and Seferino were at the front, holding the nearly life-sized statue of the Baby Jesus, the heavy one made of plaster with painted brown hair and painted blue eyes, which Dianira knew wasn't historically accurate. Jesus had been brown with brown eyes just like her and all of her cousins, or maybe even more moreno than them. Instead of a manger, the Baby Jesus laid his head on an aluminum plate with colaciones, those colorful round bumpy sugar candies. The time for the Niño Dios to be placed into the manger would come. Dianira thought of the song "Away in a Manger" and sang it in her head, replacing the word *manger* with *aluminum plato*. It really was not funny, but she felt like laughing. She asked God to forgive her, and to set her mind right.

The Baby Jesus started to slide to the left because Sef was looking behind him at his cousins because they kept whispering, "*Psst, Josefito, give us a candy.*"

Dianira whispered, "*Sef! Watch what you're doing.*" To her little cousins, she said, "*You all better be quiet or I'm going to give you all some chanclazos you won't ever forget.*" She pretended to reach for her leather sandal.

Everyone heard her, though, and her tío Macario said, "Oye, she really *is* the Queen of the Universe." Only the backsliders and the irreverent laughed, but Dianira had to admit it was a *little* funny. Why was everything so funny when you were not supposed to be laughing?

The prayer was long, and once they got started, Dianira's voice blended perfectly with Abuelita's. Her eyes were closed most of the time, but Dianira knew her little cousins, especially the girls, were watching her. In their hearts, they wished they could get the attention Dianira received from the family, all eyes on her, everyone thinking how holy she was, knowing *all* the words to the Rosary when most people just knew the Our Father and Hail Mary parts. She was glad she could give them something to look up to. In a way, Dianira believed *her* enthusiasm, *her* portrayal of the Virgin had kept the tradition alive for all these years. What would happen when she got too old to play the part? Yesenia, Michely, Lizbeth, or Lila surely could not or would not keep it alive.

She saw Aaron's eyes were on her too. He was waiting for her eyes to meet his so he could smile with his pretty white teeth. Dianira did not give him a chance. With everyone watching her, what did Aaron expect her to do?

When the Rosary was done, and all of the mysteries were spoken, the children stood in line to kiss the feet of the Baby Jesus. Although the colaciones all tasted the same, some of the cousins took their time selecting the color they wanted. They kissed the Baby Jesus's feet, got a sugar candy, and crossed themselves.

Without reverently kissing the Baby Jesus, Lila walked up and grabbed two colaciones. Dianira gave her the slitted mother-eyes. La Virgen would have *never* done that, be all selfish like her prima had been, not giving Jesus respect.

Now that the Baby Jesus was finally in the manger, and because the Rosary was so long and they'd been holding the Niño Dios the whole time, she and Seferino shook out their hands and tried to rub the numbness out of them. Abuelita handed out plastic Christmas bags of candy to the little kids. Inside the bags there were peanuts and hard Mexican animal crackers (which all the kids usually ate last if they did not throw them away), chocolates and other candies like de la Rosa mazapán, leches quemadas, Salimones, tamarindo lollipops, Chupa Chups, Duvalín cups with the tiny plastic spoons, and strawberry candies with the gooey centers. Abuelita came up to Dianira, and it seemed like she did not know whether or not she should give her candy because the bags were for the younger kids.

Dianira made it easy for her grandmother and said, "Gracias, no."

Later, they were all inside, eating tamale after tamale, some made with pork, others with beans. There was a plate in the center of the table that was stacked high with the greasy tamale husks. They were eating and laughing, having the annual discussion about whether the proper word was *tamal* or *tamale*, but no one was drinking, except for the tíos: Manuel, Lalo, Joe, and Wally.

Tío Braulio had gotten there too, was eating tamales inside, and he called out to the uncles drinking by their trucks in the darkness of the street. He said, "Oye, Four Wise Vatos, why don't you all come and eat some of this good food and put down those beers for a while?" It was a joke and everyone laughed, but Dianira knew what was behind his words. He was one of those recovering alcoholics who met in that building on Broadway across the street from the McAllen Public Library. Over its door it had a sign with a plain triangle inside a circle, and Dianira thought it was some weird kind of cult until her father explained it to her. When they'd brought out the beers, she had seen her tío Braulio's face change. Where was tía Ofelia? She was the tía no one talked about anymore because she stopped coming to the house when Abuelita had confronted her about the drinking, the way she wasn't raising Cirilo right. Tío Braulio was thinking of her now, she could tell. The way his smile quivered just a little, it was obvious.

Cirilo knew this too, because he said, "Pop, imagínate, the Four Wise Vatos on camels, todos off-balance because of Mexicans with big beer bellies riding on them."

Braulio laughed.

"And then just think about the camels' eyes popping out."

Cirilo's father kept laughing, and Dianira loved her cousin even more because he always knew exactly what to say to someone, cared enough to pay attention to his loved ones' moods and checked in on them or tried to make them feel better.

Aaron was sitting next to her, and he said, "Dianira, what school did you say you went to?" As if he did not know, as if the conversation they were about to have had not already happened the first night they spoke on the phone until one o'clock in the morning.

"Travis Junior High."

"Eighth or seventh grade?"

"Sixth," she said.

"What?"

"Eighth, menso, I was just kidding."

"So you'll be in high school next year. Mac High, yeah?"

"Yeah. I'll be a Bulldog. And you'll still be a Rattler."

"You'll like high school. I thought you were there already. I thought you were like in ninth or tenth grade."

Dianira smiled at this and stuck out the tip of her tongue, making a face like she did not believe him.

"Órale, I bet you hear that all the time. Even though I'm a junior, you're prettier and more mature than *half* of the girls in my grade."

Dianira said, "Just half?" They both laughed.

At around nine-thirty, tío Gonzalo and his family showed up late like always.

Gonzalo was carrying something tall draped in a white cloth. He uncovered it and it turned out to be a life-like statue of the Virgen de Guadalupe. Dianira felt all the blood leave her head and she felt like she was going to fall. No one noticed because their eyes were on what Gonzalo was carrying.

There she was, the most beautiful image of La Virgen de Guadalupe Dianira had ever seen. The statue wore her golden crown. She had actual hair some Mexican girl had had the honor of offering to the Virgin.

"Amá," Gonzalo said in Spanish, "all of us pitched in for your present this year. We want you to know that we thank you for making Christmas beautiful every year. This is for you too, Dianira. You have helped Abuelita a lot, and we want you to know we appreciate you." He was talking about all the times Dianira spent at Abuelita's, reading to her from the Spanish Bible, learning how to crochet with her, spending the night on the weekends now that Abuelita lived by herself. Some of those nights, when Abuelita was scared, she would have called one of her sons if Dianira had not been there.

Dianira reached forward and the Virgen's hair was so soft and delicate in her fingers, like it would come out if she stroked too hard. Her majestic cape was the blue of the night sky. Embroidered stars glittered in the Christmas lights. Her porcelain skin was so smooth and clean and dark. The Virgen's eyes were the lightest brown, the forgiveness and sorrow in them so human that surely God Himself must have touched the artist with a divine ability.

"She was made in Mexico City, near the hill of Tepeyac where the Virgin of Guadalupe appeared to Juan Diego," Gonzalo said. "And now, Amá, she will bless your home and watch over you when you sleep. And Dianira, we have all watched you play La Virgen every year and watched you become as beautiful as the real Virgen. Your faith has been an inspiration to us all." Neither Dianira nor Abuelita could speak, but the gratitude was in their eyes. Dianira could feel it welling up inside of her. No one had ever said anything like that to her, especially her father, who came home at night just to say that he did. He ate and spent most of his time at his restaurant. He never cared about his daughters' interest in religion. In fact, she thought he hated God for what had happened to her mother Dina. Gonzalo, who probably didn't even believe in the faith himself, as evidenced by his never praying with the others, had said this nice thing in front of her family, who now gathered around Dianira, Abuelita, and the Virgen. She felt so warm and happy in that ring of her family, but beneath her joy was the knowledge that this would all end. With the way Aaron and her grandmother's neighbors had been looking at her all night, and the way Gonzalo had honored her, she knew this was her last night playing the Virgen. This was what Gonzalo and the others were really thinking, that the time had now come for one of her cousins to take the role.

Dianira was tired, and all she wanted to do was lie down in Suzana's room, but everyone was in there with her. They were setting up the space for the Virgen on Suzana's old dresser. Usually Suzana's room was quiet because no kids were supposed to play in it now that Abuelita had converted Suzana's bedroom into a shrine. This happened once Suzana got pregnant by Artemio and got married. Dianira had helped Abuelita set it up. One Saturday about a year before, both of them had gathered religious items new and old: a hologram of Jesus at one angle praying on the rock at Gethsemane, at another angle naked and bleeding on the cross, and holy cards of the Virgin and Padre Pio, the father who had received the miraculous wounds of the crucifixion. Dianira had used her low-heeled shoe to drive the nail into the wall where she had hung a huge rosary.

That Saturday afternoon nearly a year ago when they had gotten the shrine to look just like they wanted it, Abuelita had gone to lie down in her bedroom where the window unit was. Dianira had then sneaked into her grandmother's bedroom and taken down a picture of herself which was slipped into the mirror. It was of Dianira the first time she had put on the baby blue dress, back when it was baggy on her. She had gone back to Suzana's room and propped the picture next to the painting of the Virgin of Guadalupe. She had whispered, "La Virgen Dianira," so quietly that only God and La Virgen María could hear her. Dianira knew it was probably blasphemous, but she had thought they would understand that it was in the greatest love and adoration that she had tried to imitate the Virgin.

Now there were so many people in Suzana's room that the wooden floor creaked and Dianira thought maybe they were all going to fall through. Gonzalo moved forward and carefully placed La Guadalupana on top of the dresser.

He said, "Later, we'll get you a glass case to protect her, just like they have Juan Diego's tilma protected in Mexico."

She was immaculate standing there, and Dianira said, "You don't have to worry about keeping her clean. I'll keep the dust off of her, and I will comb her hair if she needs it."

All the kids were packed into Abuelita's little living room now, while Abuelita sat on the couch and watched them with a quiet, amused smile at the chaos unfolding around her. Tía Melinda was passing out the One Gift from the yearly gift exchange. The kids squeezed and peeked inside and shook their presents because they were supposed to wait and open them together. Dianira thought there had to be a better way. Tía Melinda handed Dianira a present. Cirilo and Aaron were by the doorway laughing about something, and she thought maybe they were laughing about her because she was still a little kid getting a present, but she was not sure. Cirilo was too old to get a present; his name had been taken out of the drawing since she did not remember when. He had always seemed too old to get a present.

Tía Melinda said, "Okay, kids, on the count of three—"

Tía Ana interrupted her and said, "Open your presents! Open, open, open!"

Tía Melinda tried to say that they were supposed to wait to get the cameras ready, and she shook her head and sucked her teeth at tía Ana, who just laughed at the chaos in the tiny living room.

Paper went flying everywhere, but Dianira calmly opened hers. Her present was from Abuelita. It looked like a little purple aluminum lunch box. It was filled with a little vial of bubble bath and grape-smelling hand lotion and lip gloss. Not *too* bad. Last year, tío Macario had gotten her one of those artificial digital pets that you had to feed and love and take "outside" so they could go to the restroom. Not only had it been a little kid's present, but those things had been out of style for many Christmases. As Dianira made her way to Abuelita to thank her for the gift, she stepped around her cousins, because all the kids were on the floor playing with their toys. Some of them, like Macario's boy Elías, were crying because they thought the other kids had better presents. Why do kids have to be like that, always wanting what they do not have?

Dianira was tired and it was time for her to rest. Her sisters had gone to spend the night at tío Lalo and tía Marisol's. Dianira was happy that she was going to spend the night in Suzana's room where the statue of the Virgen now was. There was a small single bed where Cirilo had set her overnight bag. The only light in the room was from the red Virgen de Guadalupe and Sagrado Corazón de Jesús candles. She had said goodbye to all of her uncles and aunts and cousins even though she would see them tomorrow. After everyone had opened their presents, they would all come over and Gonzalo and Braulio would cook fajitas or carnitas outside, and the kids would pop Jumping Jacks, Black Cats, and Lady Fingers in celebration of Christmas, but also in preparation for New Year's. Seferino would probably get into trouble again for shooting Roman candles into the neighbor's yard across the fence and scaring the dog. She knew Aaron and Cirilo were still there because she had not heard Cirilo's big engine start up, and because he liked to drink beer with his uncles sometimes, but only when his dad was not around.

She lay down. Dianira thought about the Holy Family's journey, and soon the sand and wind blew through her mind and she was almost asleep.

Dianira heard someone knock on the door.

"Dianira," someone whispered.

It was Aaron.

"What is it?"

"Oye, I want to talk to you."

She did not know what to say. Aaron answered for her by walking into the room. He looked the same, like he had not been drinking at all.

"What you doing asleep already, sleepyhead?"

Dianira sat up and said, "I was just here laying down."

"Órale pues, scoot over, you're hogging up the whole bed."

She did like that he asked. Dianira was not afraid at all. She had even thought about something like this happening, the way he had written to her.

"Well, what I wanted to say was maybe it would be okay if I called you again sometime. You know, see what you're doing sometimes. I love the letters, but I need to *hear* your voice."

"Sure, but I have to be sure about my parents not knowing." Dianira tried to say it like, *You can call me sometime, but you have to leave now*, but she was not sure if she had said it that way. Dianira did not really want him to leave, but it was better for him to go.

"That's good, that's good." In that moment when he did not say or do anything, Dianira was not sure what was about to happen. She imagined two things: Cirilo walking in and beating him down, or she and Aaron kissing in front of the Virgin. This made her feel guilty even though Dianira knew all she would do was *kiss* Aaron. There was nothing wrong with kissing. Was there?

He leaned forward, and because she had never kissed a boy and wanted to and because Aaron was handsome and nice and she thought she might love him, she did not move away from his touch.

Aaron tasted like beer and breath spray, but he was gentle. Dianira felt his hands searching for her through the sheets.

It was not until he found her, his hand on her bare leg, that she started to feel uncomfortable, started to think of the Virgin watching her. She started to pull back, but he pushed himself forward. This was not okay, and it was not how she wanted any of this to happen.

She pulled away quick, and her own strength surprised her. Dianira looked into his eyes in the candlelight and said, "Please. Get out."

"I see how it is." His voice had changed, all the sweetness and flirt gone as he got off of the bed. "You want to play the Virgin, and act like you want to put out too. You're not worth anything. All you *little* girls are the same. Wasting my time. No vales una chingada." How quickly he had changed.

Aaron got off the bed, left the room, and she began to cry. Dianira cried because of what he had said, yes, but she also cried because she thought Aaron was better than that. Also, there was her mother who would not leave the house, and her father no longer cared that Dina had taken a vow of chastity, staying out late, presumably still seeing the movida he'd been caught with. She felt all alone in the world, even apart from her sisters. She cried because the Izquierdo blood was bad, and they were all cursed, and no one would ever want her in a good way. They would only want her like Aaron had wanted her. *And* was she worthless like Aaron had said?

Dianira looked up. The Virgen's eyes had been on them like she had seen them in her mind, glinting in the candlelight. Dianira was still wearing the robe and dress, and she did not deserve to be wearing them. She herself was no santita, and it was time to stop playing make-believe, stop trying to be holy and pure when she was not.

Dianira's breaths were coming in heaves, like she was choking, and she thought this was maybe how it had started for her grandfather and for her mother. This kind of breathing that led to a breakdown. She had not cried like this since she was a little girl and had heard her father and mother arguing.

Dianira had to get out, to leave, but she could not look into the faces of her cousins, tías and tíos, and Abuelita. They would all know Aaron had touched her leg, and more, how she had felt. It would be on her face like a confession. And her grandmother who knew everything would be like a priest who could not see a sinner's face perfectly in the confessional, only the dark outline of someone who had done wrong against God.

Dianira, still wearing the garb of the Virgin, climbed out through Suzana's window.

Even though she did not want to feel anything good, she welcomed how the night air cooled her flesh. She pulled the dress over her head, and it was even harder to breathe now that she was colder and shaking, the slip she still wore doing nothing to keep her warm.

Dianira fell to her knees and began digging at the ground. She would bury her virgin clothes forever, because even though she had not given her body, for a moment she had wanted to, and wasn't this the same thing as actually doing it? Aaron had touched her. Like the brujo's entierros, she had cursed the clothes with her impurity and the only thing to do was bury them.

The ground was hard and Dianira winced at the way it was tearing the quick of her fingers, how the nails she had kept pretty and painted were breaking.

Dianira bled.

A sound came from her throat. It was a groaning sound, the sound her mother had made when she had found out her father was sleeping with another woman. This and the bad Izquierdo blood were the real reasons why Dina had lost herself. Dianira bled the bad blood of her family.

Her groan became a scream as the ground refused to open for her. Dianira wanted it to swallow her virgin clothes, swallow *her* for what she had done in the presence of the blessed Virgencita.

When she knew her family was near her, gathering around her to see what had happened, Cirilo's face was the only one she saw. He was not looking at her face, but instead was focused on the blood coming from her fingertips, his forehead knitted in concern. Dianira thought he could not bear to see her, like he knew exactly what had happened. Aaron was there too. Cirilo looked at Aaron, who was shaking his head, as if he had expected Dianira to do something stupid like this. Cirilo's face then changed to understanding. Dianira could see his rage.

Cirilo threw a punch at Aaron, and he fell flat. Aaron did not have a chance. Cirilo straddled Aaron's stomach and he was swinging in a rhythm, no wildness at all, just like his father had taught him, not like the weak, untrained swings Aaron was taking. She saw Cirilo's strong arms come back, left then right, right then left. The dirt from the ground where Aaron struggled to get free came up like smoke. Aaron quit trying to buck Cirilo off. He was out cold. Cirilo had not said a word the whole time.

No one had helped Aaron, but now Macario and Gonzalo picked him up and took him to Cirilo's car, where they would accompany Cirilo to take him away from there.

Dianira did not see any of these things happen. She only heard about it afterward.

The only thing she would remember was Cirilo picking her up. She would remember how warm and sweaty his arms were. Dianira would remember the way he breathed in and out, his chest pressing into her, his strong heart beating next to her skin. This movement, this rhythm of his breathing and blood, soothed her to sleep in his arms.

Later, when she woke, Cirilo was gone, and she wanted him back, her best primo watching over her. Someone else was near now. Dianira felt a warm, damp cloth wiping the dirt from her feet. It was Abuelita. Only she would do something like that.

Through half-closed eyes, Dianira saw and wondered at the expression on Abuelita's face. It was something like sadness. Whatever it was, Dianira had caused it.

In Spanish, Abuelita said, "I know very well that you are not asleep." Even as a little girl, when she used to try and trick her grandmother into thinking she was asleep—a trick Cirilo had taught her, and she had taught Little Gonzalo—Abuelita always knew. Abuelita checked the bandages on her fingers, wiped at Dianira's face with a clean cloth, and she smiled now. Dianira knew the way it would be. Just like Abuelita had done after the miraculous event at Teresa's quinceañera, her eyes would tell the whole family that there would never be a reason to talk about any of this. Dianira was intact and blameless, punto final, she would say without saying. Once in a while, her more chismoso cousins would try to bring it up, but Abuelita would look at them, and that would be it. They would have to share in Abuelita's silence. Her grandmother pulled the covers over her, touched her cheek with her cool hand, and got up to leave the room.

"Duérmase," she said, and closed the door behind her.

As sleep was about to again take Dianira, she looked into the eyes of the statue of the Virgin. Afterward, this was all she would be certain about seeing for those few seconds before she received her vision. Dianira would never be sure if her eyes were closed the whole time the vision was happening, or if she just received holy blindness so that she might see what God wanted her to see. Eyes open or no, the prayer of her young life to receive a vision of the Holy Virgin finally happened, but it was nothing like Dianira had expected.

In the vision she received, Dianira heard a woman speaking words in a language she had never heard before. The air was dry, spiced with an unfamiliar fragrance mixed with something like roses. When Dianira blinked, Suzana's room fell away, and it was like a dream where she could see through someone else's eyes, feel what they were feeling. She was lying down on a mat on the floor, and she could feel the warmth of someone's body.

Dianira heard the woman say, "Ahuv Yosef," to the man who lay next to her, and she sensed him rolling over on his side to face her. He caressed her face and whispered, "Ahuva Miryam, ahuva Miryam," and stroked her closed eyes. Beyond their bed, she heard the child stir, His own vision of what was and what was to be fluttering inside His sleep.

Holy Weak

I t was Sábado Santo, the eve of el día de Pascua, Easter Sunday. Twelve-year-old Yesenia had lost six pounds, and the hunger in her stomach, which was all she had thought about for the first two days of fasting, was only a dull ache. Her body felt barely there. Anything she touched, a doorknob, a pen, her diary, the clothes on her body, felt only like memories, like phantoms of substance, and not the things themselves.

She had fasted throughout Holy Week because she figured it was the best time for her to receive the Five Miraculous Wounds of Christ. Yesenia wanted to join the brothers and sisters who had come before her, those saints who had yearned to connect with Christ, fully understand His suffering. In her reading done at the McAllen Public Library, she had learned that throughout history, in Europe and Latin America and even in America, mystics had bled from their hands, feet, and side, just like Jesus. Even though Padre Pio of Pietrelcina had been the most famous, Yesenia was happy and hopeful to know that the majority of the stigmatic saints had been women. The two Yesenia was most fas-

cinated with were the Saint Catherines. At the age of seven, Saint
Catherine of Siena had received visions of Jesus with San Pedro,
San Juan, and San Pablo and bore stigmata that only she could
see. Then there was Saint Catherine of Florence, who was said
to have experienced the Passion every Thursday around lunch-
time until Friday afternoon at four p.m., bearing the stigmata in
the order in which Jesus had received the wounds. She was also
known to be in two places at once, her body in Florence while
having conversations with San Felipe Neri, who was in Rome.
If God could make these miracles for the Catherines and other
women because they yearned to understand His suffering, surely
He could do it for her. Her sisters Teresa and Dianira, who had
received their own miracles of levitation and a vision of the Virgin Mary, respectively, believed it too. Though they were concerned about her fasting for so long, from their own research
they knew these stories of the saints well. If God wanted to bless
Yesenia this way, they would not try to hinder it, and would support their sister through it.

In addition to wanting to embrace Jesus and His suffering,
Yesenia wanted Him to manifest Himself with the evidence
of the stigmata because she wanted to receive a transfusion of
holy blood. The blood from her mother's side of the family,
the Izquierdos, was afflicted with sadness and fear, while the
Torreses' were prone to greed, envidia, and suspicion. Yesenia
wanted to be someone new, a girl who transcended the failings
of her families.

And her mother was the most afflicted of them all. For a year
now, she had kept herself locked inside of the house. If she was
not praying or reading or listening to music, Dina would only
peek through the curtains and say, "El Mal Ojo, the eye of the

devil himself is waiting to look at me through the intermediaries of his malice, the zanates. Poderosas, we have to pray."

Then Yesenia, her sisters, and her mother would pray the Rosary on their knees, but not all nice like it was with Abuelita. Dina would pray in this high-pitched screech that made Yesenia want to run out of the house with her hands covering her ears. Maybe if she had the stigmata and a holy blood transfusion, Yesenia would be strong enough to coax her mother outside of the house, outside of her fear. And then her parents would start to be happy again, maybe her father would not hate the Izquierdos so much or be out cheating with Iris Salazar, that home-wrecker who did the books at his restaurant. Yesenia just wanted things to be normal, for her parents to be in love again, to have hope, to want to go to the Izquierdos' pachangas. Even with all of their problems, they did throw the best parties.

When she began, Yesenia promised God she would eat only when she received the Holy Blessing with the evidence of His wounds in her hands or wrists, feet, and ribs. As a reminder against the hunger pangs and a commitment to keep fasting, she had written in black permanent marker the words *Holy Weak* on her forearm. And even though Yesenia knew she'd misspelled it as soon as she saw it on her arm, it was permanent, and it helped as she was able to abstain from food all that week, only drinking water. That Saturday, all day long, the hunger pangs grew stronger, as if her body was telling her it was finally time to eat. To focus even harder she looked at the pictures of the paintings of the Fourteen Stations, the holy card of Padre Pio, and looked at her bare feet and hands and thought about the pain and the miracle she would soon be receiving. Hopefully.

When Yesenia got into bed that Saturday night, with her

father still not home from another night of adultery, she again prayed for it to happen. "Let me receive the stigmata. Let my blood change. Let my parents be happy and come back to the family. Whichever comes first, let it be Your will." Yesenia searched the side of the bed for the gauze pads and the surgical tape she had bought at Klinck Drug Store before Semana Santa even started. "When I wake up," she whispered, "please let my sheets be stained red with Your blood. Amen." Then she said the Our Father for good measure.

On Sunday morning, the sheets felt wet. Just before Yesenia opened her eyes, she patted her body. The dull ache in her stomach was still there, and she felt an itching in her hands and feet, the same sensation almost every stigmatic saint reported in their diaries and journals. Her head still had the floaty feeling from hunger. She felt her hands first.

They were dry, and all she felt were the veins and tendons undamaged and the dampness she had felt on the sheets was only the coolness of the air conditioner blowing on them all night. When Yesenia kicked her feet out, though she would never admit it because she was supposed to have faith like her sisters, she was not surprised. The green polish on her toes she and Teresa and Dianira had applied before all of this was cracked and dull. The top of her foot was clean, a perfect surface she could paint on. All of her was unwounded just like it had been every day of her life.

"Big surprise," she said to herself.

She lifted her nightshirt and her side was unpierced, another clean surface.

Yesenia threw the white sheet over her face and wept into it. She had failed and her faith had not been strong enough and there was no miracle for her, no miracle like her sisters had experienced.

Teresa and Dianira knocked at the door and let themselves in. They sat on the edge of the bed and took one of her hands. Yesenia could not bear to look at either of them, at Teresa of the Levitation or Dianira of the Marian vision.

Dianira asked, "Sister, are you okay?"

Teresa asked, "Yesenia, are you going to uncover your face?"

Yesenia said, "Go away. Nothing happened, okay? It's like any other day."

"But it's Easter."

"Which isn't even really the day Jesus rose, Dianira."

"Yes, but He is risen."

"Yeah, but no one knows the exact date, do we?"

And regardless of how Yesenia felt, how she was crying so much her tears now saturated the white sheet over her face, she said, "He is risen indeed."

"That's our hermanita," Teresa said to her littlest sister.

Then Yesenia heard their father mumbling to Mama, who was praying in their walk-in closet.

He knocked at her door.

Teresa let him in and Yesenia uncovered her face.

"Mijas," he said, looking at the three of them on the bed, then without recognition at the bandages on the side of Yesenia's bed. He did not look into her puffy face. Just like her father not to notice: she had lost weight, she hadn't eaten dinner in over a week, she'd obviously been crying and there were dark circles around her eyes, and the sheet covered her body like a shroud.

"Get dressed, okay, girls? We're going to Bill Schupp Park." Because their father had kept them away from the family so long, the sisters looked at each other, stunned at the announcement. This was where the Izquierdos and practically the entire Río Grande Valley celebrated every Easter after the Easter Mass, but was a place where Eusebio hated going. He called it the "parque with all the drunk Mexicans," where it was so packed with kids running around everywhere, where he complained it was hot even in the shade. So, why was he taking them? They hadn't gone to the park on Easter since her father's falling-out with tío Braulio over him helping his competition and before her mother sequestered herself away at the house, and even then, it was only every other year or so. Yesenia's stomach twisted and turned just thinking about her tío Gonzalo's brisket, which took hours to cook. The sisters exchanged glances again, mouths still agape at their father's announcement, but then Teresa motioned her sisters to get ready.

⁂

THEY GOT TO BILL SCHUPP PARK in North McAllen and drove along Bluebird Street, on the side of the park where the rich gringos lived in their condominiums.

"Every year," Eusebio said, "they put signs up in their pebbled and landscaped yards saying PLEASE DON'T PARK HERE."

"Every year us Mexicans park here," Eusebio said to himself now, and chuckled as they rode in the Suburban. None of the girls spoke as they searched for a familiar car among all of the trucks and cars lined up along Bluebird Street, their windshields glinting in the sunlight. On either side of Eusebio's Suburban, the cars were close enough to touch. They drove all the way down to the end and parked in the cul-de-sac. Eusebio hopped the curb, putting the passenger wheels on the grass. It would give some kind of protection from being sideswiped. Her father just did not care about some things.

Yesenia felt herself sway as she got out of the Suburban and the heat made her face flush. Teresa and Dianira stood on either side of her, looped their arms under hers, and steadied her.

When the Izquierdos saw her father get out of the Suburban with Yesenia and her sisters, they smiled and were excited to give them their saludos, but there was the slightest pause as they noticed Dina's absence, as if they were suppressing the urge to ask about her.

The sisters made their way through the lawn chairs and park tables, side by side by side, hugging and kissing each of their tíos and tías.

Teresa and Dianira set Yesenia down at a concrete park bench while they circulated among the family members. It was from there that Yesenia watched everything. Nearby, her uncles Gonzalo and Braulio tried to make her father feel comfortable, offering him a beer from the ice chest and a plate of brisket. Dianira was over there talking to Cirilo, who had his head down, looking sad about something. Dianira looked up into his eyes, lifted his chin, said words Yesenia could not hear over the radio, and gave him a hug.

Gonzalo handed her father a beer, and the way they stood there, silent for an awkward second, Yesenia knew they were searching for something to talk about other than Eusebio's restaurants or the past between them.

"Oyes," Braulio said, "Mira, qué gentillazo," and took a swig of Big Red. His chin jerked toward all the people at the park, at the children in bright clothes on the swings, at the plumes of smoke coming from the barbecue pits. How long had it been since Yesenia had seen all of this, so many people in one place? Or seen her father talking cordially with her uncles?

Gonzalo said, "Imagínate how bad South Padre Island is right now. All those Mexican nationals over there, the island's probably going to fall into the Gulf with so many gente on it." The men laughed, even her father. He did like that kind of joke, after all. He took off his glasses to rub his eyes, something he used to do when someone made a funny remark. Yesenia had not seen him do this since her mother got sick. There was this at least, a start at reconciliation.

The heat was on them all, and to Yesenia, her little cousins in the pastel dresses seemed to glow. Before her, on lawn chairs, the women sat with plates full of brisket, rice, beans a la charra, potato salad, and tortillas. Tía Suzana was patting her new baby's back, saying, "Burp, baby, burp. Andale, Cristina, burp." A few of Yesenia's cousins played peek-a-boo with baby Cristina and giggled.

Then everyone laughed when tío Macario's daughter Lila cracked an Easter egg on her mother's head. Elvira shook her hair, and confetti came raining down on the ground where painted, cracked eggshells and confetti lay everywhere. *Esa Lila, she's bad,* Yesenia thought.

Elvira said, "Ay, Lila, vas a verlo, you're going to get it. When you least expect it, mija, expect it. Believe me, my cascarones are coming!" Elvira rolled an Easter egg in her palm. This was the kind Yesenia's mother used to make. For weeks before Easter came, whenever she made eggs for breakfast, she would just break off the top and pour the yolk out and leave the unbroken shells out to dry. Then, when she had saved a couple of dozen eggshells, Yesenia and her sisters would dip them in food coloring, fill them with confetti, and glue squares of paper towel over the top. Her mother would count out the cascarones and distribute them evenly among the girls. She used to joke with Yesenia about maybe not giving her any at all because Yesenia was the sneakiest when it came to cracking them on peoples' heads. "Ah, Malinche, no one ever sees you coming." Yesenia did not know why, but she liked it when her mother called her Malinche. It was not until later in her research that Yesenia found out Malinche was the Aztec woman who betrayed her people because of her love for the conquistador Hernán Cortés, and then she didn't like the name so much.

Tía Maggie, tía Victoria, and Little Gonzalo came to sit across from Yesenia at the park table, each of them with a plate of food. Little Gonzalo sat close to tía Victoria, and they shared a rolled-up flour tortilla. They were dressed up too, as if they had just gotten out of church. Maggie wore a bright yellow dress with a hibiscus flower print and buttons all the way down the front. She tucked a napkin into the collar, trying not to stain the vibrant yellow, red, and orange. Tía Victoria wore an off-the-shoulder powder-blue and daisy-patterned sundress. Yesenia hoped she looked as pretty as her tías when she was older. Victoria and Little Gonzalo ate and talked in whispers to each other, as if the others were not supposed to hear what they were saying.

Maggie said, "Mija, you want me to get you a plate?"

"No," Yesenia said, "I ate before I came." She did not even believe her own voice, how it spoke its practiced lie.

Victoria smiled as if she knew, while Maggie clicked her tongue against her teeth in disbelief. This was the one thing she hated about her tías. Victoria had this way of looking at you as if she knew secret things, while Maggie would always just call it out whenever her word of knowledge came. Victoria was so much younger than tío Gonzalo, but the way she seemed to know everything made her seem older.

Victoria said, "Look at your hands. You need to eat."

Yesenia's hands shook from hunger and they were splotchy and veiny. Did Victoria mean for Yesenia to look at how they shook, or did she mean for her to look at her own frailty? Or, worst of all, did she, the secret-knower, *La Hallelujah*, want to remind Yesenia how God had refused to bless her with the Five Miraculous Wounds? Yesenia could not meet their eyes because she didn't want Victoria or Maggie to know what she'd prayed for all week, how foolish she had been to believe it would come true. Instead, she focused on her unwounded hands, side, and feet, thinking how her skin was translucent and so fragile.

Victoria grabbed a fresh flour tortilla, tore off quarters for herself and Little Gonzalo, and handed the half to Maggie, who then did the same for Yesenia. Maggie raised a piece of tortilla and so did tía Victoria like it was a ceremony.

Maggie said, "¡Él ha resucitado!"

Yesenia gave her response in English when she said, "He is risen indeed."

Maggie ate her part first and said, "Se ha terminado, mijita. It's finished."

Though the miracle of the stigmata had not happened, she had been faithful to her promise. It was time to eat. Yesenia took a small bite from her quarter tortilla.

As she chewed, Yesenia thought about how in church her mother had taught her that you should let the hostia dissolve instead of chewing it. She had said chewing Communion was disrespectful to God because you were supposed to be gentle to

Jesus. Yesenia chewed some more, like her mother always told her not to, and looked out in front of her. All of it seemed so new, the bright children of the park, her father over there talking and laughing with tío Gonzalo and tío Braulio, her sisters playing with Suzana's new baby, Maggie, Little Gonzalo, and Victoria. As Yesenia swallowed the portion of tortilla in her mouth and it fell way down into her empty stomach, her illumination came. The fellowship of laughter over there with her father and uncles, and the tortilla communion here with her aunts and her cousins was a new beginning. And despite not receiving the stigmata or a transfusion of holy blood, she had sought Jesus, sought the impossible reconciliation of her family, and in this, Yesenia was a saint after all, a holy fool whose prayers had been answered.

Return, Return

The morning after Dina Torres's pesadilla—in which her envidioso former neighbor, the Brujo Contreras, dispatched the blue-black grackle birds to curse her with the evil eye—she made the decision to seclude herself in her house. By keeping herself hidden from the yellow mal de ojo of the multitude of zanates around her house and across the Valley, Dina believes she can keep Contreras's bad intentions and jealous hatred for her, her father, and her family at bay. If the zanates are encamped around her home, she reasons, they will leave Papa Tavo alone along with the rest of her family, the Izquierdos, and she herself will be safe. If she just stays inside, the Brujo Contreras cannot get back at them for their perceived offense against him of having many beautiful children, of being successful in business, and being able to leave the barrio Zavala, while most of his children died and he was still poor. To keep her mind off of the Brujo Contreras's curses and the plague of zanates with their taunting shrieks and croaks reverberating in the trees outside, Dina focuses on scripture, *The Catholic Encyclopedia*, prayers, photographs, music, and, of course, the Rosary. Her week is marked by the mysteries Joyful, Sorrowful, Glorious, and Luminous. After she reaches for the eternal with each bead, each decade, and she's grown tired of reading, Dina passes the week ruminating on better times by playing Papa Tavo's passed-down record collection of the old cantantes, the music of her upbringing in the Zavala, and looking at pictures of the Izquierdos' and Torreses' lives. She passes through her house listening to Jorge Negrete, Lola Beltrán, María Félix, Vicente Fernández, and the Christian conjunto of Paulino Bernal, while her fingertips hover over picture frames on the mantel, the Olan Mills portraits of the family, the old panoramic of the Izquierdos in front of the church when all of the sobrinos were so much smaller.

Dina spends her days thinking about the past because she has always wanted to hold on to the present, hoping things would never change. As she saw her older siblings Gonzalo, Braulio, and Marisol marry and leave home to start their own families, she knew each moment in their lives was a fleeting one and so she held on by becoming the chronicler of these moments. Dina in the middle—the last of the older children, the little mother to the younger brothers and sisters—has albums and boxes of photos she has either taken herself or the family has entrusted her with, black-and-white snapshots of her family while they all lived together at the house on Aurora.

Dina picks up the loose photographs she keeps in a Gamesa cookie box, careful not to smudge them. She tells herself she will organize each captured moment chronologically, but she never does. Instead, she shuffles the photographs like playing cards, enjoying the moments of surprise as she flips through the stacks, wondering at what memory from the Izquierdo history she will come to next. In her favorite photo, the first known portrait of the family, a black-and-white she always goes back to, she and her siblings all look so small standing in front of Papa Tavo's car. Baby Macario sits on the hood while Dina props him up to make it look like he is sitting on his own, keeping a towel in place under him so he will not burn his legs on the hot metal. Marisol holds a blurred Maggie in front of her as if she is about to run into the street. Papa Tavo wears a white button-down shirt with his sleeves rolled up, and Abuelita is in a floral-print housedress. Dina notices that they are both much younger than she is now. All of the children are barefoot and blinking into the sunlight. The only ones absent from this family portrait are Gonzalo, as he is the one taking the picture, and of course Suzana and Wally, who are years from arriving in the world. And because Gonzalo is not in this impromptu family portrait, sometimes she looks for the best picture of Gonzalo from this time period, where he stands next to Braulio, both of them with their fists up, glaring into the camera, as if in a challenge, their hair piled high with pomade. At nineteen, Gonzalo would have to quit boxing to support the family, while Braulio would go on to win a Golden Gloves boxing tournament, although Gonzalo had been the better boxer. Braulio would get to be the one to appear in *The Monitor*, a brief write-up of his tenacity and dedication above a picture of him in the same defiant stance as in the photo with Gonzalo. Dina had saved this yellowed newspaper clipping in a Ziploc bag to protect it from fading.

In the most personal album, the one devoted to just the Torres family, the first picture is of her and Eusebio when they were younger and more hopeful, holding hands at a table at someone's wedding, a can of Schlitz on the white tablecloth in front of Eusebio as he rubs his nose under his glasses. Then there are the pages and pages of a Jamaica Festival they attended years ago on a Día de La Virgen Guadalupe, which Dina had helped organize at St. Joseph the Worker. Here, she sees Teresa, Yesenia, and Dianira standing on their numbers in the Cake Walk, smiling and expectant, hoping to win the grand-prize cake, a trés leches made by one of the hermanas. A few pages later, Dina and Eusebio are wearing red charro suits Dina had made, with white embroidery on their chaquetillas, spangled pants for him and a spangled skirt for her. They are onstage and the DJ is waving his hand over them as he presents the couple for the traditional Mexican dress contest. Behind them in line are men dressed as vaqueros, a family of Aztec danzantes with matching feathered copili on their heads, and women and girls in colorful ballet folklórico dresses and huipiles. The last photo from the festival shows Eusebio and the girls sitting on a curb eating gorditas, tacos, and elotes over paper trays while they watch Dina compete in an unplanned grito contest at the end of the night. They are smiling at their mother, who is beyond the frame, proud of her for giving the traditional shout of joy and celebration, defiance, and Mexican independence. Dina didn't win the contest, but she remembers her own grito now, her stentorious, prolonged *Aaaah* followed by *Aye-aye-aye*, which sounded like laughter.

When Dina looks at these photographs, hears Lola Beltrán singing "Cucurrucucú Paloma" throughout her house, hears her own triumphant grito in her head, she remembers when she was not afraid, when the zanates did not startle her as they began their nightly cacophony in the trees around her home. When the grackles were just a part of the landscape, a part of living in the Valley.

Dina walks to a portrait of the Izquierdo family hanging in her hallway. Her brothers and sisters, cuñados and cuñadas, and all of the nietos are gathered on the back lawn of St. Joseph the Worker Church. Papa Tavo and Abuelita proudly sit in the center on white wrought-iron outdoor rocking chairs. Standing in a row behind them are Dina and her nine brothers and sisters, with Gonzalo and Braulio in the center. The older grandchildren stand or kneel in front of the parents, carrying babies or resting their hands on the shoulders of the younger brothers, sisters, and cousins sitting on the grass in front of them. To anyone looking at this portrait who doesn't know the Izquierdos, cousins are indistinguishable from siblings, and parents are impossible to match to their children. They are one family, not partitioned into immediate family units, and it is the only time when a camera captured them all together.

Today is Saturday and a day of the Joyous Mysteries. The girls are in their respective rooms reading magazines and books, and in the living room the 45 of Lola Beltrán's "Cucurrucucú Paloma" has played itself to the end. Dina has prayed the mystery and now that the music has stopped, the house is holding its breath, waiting for more canciones or whatever comes next.

Marisol, who calls every Saturday, and even comes over to bring food for Teresa, Dianira, and Yesenia, called earlier in the morning to tell Dina that she would be over around eleven o'clock and that she has a surprise for Dina and the girls.

Dina knows that whatever the surprise is, it is most likely an attempt to get her out of the house. Just like Dina, her sisters are tercas. Once they have set their mind on something, it is nearly impossible to convince them to give up. Her sisters have tried, each in their own way, to coax their sister into getting past her fear of Contreras and the evil eye of his servants, the zanates, to step outside the front door and rejoin the world. Even though Dina and Eusebio have one of the nicest houses among the Izquierdos—a bedroom for each of the girls, a backyard surrounded by a stucco wall, a heavy lava-stone façade, high ceilings, and a Spanish tile roof like the other houses in their neighborhood in central McAllen—they try to convince her that she is missing out on the present, living in a state of self-imposed purgatory. *Eusebio, his success with the restaurants, and all of your beautiful things have been a blessing,* they tell her, *but a house is a prison if you are never able to leave it.*

Dina finds their faces in the portrait, and loves them for trying. Marisol calls every Friday night, inviting Dina out for a nice dinner at a place of Dina's choosing.

Maggie tried to entice her with a free cut and color at her shop, or a church lady perm if Dina wants one even though those are way out of style. The younger sisters Melinda, Ana, and Suzana tried a group approach, offering to take Dina to the fabric store where they can each pick their own telas and make dresses or scarves or rebozos back in the comfort of Dina's home. They even tell her that they can make new matching charro outfits together. But she has rebuffed all of their offers.

Dina hears a vehicle pull up in front of the house, and she looks out the bay window. It is an older model Ford Explorer, and it belongs to her brother-in-law Lalo. It is early in the afternoon, and the zanates have not descended en masse on her house for the evening, though she sees a few in the trees and in the grass. She watches Maggie and Marisol get out of the car with Lalo, who stays behind and goes to the back of the Explorer, where he lifts the hatch, his attention on something on the floor. Maggie and Marisol look determined, their eyebrows knitted together more than usual as they walk up to her porch, past her bougainvillea, her potted succulents, her thorny maguey. Dina knows that they are there to try to rescue her from what they believe is the prison of her own home. And though they never say, Dina knows her sisters are there because they regret not doing more for their father, Papa Tavo, when he suffered his own mental anguish at the hands of Contreras's maldiciones. Now they are trying to do better by focusing so much attention on her. As the sisters get closer to the front door, Dina notices her plants, sees how they are drying out and dying. She feels a pang of longing for the mornings she spent outside, listening to the doves and the cicadas in the trees, watering her plants with the manguera, the water splashing onto her chanclas, leaving little rivulets of mud between her toes.

Once they are in the house, and without being invited to, the sisters sit down on the velvet couch in the sala, the ornamental sitting room to the left of the front door where no one actually sits. Though Maggie is younger than Marisol, she has always been the spokeswoman. She says, "Hermana, we have something good to tell you." Dina sits on the matching armchair facing the window where she can see Lalo is still focused on something in his Explorer.

Dina decides to speak first to take control of the conversation, because she knows that once her older sisters start, she won't be able to get a word in, either in English or Spanish. "I know what you are going to say, hermana."

While Dina is still speaking, Maggie says, "Oh yes? Well, then what am I going to say?"

"You're coming to try and take me to eat or to take me to

get my hair done." Instead of saying, *You think I'm chisquiada and you're here to extricate me from my locura*, Dina finds these words much easier to speak.

"No, hermana, that is not it. Even though we could do those things too."

Marisol interjects, "We have something to give you." She begins to rummage through her purse, but Maggie rests her hand on Marisol's, and shakes her head that it is not time to present Dina with whatever it is they want her to have.

Dina turns her head and, without breaking eye contact with her sisters, calls to the girls in their rooms to come and give their saludos. Dina does this because she wants her daughters to be respectful, but also because it will give her sisters someone else to focus on, and perhaps maybe the conversation will turn to pleasantries.

Marisol says, "Ay, chulas, I'm glad you're here too. You are a part of this."

The girls hug and kiss their tías, then sit on either side of them on the couch, and though it is not their intent, they are all facing Dina, who sits by herself across from them. The sisters remain quiet, as they can sense the gravity of this situation, and like their cousins, they have been taught to hold their tongues when the adults are talking, interrupting only when an adult has acknowledged them as they stand or sit in silence waiting to speak.

Maggie notices their sitting arrangement and says, "Ay, Dina, I'm sorry. Parece intervention. It's not like that, all daytime-talk-show-style." This is her sister Maggie, never holding back what she knows the others are thinking but are too civil to say.

"Well, then, what is it, hermana? I love that you are here, but I can tell you got something on your mind." It is the fear of Contreras's malice and his curses by proxy that are driving her curtness, and she hopes they will just leave. Dina manages to stay strong, unfaltering in her belief that today is not the day her sisters will win.

Maggie says, "The reason we are here, manita, is yes, we want to take you somewhere, but before we do, we also want to remind you of something. Do you remember when we took Braulio's fishing pole and went to the canals to catch a fish for Papa Tavo?"

Dina says, "Of course, sister, how can I forget?"

When McAllen was mostly farmland and canals and levees, one of the things Dina and her brothers and sisters liked to do was to go exploring. However, Papa Tavo and Abuelita always told them never to go near the irrigation canals for fishing or swimming. *Se pueden ahogar*, they would say.

One day, Dina convinced Marisol and Maggie to accompany her fishing because she wanted to bring a fish home for Papa Tavo, something that would cheer him up.

While Dina was fishing, Marisol and Maggie tried to skip caliche rocks on the water. The water was rushing, and the rocks were the wrong kind for skipping and they only plunked onto the surface of the canal and dropped to the bottom.

Dina tried to tell them that they needed to use flat rocks only. Because she was distracted trying to find the right rock while also casting, she dropped Braulio's favorite fishing pole into the water. Since Dina was so terca, she wasn't going to let that pole go. Her sisters' pleas didn't stop her and neither did the past regañadas from her parents. Even the stories of La Llorona, who was said to be hiding beneath the water and dragged down disobedient children, didn't stop her. She dove right in.

There was a current, as they were irrigating the fields that day. It started to push her along, and though she could swim, she could not make it to the canal bank no matter how hard she tried. Her sisters ran down the caliche road along the canal, wailing and calling Dina's name. Marisol had to stop Maggie from jumping in. Maggie had to stop Marisol from jumping in. The sisters, running and holding on to each other, knew that at the end of the canal there was an open valve that would suck Dina in and she'd drown for sure. But Dina, la más terca que terca, wasn't going to let herself drown. She gave her sisters the okay sign, took a deep breath, and went underwater. Instead of trying to swim to the bank, she went all the way down to the bottom. She grabbed fistfuls of grass and mud and thorny huisache branches and she clawed her way up the side of the canal until she reached the top. She lost Braulio's fishing pole that day, but being so terca and refusing to give in had saved her life. As Maggie and Marisol cradled the sopping-wet Dina in their arms, wiped away the streaks of blood from Dina's face and wrists, they told her how scared they were, but they also assured her that they would have followed her to the end of the canal, doing everything they could to get her out. They never would have given up on her.

Maggie says, "Sister, just like that day, we are here ready to pull you out, but you have to help yourself just like you did then." Maggie looks at her nieces and says, "This is something your mother has to do, chulas."

Dina clutches at her lap with both hands, remembering the feeling of grass, the thorns puncturing her fingers, scraping her face and wrists. She blinks fast and opens her mouth as if to speak, as if she thinks to explain why she cannot leave, but the words do not come. She raises her hands and turns her palms upward, as if to ask why today is different from all of the other days of her solitude.

Maggie says, "Apá is not doing well, hermana. I mean, he has his good days and he has his bad days, but for the past couple of weeks, he has been asking for you. He goes '¿Donde está, mija?' and we all know he's talking about you. He misses you big-time."

At this, Dina breaks, and the tears start to flow and she tries to wipe them away with the backs of her hands. She feels guilt come over her for all the time she has been absent.

Dina says, "Apá," but can say nothing else. Her dry lips are stuck together.

Marisol says, "Sometimes he thinks it is the day of their anniversary party, and that you will be showing up with the girls. I just don't know what to say to him when he gets like that."

"Te extraña mucho," Maggie says. "I don't mean to guilt-trip you, sister, because, believe me, that's the last thing I want to do. You know I only like to edify. Or drop a word of knowledge here and there when the Holy Spirit me da la gana. But this has to be said."

Maggie nods to Marisol, who then pulls out a blue piece of fabric from her purse. She shakes it out, and it is a lace embroidered mantilla, the blue of La Virgen, the kind of veil worn to Mass on Marian feast days.

Dina's fear turns to confusion as she narrows her eyes to confirm what she is seeing.

Marisol says, "It's a blessed velo, Hermana. We took it to church and had Padre Guerra sprinkle it with holy water."

Maggie nods in understanding, if not in approval. Though

she is a hallelujah holy roller, and they don't believe in holy water at their church, she, bautizada and confrimada, still goes to Mass when she's invited and takes the Eucharist whenever she does, not crossing her arms in front of her for a blessing like someone outside of the sacraments would do.

Then Maggie says, "We promise that with this you have protection from ojo, from every weapon formed against you in the spiritual realms. If you go outside with that velo, and you cover yourself with prayer, the grackles can't pass along any bad intentions. You will be protected."

Marisol then pulls out red earmuffs. "These are Lalo's. He uses them when he cuts leña with the chainsaw. We had them blessed too. That way, if the zanates start being necios, you won't hear them."

Maggie shakes her head and quickly slices her hand back and forth in the air in front of her neck to tell her it is not needed, telling Marisol that it's too much.

Dina can only croak when she says, "But why?"

Maggie says, "I know this is hard, sister, but we need you for something important. We managed to get all of the family together and Gonzalo talked to the administrator at the Shrine Nursing Home. They are going to let us take a family picture in the dining room. Papa Tavo's been having some good days, and I know if he sees you, he'll be all lit up. Apá needs you to lift his spirits."

Marisol says, "We are with you, and we are not leaving without you." She flashes the okay sign and nods.

Maggie says, "And if you don't leave, I'll just have to move in. Believe me, sister, I'll do it. Soy soltera. I got no husband waiting at home for me, not even a puppy or kitty, and believe me, I've slept in worse places. Before Diosito got a hold of me, of course." Marisol and Dina avoid her eyes, Maggie's smirk. They do not comment or ask her to clarify what she means with the last statement, knowing Maggie is so exagerada, saying things just to shock others, that if they give her the slightest indication that they want her to clarify, she will go into some story from her carousing past to make her point.

Dina looks to her sisters, then to her daughters, and they are in agreement. They are all resolute, confident, their eyes meeting hers, telling her that she can actually do it, that she can leave the house and that they will protect her. With their same full lips, the high cheekbones, it is obvious from their facial features that her sisters are her daughters' aunts, that the Izquierdo bloodline is strong throughout the generations. Other than her daughters' auburn hair from the Torres side of the family, it is only their eyes that are different. Dianira has the Izquierdo eyes like Marisol and Maggie, slightly hooded and dark brown, while Teresa and Yesenia have Eusebio's wide-set tan eyes, their brows forever arched in a look of mild concern. Their resemblance makes their determined expressions so much more alike, and that much harder to resist.

Dina licks her lips and they feel dry, thinner. Her mouth is parched, as dry as a caliche road, and she doesn't know if she could speak even if she wanted to.

Marisol breaks the silence. "Sister, no pressure, but this could be the last time we all get a picture together." For effect, she crosses herself.

Dina crosses herself in response, but then clutches at her legs, and as she does so, Maggie and Marisol leave the couch and kneel in front of her. Maggie takes a brush from her purse and begins stroking it gently over her sister's thin and brittle hair. Dina closes her eyes and tilts her head back and then to the side as Maggie lifts her hair to brush underneath. Maggie pulls her hair back and asks Dina if she wants it up or down and when Dina doesn't respond, she drapes it over her shoulders to hang loosely. The tears begin again, and they streak down Dina's cheeks, into her ears. When Maggie is done, Marisol raises the Virgin blue velo in the air and lets it float down over Dina's head, sets it an inch behind her widow's peak, sticks a bobby pin through the lace pattern above each temple. Dina's daughters close the space between them and their mother and huddle against her.

When all the cajoling and encouraging has ceased, they sit in silence, sometimes looking at each other, sometimes looking out the window. But then, without notice, without giving them any indication of where she is going, Dina walks to the front door and presses her hand against it. Surrounded by her daughters and sisters, she opens the door and steps into the sunlight. Maggie rests her hand on her sister's veiled head, lowering it as Dina tries to look up into the trees for the zanates. Her eyes meet the clear blue sky, the same color as her veil. She sees that Lalo's Explorer is running and the windows are open. As if on cue, Vicente Fernández's "Volver, Volver," starts playing; the opening organ and the trumpets and Vicente's grito blare throughout the neighborhood, Vicente's petition for his love to return, return, drowning out all other sounds in the neighborhood, even the zanates who've begun to call for Dina. Lalo holds up a Roman candle he's taken from the back of his Explorer and a Zippo lighter to show his sister-in-law what he is willing to do, ready to aim the Roman candle up into the tops of the mesquites, to expel the zanates from the yard if she commands it. Dina squeezes

Lalo's shoulder and lowers her hand to tell him this will not be necessary, and so he puts the fireworks back in his truck.

There will not be a picture of this moment, her re-entry into the world, adorning the textured drywall of Dina's home, on the mantel of the fireplace they have never used, or in her picture boxes. However, this is the moment that makes the next one possible: the hastily arranged portrait taken by the nursing home administrator. And just before it is taken, Papa Tavo recognizes Dina and calls her mija and holds out his sagging but strong-in-this-moment arms to embrace her. "You came back to me," he says.

The last portrait with Papa Tavo—where every apellido—Izquierdo, Buentello, Torres, Cárdenas, Alaniz, and Gallardo—is represented, will be found in every family's home. They will stand gazing at the sixteen-by-twenty-four print in their hallways in houses across the Valley and San Antonio, pause at the refrigerator door to glance at smaller reprints, touch their fingertips to its metal frame on their end tables. They will see themselves positioned to be near Papa Tavo and Abuelita, see Dina, standing behind her father, her veiled head tilted to one side, her hand on his shoulder, his hand crossed over his chest resting on hers. They will remember the last time the whole family was with Papa Tavo, and agree she was the one that made it possible.

The Seven Songs

Zanate (Quiscalus mexicanus): *The Mexican grackle, or great-tailed grackle, is a bird that is native to Mexico, but is common along the border and throughout Texas. The males have a glossy blue-black plumage while the females have an earthen hue. The zanate is distinguishable by its piercing yellow eyes, and its wide array of sounds that alternate between high-pitched whistles, squeaks, croaks, clicks, a mournful cry that evokes a question that cannot be answered, and a sound that mimics a rusty gate opening between worlds.*

Pay attention, my Poderosas. I need you to listen and remember so that you will tell this story to your children and they will tell it to theirs. This is the cuento of a brujo, the devil, and the zanates we think we know so well. You are ready for this, my daughters. Each of you, my Poderosas, are living saints, too wonderful and beautiful for the anxieties and tribulations of this world, and you have overcome so much. I am so sorry I could not always protect you from your trials, but you are stronger because of them. This is why I call you my Poderosas, my powerful ones. I share with you this story because the veil between what we see and what we cannot has parted for you.

Now let me begin.

As you know, the time of my sequestering began with a dream or what you could call a nightmare. My reclusion was not because of agoraphobia like you read about in your encyclopedia, Dianira. Or because I have bad Izquierdo blood like your father wants you to believe. The origin of my being an ermitaña began with a terrible dream, and although it was not like the signs and wonders that visited your life, I find comfort in what every parent knows. We are to rejoice when our children do better than us. I only wish that you had not experienced the pain that preceded each of you receiving your miracles.

I saw the devil in a nightmare, mis Poderosas. It was terrible and ugly and will always leave a mark on me like a hidden wound. Like I said, these are not the signs and wonders I prayed for. I would like to say that I saw La Virgen like you, Dianira. Or that I made a proclamation of faith like you, Teresa, with the evidence of levitation, just like Santa Teresa herself. Or that I wished and prayed and fasted for the authentic stigmata of Padre Pio like you, Yesenia, only to discover that the prayer to see us all come back together was the true miracle worthy of sainthood and you were a saint all along. Lamentably, these things were not meant for me. Even if the pesadilla I experienced was meant for evil, it was used for good, as I will share with you now. There is a happy ending in this, I promise. We could all use a happy ending, no?

In this vivid nightmare that occurred in a shadow version of the old barrio, I saw El Diablo with the Brujo Contreras. As every Izquierdo knows, he is the man that let his hatred and envidia for our family and all that is good poison his mind.

Contreras appeared as he does in life. An old, overweight balding man with thick glasses, nothing much to look at and certainly not one you would think had the power to bring an entire family to their knees. The devil was an exquisitely dressed man with the left foot of a rooster and the right hoof of a goat. His suit coat and pants were black, with a blue that shined at different angles, like the feathers of the male zanates you see throughout our homeland. He had the handsome, unshaven face of a man. I'm not going to lie, Poderosas. He looked a little like the actor Antonio Banderas. Don't act surprised I know who he is, mijas. No se hagan. I know you watch him in those cochinada movies when you go to the dollar movies with your cousin Cirilo.

In Contreras's front yard, the devil stood face-to-face with the brujo. I stood on the sidewalk looking at them across the street through some branches, hiding behind some pink bougainvillea. I could tell they were conspiring or spreading chisme; they both kept looking over in my direction as they talked. I knew they did not see me, as if I were invisible and not fully in this realm of dreams or really well hidden by a neighbor's plantitas.

The devil called up into the trees, and it was not the voice of a man that I heard. His voice was that of a flock of zanates, except the only sound was the terrible scratchy call they make, the one that sounds like a rusty hinge.

Then I saw the zanates, flying in and out of Contreras's mesquite tree. One landed on his wide shoulder, then another, and then another. He was not afraid of them, but laughed, as if they were children who were giving him cosquillas.

Mijas, it's okay. I can see by your eyes that you are scared as I share this with you. You know that, thanks be to God, the zanates have fled from our property, even though they are still out there in the world. Thanks be to you and your tías for getting me out of the house.

As the zanates landed on Contreras's shoulder one by one, he whispered something to them I could not hear. All I comprehended was that they were human words and not the language of the zanates that the devil could speak. And in my spirit, I knew that Contreras was whispering a curse for each Izquierdo, for your Papa Tavo who has been through so much already. Whether by blood or by marriage, there was something awaiting each member of the family, and the devil stood there, nodding in approval.

When I awoke in the morning, the zanates had flown from my dream and had arrived in my life. They were in the trees around our house, and I could hear them beckoning me to come out. They wanted to fulfill their mission and utter maldiciones against me, cast their yellow mal de ojo over my appearance. Because they were extensions of Contreras's will, it was as if the brujo himself were outside calling to me. The worst fear for me was—

I don't want to say it.

But I will utter these words, because you have to know. My Poderosas, I worried that they would pluck out my eyes like the accusers did to Santa Lucía when they came to take her away.

Remember her story, hijas. Even though they tried to take Santa Lucía away for refusing to renounce her faith, they found that she could not be moved and was as heavy as stone. And then when that didn't work, and her holy heaviness kept her there bien plantada, they gouged out her eyes. But what happened then, hijas?

She could still see.

That's right. Even though she was eventually martyred, no matter what they did, they couldn't take her down.

In this way, mis hijas, I am like Santa Lucía. Contreras could not take me down and he could not prevent me from seeing. He kept me in fear for months, and you all have been so patient with me. You and your tías never gave up. I could only leave the house with Marisol or Maggie for short trips in the car, but after that day when they came for me, I managed to do something amazing.

I left the house today with your tía Marisol and went somewhere I never thought I would have the courage to go.

Yes, Poderosas, your tías made it possible, but I have to tell you, each of you inspired me with your faith and your strength. I was finally able to end my self-imposed exile. I put on my blue Virgen's velo, not to hide my face or beauty, but to shield myself from the zanates giving me ojo and to show them that I'm a woman of the Holy Sacraments. I did this while you were at Abuelita's because it was something I had to do alone. As soon as your primo Cirilo picked you up, I equipped myself with symbols of your powers. From you, Teresa, I armed myself with your quinceañera corona. From you, Dianira, I took your First Communion rosary. And from you, Yesenia, I chose your Padre Pio scapular. I put them all in my purse along with holy water Marisol had given me and a vial of anointing oil from Maggie. I was confident God would protect me, that His angels would spread their wings in a canopy all around so that Contreras's bad intentions could not reach me through his intermediaries, the zanates.

When I heard Marisol honk, heard her blasting Selena on her car stereo with the windows open, and I walked out, I half expected to see the zanates, hear their clicks and croaks ringing out against me, see their yellow eyes fixed on me. But no, Dios Todopoderoso, your tía Marisol and your tía Maggie with their prayers of protection had made sure that they would not return. Still, I prayed the presence of God the All-Powerful and the blue veil would protect me from any evil intentions as I walked out to her car.

If the zanates were out there somewhere waiting to sing their songs against me, they would have no effect and would just bounce off of the protective barriers surrounding me, and their cursed voices would get lost between the sound waves of "Bidi Bidi Bom Bom." If they tried to give me mal de ojo, it would make no difference. I was protected because I had something very important to do to help Papa Tavo, que Dios lo guarde, and greater is He that is in me than He that is in the world. You will see. Marisol just put that car in reverse and drove away en friegas, intent on helping me fulfill the task I had been given.

No, I did not go to church, mis hijas. I had to go into the enemy's camp: the place of evil and idolatry, of greed and charlatans, that den of vipers where I knew I would find the Brujo Contreras.

We went to the flea market.

Yes, the Pulga, my Poderosas. Your tía and I went to the Pulga.

I had her take me there because I knew it was where the curanderos sell their remedios and do limpias and read cards for people. This is where Contreras does his consultas and trabajos.

I crossed myself as we went through the turnstile entrance. Marisol paid our fifty cents to the señora who looked at my velo and only raised her eyebrows a little, as if she had seen everything come through that gate, even a woman with a pre–Vatican II head covering.

People were all around us, some stopped at stalls, looking at tools, machetes, wallets, belts, and clothes. No one seemed to pay much attention to us.

We walked by the stalls of clothes resellers, the food and beer corner where they sell elotes and cucumbers with chile, chamoyadas, and micheladas. Though your tía Marisol wanted a corn in a cup, I convinced her to follow me to the covered booths where the more prosperous vendors had their businesses. This was where I would find Contreras. I think she was stalling because, even though your tía is brave in so many ways, she has always been afraid of conflict, not wanting to confront people when something needs to be said. Her coming with Maggie to get me to leave my exile took a lot out of her.

As your tía paused there, I gestured that it would be okay, and she shook her head and pursed her lips because she knew I was using Papa Tavo's sign just to persuade her. What she did not know was that I was actually trying to persuade myself to move farther, into the darkest heart of the Pulga.

Just as I predicted, he was in the central section of the Pulga, the darkened indoor area where you could find air-conditioning and mini-shops with mismatched doors. I saw his sign between a hair salon and a TV/video store: CONTRERAS CONSULTAS.

Marisol said, "Ay, sister, I just don't know about this."

I opened my purse to her, then reached in and showed her your symbols of virtue, my Poderosas, to give me courage. I held

her hand, said another prayer, hoping that the angels would follow us into Contreras's store.

A single zanate puffed out its feathers, blocked the entrance,
and started to hop toward me, making its warning screech for
me to go no farther. At first I froze, as I had never seen one so
close, and here was one of Contreras's very own threatening me.
As Marisol gasped, I found my coraje, pulled the chancla off of
my left foot, and waved it at the zanate. I also reached for the
holy water in case the sandal was not enough. Was it a regular
grackle or one of Contreras's messengers? Either way, I was not
going to let it stop us and I would throw the chancla if I had to,
or spray its eyes. The zanate must have been a regular kind and
not one of Contreras's servants, because it flapped its wings and
hopped out of my way. It did not utter a curse or keep its yellow
eye fixed on me. And if it was one of his, the zanate got out of
my way because the angels were with me.

I looked at Marisol, crossed myself, and we walked through
the door.

I had never been inside a tienda botánica, or a store for brujos. It was too much to take in at once, Poderosas, I'm not going
to lie. There were charms and amulets, statues large and small of
La Santísima Muerte and Jesús Malverde, black and red candles,
some in the shapes of men and women. Behind the glass counter
on shelves under a sign that said LISTO were jars of dark things,
decaying things, cursed things floating in a cloudy liquid I knew
to be urine. These were the entierros meant for burying, meant
for ruining peoples' lives. The last thing I saw before I stopped
looking around was two red canvas dolls tied together with red
ribbon, a padlock piercing through the groin of one of the dolls.
I figured it was an hechizo meant to bond two people together,

when only one person wanted to be amarrado. I had to look away. Marisol had her eyes on the floor and kept them there. She stayed by the door and I beckoned her farther in with me, but her feet were planted on the floor. It was okay, because she had gotten me this far. I stroked her hand, looked for her eyes, and told her it was okay.

I had never been this close to Contreras, but there he was, sitting in a chair at a card table, not even paying attention to me. He had his head down low, his eyes peering over the glasses on the end of his nose, reading those little vulgar comics from Mexico, those cochinadas the malcriados like to read, the ones with half-naked women on the covers. *Cochino*, I thought, even though I didn't want to be judging him.

Contreras was much smaller than I had thought he would be, even smaller than he had appeared in my dream. He was bald, more gordito than I imagined, and had thick glasses. He wore a dark brown guayabera that was tight around his stomach. I checked his feet to make sure they were not that of a gallo or chivo. All I saw were an old man's huaraches stuffed with dry crusty feet and toenails like wood chips, not the rooster foot and goat hoof I'd seen on the devil of my dreams.

I pulled my velo closer to my face, as if I could block the faint smell of patas and death and other things I did not know about coming from the shelf where the curses were awaiting to be planted in the ground.

Without looking at me, his eyes still on the pages of his comic book, he said, "Are you in the right place? I've never seen you here before. And why are you wearing a veil? This isn't misa. Did someone die? Are you in mourning?" There was a smirk on his face as he said this.

"I am a woman of God, and He is everywhere, and misa is not the only place to humble yourself before Him. And no one has died. Besides, someone doesn't have to be dead for you to mourn them, to mourn what you have lost."

There were so many other things I could say, how, as my father slipped away more and more every day, I was mourning him. We all were. All these thoughts ran through my head just then, so I decided to just come out with it. I had to be brave and powerful like each of you. I had to speak up for the Izquierdos.

In Spanish, I said, "I am Dina Torres, but you know my family." This was the line I had practiced in my head all the way to the Pulga. It wasn't much, but it was an effort.

With this, he looked up at me, pushing the glasses up on his nose.

"Who is your family." It was not a question, my daughters. It was a statement, I could tell. And the way he spoke, Poderosas, so low and deliberate, his Spanish so superior to mine, like from the older time when there was no border and the river only had one name.

"I think you know, but I will tell you anyway. I am Dina Torres, daughter of Octavio and Valentina Izquierdo. I want you to leave my family alone. You have to stop cursing us."

He didn't listen to me, Poderosas. It's like I had not spoken even though I had said this as forceful as I knew how.

Instead, Contreras said, "I know you know that Izquierdo means *from the left* or *left-handed*. But did you know that to have the name of Izquierdo means you have always been cursed? In Latin, the word for *on the left-hand side* is *ad sinistrum*, which in Spanish is *siniestro*. That is another word for evil. It is the same in English. That is a curse in at least three languages.

That is what you and your family call yourselves every day, what your brothers have painted on their van, as if this is something to be proud of. And you may be surprised to know I read more than these comic books, señora."

"All I am saying, Contreras, is that you have done what you wanted, and you can leave us alone now. My father is sick and we have all suffered enough, each of us in our own way."

"You are a woman of the church, so I will tell you this because maybe it is something you can understand. This can even be seen in the Bible. But it is always the lambs on the right and the goats, the ones who are condemned, on the left. I know you know about goats." He smiled and waited for my reaction.

"You will leave us alone."

"What surprises me is that you come here asking me to stop making hechizos against you when you have no proof, only these suspicions because I was once your neighbor. And all along, your whole family, your father, your mother, all of your brothers and sisters, have proudly been using the name of Izquierdo, calling yourselves condemned. And you somehow expected your lives to be anything more than cursed. You just want someone to blame. Well, you should blame yourselves. Blame God. Blame your father for raising malcriados. Blame your oldest brother for what he did to my daughter. Anything that comes to you and your family was started before I even knew any of you. If you only knew the half of it."

Poderosas, I'm not going to lie. My strength was failing me, and doubt was starting to set in, and his words had me even questioning my father and brother and the way we were raised. I didn't know what else to say. I looked over at Marisol, hoping she had something to add, but she shrugged her shoulders and had nothing to say. I could hear the wings of the zanates flapping in the entryway, with their croaks and cries as they gathered there for me, in expectation of us leaving in shame.

Because I had nothing else, and because I know that people who do the most evil things can still love their children, I said, "I know you had family, your daughter, sons, and your wife, that they rest in peace. And I know the only one you have left is your younger daughter. I am asking you this as a daughter who loves her father and her family, just like your very own daughter must love you."

Contreras continued to look at me and said nothing.

I turned to the door, defeated, knowing I had failed. I paused and looked through the small window at the zanates gathering outside.

As if he did not want me to leave so he could taunt me some more, he spoke a little louder and said, "Did you know the zanates have their own songs? Oh, I know about them too, about the old stories of our antepasados. They sing the passions of our lives: sadness, anger, hate, and fear. They sing these for you, Dina Torres of the Izquierdos." And by saying my full name, I knew he was attempting to proclaim his power over me like the demonios did to Jesus when they asked Him His name.

And then the Holy Spirit gave me the words to speak and, as your tía Maggie says, I got a word of knowledge. I had Maggie's and all of your combined strength within me, my powerful ones. Even though Marisol was timid and said nothing, she was brave enough to be there with me, giving me strength too. And then I could also feel my mother's fuerza. Then, it was like all your tías, Maggie, Melinda, Ana, Suzana, Victoria, Elvira, and even Ofelia were all in the room with me and Marisol. I'll even go so far as to say I felt the strength of Santa Lucía, making me an unmovable force until I said exactly what he needed to hear.

"Your forgot the other songs, Contreras." Just like that, I said it.

He squinted at me, and whether he had never known or satanás had clouded his mind, this was new to him.

He opened his mouth as if to speak, but I interrupted him before he could.

"Yes, Contreras, I know our stories too. You're not the only one with ancestors who passed down our stories or even a library card. You didn't mention the other songs of the zanates. You forgot courage, joy, and love. Especially love. As the story of our ancestors goes, when the zanates stole these songs because they had no voice of their own, they also learned the good ones. Do you see? They also learned to sing songs that brought good into the world. And there were seven songs in all, the number of perfection, the number of God Himself."

Contreras still could not respond, and whether it was because he didn't know what to say or if the feathers of San Miguel Arcángel were covering his mouth, I'll never know. He kept licking his lips, inhaling as if he were about to say something, then spitting as if feathers were stuck between his teeth, but the words would not come.

And then, my Poderosas, I was even bolder, and now even the zanates outside the door were silent. Because now the flapping I heard was not the small wings of the zanates, but the angels hovering inside and outside, flapping their giant angelic wings, as they were there going before me and behind me in this battle. What I said next was what he desperately needed to know, what I hoped would carry him through the rest of his days and bring him to a place of forgiveness where he could leave the hatred behind.

For dramatic effect, as if I were a singer of old, like Vicente Fernández taking off his sombrero, I removed my blue velo and uncovered my head. I let my hair fall free to my shoulders, got out your quinceañera crown from my purse, Teresa, and put it on. In spite of the spiritual battle we were in, I heard Marisol snort behind me, like she used to do when she was trying not to laugh in church. I turned to look at her, but she wasn't making fun. She was just laughing with me at how I was being so exagerada, doing something only Maggie would do. She nodded assuredly, as if to say, *Dile, sister, you tell him what's what.*

"You are loved, Contreras."

And then, like a sin vergüenza on the streets or in a cantina, I was singing it, Poderosas. I was singing it to the tune of Lola Beltrán's rendition of Tomás Méndez's "Paloma Negra." I had her strength too.

"*You are loved, you are loved. You are loved of God.*"

It was true, and it was not too late for him to know it. Then I felt Marisol's hand on my shoulder, and I thought she was trying to silence me, but no, Poderosas, she was encouraging me. *Sing, Dina, sing.*

I was a woman with no shame and I didn't care how many people at the Pulga heard me as I opened the door and scared the zanates away with my singing voice, one that was louder than I ever used in church or when I sing along to Papa Tavo's records when I am feeling blue and want to think about better days.

There in Contreras's open doorway, I stood with Marisol's hand of support on me, Teresa's quinceañera crown on my head, and I gave the most passionate grito that would have won any contest, even ones I entered years ago when I was much younger. A crowd was gathering, watching me with mouths agape, as I courageously sang my own irrepressible song of love. Although I was no Lola Beltrán or María Félix or Linda Ronstadt, I was singing a joyful noise as the Spirit gave me utterance. All Contreras or anyone could do was listen to my song of love, listen to my gritos louder than any zanate from legend or from this world or the one below us.

Part 5

Sueños, Viajes

1987

With so many Izquierdo children and in-laws, it was important that there was an understanding of when the children and grandchildren would spend time with Papa Tavo and Abuelita. It was an agreement, unspoken but unbreakable, that following church, Sundays were reserved for Izquierdos. A compromiso was also in place for holidays. The Izquierdos kept Thanksgiving lunch, Christmas Eve, and Easter Sunday, while the in-laws' families got Christmas Day, the brindis and eating of the twelve grapes of luck on New Year's Eve, and Thanksgiving dinner. This was the way of it, and even though Papa Tavo had never made a pronouncement, his annual invitations for these days were never challenged.

On these Sundays, each of the families brought a dish: a box of fried chicken from Church's, tamales if it was that time of year, and someone, usually Marisol or Elvira, would make caldo, regardless if it was soup weather or not. For sweets, there was always pan dulce from De Alba's, Gamesa cookies, and even Little Debbie nutty bars. Some days, there were gallons of ice cream from the Hygeia truck or ice-cream paletas from the neighborhood heladero.

One Sunday, Papa Tavo stood in front of this ice-cream van trying to take orders from his nietos, who were pointing at pictures of ice cream taped to the van's door: ice-cream sandwiches, Neapolitan and regular Drumsticks, Bomb Pops, and orange sherbet Push-Ups, and paletas of assorted cartoon characters, which were always a disfigured representation and disappointment when the children opened them. Inside the van, the heladero sat on his stool, listening intently for the order among the children's raucous voices and the music of "Pop Goes the Weasel."

Papa Tavo leaned over and looked at Seferino, Teresa, Dianira, Yesenia, and even his oldest nieto Cirilo, who stood behind them, trying to get his younger cousins to quiet down. Cirilo was his little hombrecito, so serious, his ojos borrados always studying the world around him.

"Listen, mis babies, one at a time. You, Seferino, what do you want?"

"A Push-Up and an ice-cream sandwich."

"Hijito, you can only have one."

"Okay, then an ice-cream sandwich."

And so it went with each grandchild. Braulio, Gonzalo, Macario, and Marisol sat under the carport on benches and chairs and smiled at Papa Tavo and his predicament. They laughed at how every time he got frustrated, he rubbed his forehead, pushing his Stetson higher and higher until it was practically on the back of his head like the cowboy Will Rogers from the old days.

After all the grandchildren had received an ice cream, they

went back to the kitchen and resumed the game of dominoes they always played after lunch. Papa Tavo again explained the rules, though he knew he had lost their attention because the children were focused on their ice cream.

"Lila, you have to hide your pieces. Turn them facedown, hijita. Everyone can see. Cirilo, help her, please."

Cirilo, who was sitting next to her, turned them over, as Lila could not seem to be bothered.

When Papa Tavo saw that they were dripping ice cream over the domino pieces, and were no longer listening to him, he called to Valentina, who was at the coffee maker breaking sticks of cinnamon into the brewer and sprinkling coffee grounds over them.

"Vieja, por favor," he said.

"Andele," she said. "You can run a crew of men, but give you your nietos and you can't keep them from getting the dominoes sticky. Andele, jefe, patrón, tell them what to do." A look passed between them as they shared a memory of when their own children were young and he was the disciplinarian. But with his grandchildren, Papa Tavo found he could never yell at them, nor give them nalgadas when they deserved it.

"Babies," Abuelita said. "Now that you've finished your ice creams, go to the restroom and clean your hands, and Papa Tavo will show you his maps."

The nietos ran to the back bathroom, stumbling over each other to get there, because this was one of the things they liked to do most.

Papa Tavo only had one hobby: collecting maps. He had fold-out maps, Rand McNally road atlases, colorful cartoonish maps to theme parks like Fiesta Texas and Six Flags, and maps of the River Walk in San Antonio. Other than Mexico, Papa

Tavo had never been outside of Texas for work or vacation, though he had always talked about it. Anytime his children took trips for vacation, they always brought him maps from each state they drove through, and Papa Tavo's goal was to have a map from all fifty.

Papa Tavo kept them in a wooden cabinet, locked behind a glass door. His nietos followed behind as he went to this cabinet.

"Where do you all want to go today?"

Though Papa Tavo was not the best reader, he had memorized each of the fifty states.

Seferino said, "Wherever you want to go, Papa Tavo."

"Pues let's go to the coast, see the Pacific Ocean, and then we can go to Canada. Visit the other border."

Papa Tavo pulled out the Road Atlas, their favorite one because this was the only one he let them handle themselves; they could never fold the others back correctly. He also took his map magnifying glass, a white one with a battery in the handle for the little light.

With his nietos leaning over his shoulder, he traced his finger west, pausing when he got to El Paso. He let each of them look through the cup of the magnifier, which illuminated and enlarged the city.

"Did you know that it takes over twelve hours just to get out of Texas? Texas is like its own country. If we drove straight through we could make it there in one day, but Cirilo, you'd have to help with the driving. The rest of you, if you want to drive you're going to have to tie cookie boxes on your feet to reach the pedals." They all giggled at this, as he reached to tickle their feet.

He continued tracing his finger. "Then from Texas into New

Mexico and the desert, Utah, then pass through the little corner of Idaho where all of the potatoes come from. Through Oregon, then into Washington. One of my workers who used to work la pisca up there told me he had been to the coast and the water is actually freezing. Can you believe that? It is not like here at South Padre where the water is mostly warm. It is cold. You put your feet in it, and they freeze like paletas." He reached for their feet again, and they laughed at this.

"Hijitos, hijitas, my babies. I may never go to these places, but you will. Get to studying, working hard, keeping your Spanish, and you can go anywhere you want, be anyone you want to be. You always give it ganas, right, babies? And what is ganas?"

Seferino said, "Ganas is when you want something and you never give up."

"Yes, papito. ¡Échale ganas! You have ganas because you are an Izquierdo, even if Buentello is your last name." Papa Tavo passed his eyes over each of his nietos, made sure theirs were locked on his as he said, "Because whatever last name you all have, you will always be an Izquierdo, have our blood running through you. And when you have babies of your own someday, and you go anywhere on these maps, you will teach them this, what it means to have ganas, what it means to have our name."

A Map of Where I've Been

When my parents were happier and not drinking as much, Sundays meant church and driving to Papa Tavo's and 'Buelita's house. Now, in the middle of the junior year of my life, Sundays meant driving to my grandparents' house without my parents. Pop had bought me my Impala at an auction in San Antonio. It had a clean body, but needed some work. He said that I would need to get a job to make payments to him, that the only reason he had gotten it for me was because I needed to drive myself around, but I knew he was just trying to bribe me into not complaining about having to go to a new school. Or maybe he was just trying to make up for all I had lost.

Besides my ex-girlfriend Llorona leaving for somewhere up north, there was other stuff that had gone down with my friends Ángel and Smiley, and I'd lost them both to gang violence, because of some beef with vatos from Pharr. Because I'd been friends with other dudes in the Hispanics Causing Panic crew, Pop moved me to Sharyland High School for my junior and senior years, saying I needed to get away from the vagos at

Dennett High School. He wanted me to make some new friends, which I really hadn't, friends I could trust anyways. So now my Sundays weren't about Westside Park and checking out the other ranflas, but all about having lunch with 'Buelita: her guisos, mole, or chicken and rice, and always her tortillas. Other times there were pachangas, parties for my little cousins' birthdays, or get-togethers just because. Ever since Papa Tavo's breakdown, Sundays also meant going to the nursing home. It was a way to not be alone, but also a way for me to remember how it was before everything had happened.

This one Sunday, I especially wanted to go to 'Buelita's because my cousin Erika, tía Marisol and tío Lalo's daughter, was having her second birthday party. Almost all of the Izquierdos were going to be there. Even a few of my tíos and tías had come down from San Antonio for the weekend. My little cousin Erika was something else. At two, she had attitude walking around with a toy purse and telling us "No" anytime we tried to hug her or get some besitos. She also danced like Selena whenever one of her songs came on the radio.

'Buelita's neighborhood wasn't East Los, and the Zavaleros wouldn't blast you if they didn't know you, but the locos still looked at you gacho if you didn't belong or they had never seen your car before. The only times they'd mess you up is if you came in throwing colors or signs, just asking for trouble like some junior high wannabe. This was my father's barrio, where he used to run around with his brothers, causing panic around town. He and my tío Gonzalo were in an old-school gang called Los Diggers, which was short for grave diggers. They weren't that gacho, but they had a reputation and you didn't mess with them.

Me, they knew I was all Dennett, but they also knew who my

pop was and that I was an Izquierdo and that I had been coming there since I was a kid. We'd all seen each other since we were little, me and my cousins walking to the corner store or to play on the swings behind St. Joseph's Church. I'd even played with some of them back then. So I'd drive up Aurora Street in my old-new Impala and none of them threw me even a sideways glance. Only the younger ones without respect, little junior high escuincles trying to act all bad, would stare me down as if it would scare me. I had to laugh. They had no way of knowing the things I had seen, the things I had done.

As soon as I rolled up, I could smell the smoke from the barbecue pit. With this smell of mesquite and fajitas, and the sounds of my tíos laughing, my tías talking inside, behind the burglar bars, and my little cousins running around my legs, I forgot everything that had happened in my life and how my Papa Tavo was sick and would not last much longer.

When I walked in to 'Buelita's little house, everybody said, "¡Mira, Cirilo!" Everyone was excited I was there because me, Pop, and Mama hadn't been to 'Buelita's together in several months. They were glad I was representing my family, because it was important to have at least one person from every child of Papa Tavo and 'Buelita's families come to the get-togethers or parties. The last time my parents had come together, 'Buelita had again told Pop and Mama they were spending too much time in the bars and not visiting Papa Tavo in the nursing home and taking care of me like they were supposed to. 'Buelita had said, *Maybe Cirilo wouldn't have gotten into all of that trouble if you had paid more attention to him. You could have lost him all because you two are so lost in yourselves.* You couldn't tell Mama something like that to her face and have her take it. Once you told her anything or did her wrong, forget it. She would never let it go. Even if she talked nice to you afterward, this thing would always be there, behind her eyes, in the way she said things to you. If you said them behind her back, maybe she could ignore it, but this, those words to her face? It would be years before she came around again. And because Mama was back at home and Pop was trying to keep the peace, this time my pop stood by her and hadn't come around either.

My parents hadn't spoken to 'Buelita since that argument, but they didn't care if I went to her house. This silence between them was not just because of the argument, even if that's what Mama said. It had been building for years. They'd never gotten along. Before they got married, Pop messed up by telling Mama what 'Buelita had told him about her. *That woman, she is going to be very expensive.* Mama had never really forgiven 'Buelita for saying that. With the way Mama bought gold jewelry all the time, and got her nails done downtown, 'Buelita had pretty much been right. Anyway, if my parents ever got mad that I was here at 'Buelita's, I'd still go. They couldn't stop me.

I went into the kitchen, which was elbow-to-elbow full of my tíos. They were cutting more fajitas, laughing with pink meat and fat in their hands. They held the meat in front of my face. My tío Manuel from San Antonio gave me his elbow to shake since his hands were full. My tío Lalo laughed his big belly laugh, said, "Good to see you, mijo!" and patted me on the back in his rough way. When I was smaller and he used to do this, it almost knocked me down. Now, at seventeen, I could stand there and take it without losing my balance. I was getting taller than all of my tíos, even though everyone said I was so skinny I looked like a palo standing next to them.

Tío Gonzalo shook my hand, smiled, and took a plate of raw, seasoned chicken out to the barbecue pit. It wasn't perfect, but things were better between us now.

My tías were sitting at the table, drinking wine coolers and coffee, even though it was so hot, especially in the kitchen where there was the pot of charro beans on the stove.

I bent and kissed my aunts on their cheeks, one by one. When I got to tía Marisol, I said, "Tía, are you losing weight?" I said this every time I saw her, but it was rarely true. She was good to me, and it made her feel better. Anytime she saw me, she didn't say things like, *Long time no see, stranger* or *Where have you been?* or ask about my parents. She didn't judge or give me the evil eye because of what my parents had done. She was just happy to see me.

"Ay, mijo, gracias for noticing. I'm on ese low-carb diet where I can eat a lot of meat and bacon and barbacoa, but no bread or tortillas. Why don't you tell your tío I've lost weight, mijo? He don't seem to notice." She said this last part, pointing her eyebrows at tío Lalo, who was chopping at the chicken, cutting it down the middle and laughing the whole time.

I winked at my tía and said, "Oye, Tío, have you noticed my tía's losing weight? She's looking fine. You better watch out the next time you go to a dance or a concert." All my tías laughed and tía Marisol said, "Ay, mijo, you're crazy."

Tío Lalo lifted his shirt and patted his own big, hairy stomach. "Hey, vieja, look right here. Mira. You know what? You can never leave my beauty. Aquí te tengo under my power."

"Power, ni que power," my aunt said, rolling her eyes.

I looked around for 'Buelita, but I was sure she wasn't in the room since tío Lalo would never do anything like that in front of

her. He loved and respected 'Buelita as much as his own mother.
I also looked for tía Victoria, which was another reason I liked
to come around. Who doesn't like to talk to a pretty woman? At
thirty-four and as good-looking as she was, she could have gone
cruising with me and my friends and no one would have thought
anything about it except that we'd done good for ourselves. I
was still careful around her, though, because of the looks tío
Gonzalo sometimes gave me whenever I stopped to talk to her,
because of what had happened, when he'd thought she'd been
flirting with me.

"Where's 'Buelita?" I said.

"She's in Suzana's room. Go say hi, mijo, she'll be happy to
know you're here." This was where she went to pray for Papa
Tavo, always hoping that he would get better and come home.

After Charter Palms, his liver got sick from all the nervous
anxiety medication he was taking. Then he moved from nursing home to nursing home, to the place where he was now, San
Juan Nursing Home at the San Juan Shrine. 'Buelita prayed for
Papa Tavo in Suzana's room, but she also prayed because she
was afraid. Back when they were still talking, she would call my
pop in the middle of the night so he could come check around
the house. She said bad kids in the neighborhood were always
crossing through her yard, looking into windows for something
they could steal. Whenever Pop or one of my tíos got there, they
never saw anything; no gangsters, or any sign the gangsters had
been there. This was also another reason why Mama didn't like
'Buelita. She thought 'Buelita did it for attention.

There was a little black-and-white TV screen in the living
room. It had four different pictures, and when I looked closer, it
was four different angles of her yard.

"Po'recita," I said to myself. The TV screen was hooked up to surveillance cameras tío Gonzalo had installed outside. I imagined 'Buelita sitting there at night, next to the phone, just waiting to see some kids jump the fence. I mean, what kind of barrio was it where kids from the neighborhood were trying to steal things from an old woman in the *same* neighborhood? Messed *up*. It was never supposed to be this way, even though I'm sure it also happened in Dennett.

I heard her whispered prayers. Her prayer voice calmed me like it did during all those Christmases when she prayed the Rosary and all I could think about was opening presents.

Her back was to me and she was kneeling down. She could stay that way longer than anyone I knew. She would say the Rosary, not moving at all, her eyes shut tight, her spirit somewhere far away from us, whispering every bead. Once, inside the church at San Juan, after all of us had visited Papa Tavo, she had walked on her knees all the way from the back to the altar in the front. All the way, on her knees.

I stood there by the open door, watching her, noticing how her ponytail had more white hair in it. I didn't say anything.

"Come in, mijo," she said without turning. In Spanish, she said, "I want to talk to you."

"How did you know it was me? Did God tell you I would come?"

"No, mijo, I heard everyone when they said, '¡Mira, Cirilo!' Also, I heard you driving your old car."

She stayed on her knees for a little too long, like she wanted me to get down on the floor with her too. I stayed standing by the door because I wasn't ready for that.

I felt better when she motioned for me to help her get up. 'Buelita held out her arms and I gave her my abrazo, the kind of tight hug I saved for my grandmother, and inhaled lavender and lotion, the clean beautiful smell of my 'Buelita. In Spanish, she said, "How are you this week, mijo?"

"Sí, 'Buelita, I've been good."

We were still hugging each other when she said, "Qué bueno, qué bueno. It is so good to see you, to hear you are doing better and that you are okay," sounding like she was about to cry. I was glad when she didn't. I could stand to hear anyone but my grandmother cry, even Mama.

"What I wanted to tell you was I have been praying for you and your father and mother, and I know it is all going to get better. God told me your father is going to change."

What about my mother? I thought, but didn't ask. I just said, "That's good, 'Buelita, that's good."

"No, mijo, I know it is good, but you have to believe it. And I am not saying this to make you feel better. I am saying this because I know. But your mother? I do not know."

After a couple hours, when more people showed up, they decided to put up the piñata. Because I was pretty skinny and didn't weigh that much and was old enough to go on the roof, they asked me to control the piñata, a clown with a big balloon stomach, the big kind you bought in Reynosa and not one of those cheap little ones from H-E-B. This was going to be fun, being on the other side of the piñata, the one teasing the little kids.

My little cousins had tried to bust the piñata already. I had been good to them, but sometimes piñatas were very thick, and no matter how hard they swung the broomstick, the little kids couldn't bust it.

Seferino, the oldest kid there, was up to bat last, and since he was big and strong enough, he had on a blindfold. Sef looked like a little tío Lalo with those small eyes and that big stomach. He spit on his hands, rubbed them together, and said, "Bring it on, cachetón!" Sef swung the broomstick wild and I pulled on the piñata. It went rolling through the air, and everyone went, "Oh!" He was swinging wild, not even coming close, and everybody kept moving to give him room because he had a lot of weight behind his swing. Somebody could get hurt.

When Sef stopped, I put the piñata on top of his head and lifted the clown as soon as he tried to hit it.

Sef said, "*Ya güey*, don't be like that."

Tío Lalo said, "Sef," because he'd said *güey* in front of 'Buelita. It was okay for Sef to say it in front of him, just not in front of 'Buelita, even though *güey* wasn't that bad of a word. It was like saying *man*, but it was a respect thing not saying it in front of people older than you.

Finally, because I could tell everyone was getting bored, thinking, *Ya, let him hit it already, our kids want some candy!* I kept it from moving, and Sef took this big swing. Candy went flying everywhere, but Sef kept going.

All the grown-ups said, "Wait, wait, *wait!*" but Sef kept on anyway, and Little Gonzalo ran in. You see, when you're hitting a piñata or standing around the circle waiting for candy, something takes over you. You can't hear what the grown-ups are saying. All you're thinking about is busting that piñata open or running and grabbing as much candy as you can. It's like when somebody's getting jumped, and nobody wants to stop, even when the teachers and chotas finally show up, break through the crowd, and are yelling and pulling you off of each other. It was like so many fights I had seen or been in.

I was above everybody, and I saw it happen all slow-motion before everyone else. The broomstick came back as Sef was going for another swing and—*Zas!*—Little Gonzalo's head was there. He was on the ground now and stupid Sef, all crazy with thoughts of candy, couldn't hear the grown-ups screaming, "Stop! *Stop* it!" Finally, he stopped because my tío Lalo slapped him on the back of the head. Tía Victoria went to Little Gonzalo. The kids didn't care. They were making candy bags out of their shirts, holding them out with one hand and throwing candy in with the other.

Tía Victoria was sitting there, and she wasn't treating Little Gonzalo like a baby, even though he was screaming and rolling around in the dirt. She was saying, "It's okay, mijo, you're all right. You don't need to cry." His head was going to have this big chipote, but there wasn't any blood. Little Gonzalo just kept sucking air and trying to bury his face into tía Victoria, saying, "Mama, Mama, Mama." When I saw her face, and her eyes were looking into mine, I felt bad about making Seferino have to work at hitting the piñata. Maybe if I'd made it easier, Seferino wouldn't have gone so crazy with the stick. She smiled at me and shook her head as if to say everything was okay.

Tía said, "Sana, sana, colita de rana, si no sanas hoy, sanarás, mañana." Our mothers say this when we're hurt, but not too bad. It means, *Heal, heal, little frog's tail. If you don't heal today, you'll heal tomorrow.* It doesn't sound the same in

English, though. Little Gonzalo would not get up or look at any of us. Like I thought, it looked like this big avocado pit was growing inside his head, but he was going to be okay, if he ever stopped crying.

Tía Victoria said, "Go play, mijo, go play. You're all right. Be a tough little man." She wasn't treating him like that because she didn't care about him, but because she didn't want him to be a mama's boy. Everybody knows mama's boys get jumped. I hoped Little Gonzalo got over this before he went to junior high, because the first time he cried like that at school, it would be all over for him. The other kids would knock him down just to watch the show.

Sef went up to Little Gonzalo with his shirt full of candy, his big panza showing to everybody, and told him he was sorry. "You want to share my candy?"

Later, we were all sitting down at the table in the kitchen eating. The little kids were in the living room watching a cartoon video someone had put on. I was eating with my tías and tíos. We were eating serious, no talking at all. You could hear the sound of ice in our glasses of Coke and the sound of our arms sticking and unsticking to the plastic cover on the table. Once in a while, someone would ask if there were more tortillas and someone would get up to heat more.

I was sitting across from tía Victoria, and Little Gonzalo was on her lap. This was the way they were, always talking to each other real quiet, like they were telling secrets, always praying together before they ate.

"So, what's up, LG?" I said. "You break any hearts yet?"

Little Gonzalo smiled real big, and lowered the bag of ice he held on his forehead.

"Ay, Cirilo," tía Victoria said, and put the ice pack back on the chipote. "Don't encourage him. That boy is pure Izquierdo. Still the same." She meant that all us boys and men with Izquierdo blood were dogs. We could always get pretty women without even trying too hard.

"Do you remember what they caught him doing back when he was at day care?"

"Oh, tía, how could I forget?"

Tía had told me this story before, and I always liked hearing her tell it. The conversations at the table had stopped, and everyone was listening to her, as they liked this story also.

"They found him and this little girl hiding in the gabinetes underneath the sink. I remember saying, 'Mijo, your day care's called Little Friends, not Little Kissy Kissy Friends, so don't be kissing girls in any cabinets!' Now when I do his laundry, I find notes from the little girls at his school. This one's going to be bad. Va ser terrible." My tíos and tías all laughed at that one.

Little Gonzalo smiled bigger at the word *terrible*.

"Little man knows. Ain't that right, LG?"

"I like girls," Little Gonzalo said, lifting his shoulders and smiling.

"I know you do, mijo. Just like your father and your uncles and your cousin Cirilo. Y tú, Light Eyes? Got any girlfriends?" As she asked this, everyone at the table went back to their own side conversations.

Even before she finished her sentence, I thought of my Karina who had gotten away, leaving me here to wait for her, to look for her around every corner, to walk to the mailbox hoping to see one of her illustrated letters or poems. Even though we weren't together anymore, and I didn't even know where she'd run away to, she was my first girlfriend and I had not gotten over her. She was my Llorona, my ghost woman I desperately wanted to see again, even if it meant she'd drag me under dark waters to be with her.

Tía Victoria didn't need to know I still thought about her every day, so I said, "No, Tía, I don't."

"¿Y porqué no? How can that be?" She said this looking at the tiny black knitted cross around my neck. Karina had given it to me before she left, along with a book of her poems, and I was rubbing it now.

"Better being alone. I can go out with my friends without some girl telling me what to do."

"And school, how is school?"

"I'm behind in credits, especially in English."

"Are you hoping to graduate on time?"

"I hope so. My English teacher told me that I can do a five-page book report or a personal narrative for extra credit and I should be okay and not have to go to summer school again."

"You're smart, mijo, you just have to apply yourself."

I smiled, and something on my face made her say, "I sounded like an old lady just then, didn't I? Like some guidance counselor who's run out of things to say."

"A little bit, Tía, but it's okay." She laughed and shook her head. Tío was lucky to have her.

"¿Sabes qué, mijo? I'm going to tell you something. And if I sound like a counselor who should retire, I'm sorry. But it needs to be said. Those colored eyes of yours, some girl's going to look into them and see there's something special about you. I go to the mall and to Peter Piper Pizza, and I see all these little gangsters, and in a way they look just like you, with the shaved heads and the baggy clothes. But, you don't want that life. I see something better for you."

"You think so, huh?"

"No, mijo, I *know* so. I know you've probably heard it all before, but listen. Tus ojos borrados, those eyes of yours see things others don't. Why do you think you can draw so good? It's not in the hands. It's in the eyes. You look deep into things and see how beautiful they are. Así, with your art and your words, you just have to share what you've seen, tell everybody what you know."

⁂

AFTERWARD, AS PEOPLE WERE LEAVING, I drove over to San Juan Nursing Home because I was supposed to meet Pop to visit Papa Tavo.

I walked into the yellow halls and it made me sad. This old lady named Margarita was sitting by the TV on her big rolling recliner. She was banging the tray like I'd seen her do every time I'd visited. If you didn't see Margarita, you could always *hear* her, knocking the tray with her fists three times and then clapping three times. She'd sit there, her toothless mouth open, her empty eyes looking up into space: knock, knock, knock, clap, clap, clap. Every time. If I ever came in and Margarita wasn't doing it, it'd be because she was gone.

I never liked coming here, but came anyway, out of respect and love for Papa Tavo. All my tíos and tías made their kids go. None of the little ones wanted to be here because the only Papa Tavo they knew was this sick old man in a nursing home, the one who only talked to us sometimes when he was having a good day. Other days, Papa Tavo didn't even know who we were, or he just asked us for cigarettes we couldn't give him. Now that the cirrhosis caused by his medicines had gotten worse, we had to spend as much time with him as we could.

Pop was sitting by the bed, combing Papa Tavo's hair, doing it real slow, making sure to not scratch his head. Even though Papa Tavo's mind and body were dying, he had this real long gray greña that kept growing, which my tía Maggie came by every month to cut. Why didn't anyone at the nursing home ever comb his hair? His fingernails were the same way, growing and growing and growing.

The Papa Tavo lying there—his thick fingernails like wood, his mouth open, his eyes staring out the window, his skin loose like a paper bag, not saying much of anything we could understand— was the only abuelo my little cousins had ever known.

They didn't know the days before when he used to go play dominoes down on Seventeenth Street, or how he would buy us something from the ice-cream truck whenever it came by. They couldn't know Papa Tavo showing us his beloved collection of maps or sitting at the kitchen table teaching me, Teresa, Dianira, and Sef how to play dominoes, ice cream dripping all over the pieces and Papa Tavo not even caring, just laughing with us. The grandpa that danced cumbias with 'Buelita at weddings and quinceañeras, his Stetson hat tilted at a cocky angle, back when he still had muscles on him. The only way they could know this Papa Tavo was from pictures.

I got near the bed and Pop said, "Mira, Apá, Cirilo."

Papa Tavo looked at me without any kind of understanding of who I was.

"Es mi hijo, Cirilo," Pop yelled. "Tu nieto." He didn't seem to understand I was Pop's son or that I was his grandson. He just stared at the ceiling with his mouth open.

I reached out to shake his hand, and he didn't move at all. I took his hand anyway. It was bigger than mine and cold. Sus manos. These hands that had hung drywall and painted houses, and rubbed Vicks on my chest when I was a little kid and sick. These hands that had shuffled dominoes. These hands that had folded and unfolded maps from his collection to show me and my cousins on his kitchen table.

Just then, tío Gonzalo, tía Victoria, and Little Gonzalo walked into the room.

Pop and tío Gonzalo barely gave each other saludos, just a little lifting of the eyebrows and that was it. Pop pretended to wipe some spit away from Papa Tavo's face. Tío Gonzalo was still mad at Pop for the way he was acting with 'Buelita. I didn't blame him, even though brothers were not supposed to act this way.

Tía Victoria said, "¿Y cómo están todos?" She was asking us how we were all doing, as if no one was mad, as if I hadn't just seen her earlier.

"We're good. Busy with everything, you know how it is."

She said, "Ay, tell me about it."

You could feel things change between Pop and tío Gonzalo, and they gave each other this nod viejos give, one mixed with respect and regret and a looking forward to a time when things will be different. She told me, "Long time no see, stranger," and we laughed. It was great how women could do this, make things better just by being there.

Tío told Little Gonzalo to go give Papa Tavo his saludo. "Saludale, mijo. Go say hi to your grandfather."

Little Gonzalo reached forward and picked up Papa Tavo's hand. He was not scared, unlike my other little cousins, who would act bored to try and hide it, and then not even walk into Papa Tavo's room. He turned Papa Tavo's hand over and over, and looked at all the wrinkles, the bruised veins, and the brown liver spots. He said, "'Buelito, what's all this?"

We all kind of laughed at how Little Gonzalo didn't care what he said, at how he was the only one who talked to Papa Tavo that way. I thought all that stuff about him being a chillón mama's boy didn't matter because Little Gonzalo was brave in his own way, in a way none of the rest of us were or ever would be.

It was quiet and none of us knew what to say. Then, after a little while, Papa Tavo looked down at Little Gonzalo and he actually smiled. I couldn't understand him real good because whenever he talked it sounded like he was half-asleep, like he had glass marbles in his mouth or something. He said, "Esto, mi nieto, es un mapa de dónde he estado, dónde he vivido."

This, my grandson, is a map of where I've been, a map of where I've lived. I looked down, and I knew what he meant about his hands. On his hands, I could read where Papa Tavo had been: the large spots were places he had stayed, the smaller ones the places where he had visited, every wrinkle a dusty sendero he had taken to get him and 'Buelita here across the river, every vein a street he had used to get himself to work, the clear spaces in between were places he had never been and never would go.

I turned my own hands over and held them out. The map was mostly blank, with large open spaces I would claim for the Izquierdos, with undiscovered trails and roads I would map out for Papa Tavo and the rest of us. Along the way, I would meet others and tell them about what I had seen and what I knew. I would tell them what I had learned about life, about how even when you are alone or have lost someone, you can find hope, even in the smallest things: moments like this, a tiny black cross, a book of poems, a goodbye that might not really be a goodbye from a girl who taught you how to love.

Part 6

Padres, Madres

1985

Papa Tavo was never a big believer in what the curanderos did with their limpias and hierbas, but on the third day of Little Gonzalo's fever from the flu, when all the doctor had said was to make sure he got fluids and alternate between one kind of fever reducer to another every four hours, he found himself willing to try anything if only his nietito would get better. Even if he didn't have the gift of healing like a true curandero, it did not hurt to try.

"Tenemos que hacer algo, mi Capitana," he said, waving over the baby who lay in his car seat on top of Suzana's bed.

In Spanish, Abuelita said, "He is a little one, and they get fevers all the time, especially when they have teeth coming in."

"Yes, but this is different. He has had it for too long." Papa Tavo fussed at the blankets, trying to find Little Gonzalo's foot to see how warm it was. For too many days, he thought, Gonzalo and Victoria had been taking turns dropping him off every day at their house, because the day care would not take the baby sick, and they had to work, after all. Papa Tavo knew this was a job abuelos retirados were supposed to do—take care of the nietos when they were sick while the parents worked—but still Little Gonzalo had been sick for too many days.

Abuelita said, "Ay, mi Viejo, I know, he is a baby and it scares you, but it will pass. When you were off working and it was Gonzalo, Braulio, Marisol, Macario, or any of the others, I stayed home with the babies. And they always got better. You did not worry then, and you should not worry now." She narrowed her eyes when she said it, shook her head slightly, and clicked her tongue. Papa Tavo knew the way of it, that he was being an old fool, worrying about his grandson when he had not done the same for any of his own children when they were sick.

Papa Tavo unlatched the car seat and carried out sleeping Little Gonzalo, cradling his head. His nieto was warm, too warm. He carried the baby out in front of him, as if he were about to present him for a baptism. They were in Suzana's bedroom, where his own children had all slept, where they had taken turns sleeping on the bed or on the floor, all the colchas laid out to make the wooden floor comfortable. All those days ago when he would come home from a job and his children were already bathed and asleep, he would step over them in his sock feet, leaning over each one to make the sign of the cross on their sleeping foreheads and bless their dreams. The blessing went both ways. As he extended his right hand of provision over them, he felt a sense of peace flow over him, knowing that his children went to bed with full stomachs made possible by his labor.

He held his nieto in one arm, and with the other laid a baby blanket on the bed. Papa Tavo unwrapped him, unbuttoned his onesie and pulled it up over his head, and the baby hardly stirred.

Little Gonzalo was smaller than his other nietos at this age, and smaller than Gonzalo and Papa Tavo's other boys had been.

He whispered to Abuelita, "Bring me an egg for this pollito," which was what he sometimes called Little Gonzalo because of his skinny chicken legs. Despite his worry, he laughed a little at his joke. She clicked her tongue louder than usual so he was sure to hear her disapproval. "And a coffee can, bring me a coffee can." When she walked away and he didn't immediately hear the refrigerator open behind him, he said, "Por favor, Capitana."

She came back and handed him the egg and set the empty coffee can next to him. "Do not call him that anymore. If anything, he is my Little Goose." Abuelita leaned over Little Gonzalo, stroking his fine hair. "Un angelito, mi Gansito," she said, and then asked, "Do you really think this will work?"

"I don't know what else to do, Vieja. If I could take it from him I would. I don't know if I have the gift to heal, but I will try." Papa Tavo remembered his own father doing a limpia with an egg over him when they lived on a rancho in Montemorelos, Nuevo León, because there was no doctor nearby and their family was too poor to afford one anyway.

Papa Tavo held the egg, his cracked and calloused palms gentle as he rubbed it around Little Gonzalo's forehead and earlobes, down the arms and the tips of the fingers, outlining his body down to the soles of his tiny feet. The egg was supposed to pull out the sickness and put it all in the yolk. As he did this, Abuelita recited the Rosary, thumbing the beads as she moved through the order of the mysteries.

When Papa Tavo was done, he took the egg, cracked it on the edge of the can, and poured it out. He had heard stories about yolks gone black because they had absorbed illness, or *maldiciones, and sadnesses. There was nothing off in the color of the yema and it looked like he could cook it even though you were never supposed to, as you would be taking the evil into yourself.*

Papa Tavo looked into Abuelita's eyes, which were soft without any doubt of his intentions in them. "Do you think it worked?"

"I don't know, Viejo, but what matters is that you tried."

Host

These are the dawns
that King David sang of
To the pretty girls,
we sing of them here.
"Las Mañanitas"

—AUTHOR UNKNOWN

This was Victoria's first time hosting the eve of Mother's Day at her home, and thankfully everyone had said they would pitch in to help her. Victoria's brothers-in-law offered to get the fire ready, trim the fajitas, and season the chicken. Her sisters-in-law would bring the sides: beans, rice, potato salad, and green salad for those who wanted it. Melinda was even making chicken mole, which was one of Abuelita's favorites. Cirilo would bring ice for the coolers and Gonzalo would pick up Abuelita on his way home from work.

Papa Tavo had always made Mother's Day a special event for Abuelita. He hired mariachis for a midnight serenata, made sure she had all of her favorite foods, and saw to it that she didn't have to cook a thing. But Papa Tavo was living in a nursing home, and the children, worried that their mother would feel his absence too sharply if they celebrated the day in the home they'd shared, and worried about how Abuelita would be alone after everyone left, agreed to move the annual party to Victoria and Gonzalo's house on the north side of McAllen. They were doing their best to help Abuelita focus on the blessings of family she had, and not on what she had lost.

On the eve of Mother's Day, as members of the extended Izquierdo family arrived and Victoria welcomed them into her home, she found herself with mixed feelings they had come. The sound of their saludos, their boisterous laughter, and the cumbias on the stereo imbued her with some sense of peace, keeping her in the present and muting the annual melancholy she felt, which had started her first Mother's Day when Little Gonzalo was just weeks old, born premature. The memory of her younger self, the new mother with her frightening postpartum thoughts that were louder than prayers or reason, visited every year like an unwelcome soul on the Day of the Dead. Thankfully, this shadow of who she was left as quickly as she arrived or floated into a periphery of memory that was bearable. But now that Victoria was the one in charge of hosting the Mother's Day celebration, the feeling that she was all alone in the world, and the stress of everyone depending on her, was pushing down on her shoulders, threatening to immerse her in the pain and loneliness she wanted to forget. The shadow Victoria threatened to move away from the edges into the center, where she could not, would not be ignored.

Little Gonzalo heard his father's pickup pulling up to the house, and came running into the kitchen with his cousin Michely trailing behind, saying, "Apá's here, Apá's here!" Victoria was glad for the distraction, glad for how it made her shadow self recede.

As Gonzalo walked in first, holding open the door for Abuelita, his brother Wally said, "¿Qué pasa, mi carnál?"

"Nada, nada, hermano," Gonzalo said as he put his hand on
Abuelita's shoulder and motioned her to come in.

Abuelita walked in and waved at everyone and nodded
her head, which was her blessing to them as much as it was a
saludo. Everyone stood or dropped what they were doing in the
kitchen. They gathered around her and took turns hugging and
kissing her.

"¿Donde está mi Gansito?" Abuelita said from amid the
throng of the family, exaggerating the search for her Little Goose.

"I'm here," Little Gonzalo said from behind his father.

She reached for him and he pulled back, playfully, but not
disrespectfully.

While Victoria nudged him toward her suegra, Gonzalo
said, "No seas así. Say hi to your Abuelita."

Little Gonzalo let her squeeze his face and kiss him.

"Estás creciendo, Gansito," Abuelita said with pride, but
also an acknowledgment of how far he had come.

Little Gonzalo rolled his eyes.

"Sí, he's getting big," Victoria said, recalling with her suegra's words how small Little Gonzalo had been, how skinny, when
most of the Izquierdo babies were pudgy and Papa Tavo called
them his llenitos and llenitas. When he had first seen Little Gonzalo, he'd instead called him a pollito because of his scrawny
legs, and Abuelita had corrected him later, giving him the name
of Gansito, a sort of compromise with Papa Tavo. In this flash of
memory she didn't welcome, Victoria returned to those terrify-
ing first days when Little Gonzalo would sleep only an hour at
a time, and no matter how much she tried, he would not nurse

properly. He'd been jaundiced too and needed to be wrapped in
the blue glow of the bili-light machine, which would break down
the bilirubin and bring his color back to normal. In those first
days of her motherhood, Victoria had been on her own here in
McAllen, far away from her mother, who would have stepped
in and helped her with the baby. Victoria—a nurse who knew
better—should have told her mother the truth when she came to
visit for a week, or said something to Abuelita and her sisters-in-
law about what she was feeling. Something was not right, and it
was more than just the stress of a premature baby or the sleep-
deprived miasma and typical hormonal imbalance that every
new mother has to adjust to. She should have shared her struggle
with them, but how could she have explained it? What words
could describe how, in the middle of the night, when insomnia
wouldn't let her tired mind and body fall asleep and the whisper
of, *Just kill yourself and you won't feel this way anymore*, would
cause fear to encase her body, her heart racing and her breathing shallow as she felt trapped, her soul buried in her own body?
And then, when she had managed a feeble prayer and the rush of
adrenaline had passed, she would sink to the floor, tears washing
uncontrollably down her face, the feeling of hopelessness interrupted only by the sound of her newborn son crying and needing
her. She would drag herself up for Little Gonzalo, and as night
turned into day and the adages of *Sleep when the baby sleeps* and
It'll be better in the morning mocked her, she would stare out
the window, numb, feeling this existence would last forever and
she would carry it with her into heaven. But she had kept it all to
herself, and hadn't asked for help. Victoria had not wanted them
to think less of her or compare her with the cuñadas, or even with
Abuelita, who had managed to raise ten children, while she was

struggling with just one. Only Gonzalo had known, and when she thought now of how he'd been with her during this time, more tender and compassionate than she had thought possible, she said, "How was work, my viejo?"

"Hard," he said in his way that sometimes made Victoria feel as if Gonzalo regretted his decision to sell his part of the family business to his brothers to work shingling roofs at someone else's company, when he had been his own boss.

"Go take a shower. The others should be here when you're done. I left you a clean towel on the seat and I got some new soap."

When he only gave her a tired sigh, she said, "Okay, Viejo?"

"Thank you, Amor," he said as he squeezed her hand, and went down the hall to their bedroom. After their fight on the Fourth of July and subsequent separation, and after that awful night when Gonzalo had witnessed his father's frightening final breakdown, Gonzalo had softened somewhat, gone back to the man he was during her first few months of motherhood. He was more affectionate toward Victoria, trying to show his appreciation of what she had done and continued to do for him. Victoria proved she could support herself and Little Gonzalo, and she had shown him she was not afraid to leave him. Gonzalo was on an unspoken probation, and any drunken pendejadas, harsh words, or worse, and she would leave him for good, and he knew it.

She called to Little Gonzalo, who was lost in the crowd of family still gathered near the door around Abuelita. She wanted him to eat a little now before all of his cousins arrived, because she knew he would soon be too distracted to eat. Then Little Gonzalo would wake her up at seven tomorrow asking for pancakes, French toast, or toasted bisquites from Rex Café.

Gonzalo had showered and changed and was outside by the

garage with his brothers. Victoria could see him through the window in the kitchen door, laughing at some joke Lalo had told. It was a dirty one, because Braulio, who had recently quit drinking and started going to church at Baptist Temple, was looking down at the dirt, trying to hide his smile. It was good to see him back with the family, even if his wife, Ofelia, would not come. She liked to watch them this way, like a TV with the sound turned off. Gonzalo stood among them, and she noted again that he was still slimmer than the others, and his panza didn't hang over his belt. Even Braulio was getting a gut, which he hid well under his silk shirts and his fancy embroidered guayaberas. Gonzalo had always been thinner than his brothers, but in the last year or so, as he cut down on the drinking and ate more desserts to compensate, he started wearing size-thirty-six pants. He still looked good in his jeans and Ropers, but was slightly thicker in the face.

Younger women still looked at him, though he didn't dress all rico like Braulio and didn't look like he had a lot of money. At the Christmas party last year for Amistad Home Health, which Victoria attended with Gonzalo, the LVNs, and even the older RNs, had watched him when they walked in together. She had thought it was ridiculous how some of them who did not even talk to her at work had made sure they were introduced to Gonzalo.

Lily, sounding drunk, had said, "And who's *this?*"

"Gonzalo. My husband."

"You didn't tell me he was such a papacito."

Victoria had smiled, killing the urge to ask her where her mujeriego husband Ramiro was, who picked up women at the Gaslight without shame or guilt. But she had walked away instead, holding fast to Gonzalo's hand even though he was not a flirt with other women and never had been. Afterward, on the drive home, Gonzalo had not said anything about it. He hadn't rubbed it in like a couple of guys she had dated would have. He had many faults, but Gonzalo was never one to throw his good looks in her face, and he was no womanizer. She had to give him that.

"Can I go outside now?" Little Gonzalo was asking, shoveling the last of the rice into his mouth.

"Yes, mijo. Go play with your cousins."

He grabbed a red plastic cup of Cool Whip fruit salad and ran outside, and got lost in the mix of cousins who were running around. Now that the sun had gone down, the house, garage, and driveway were full of family. Victoria loved the chaos of it all, but was not used to it, as she only had one married brother. Her mother and father, Rolando, his wife Yvette, and their kids were in San Antonio, and their get-togethers were never like this, like all-out pachangas. She had called her mother before the others started arriving, and they were all at her brother's apartment, barbecuing. Her mother had sounded happy as she told Victoria of her grandchildren splashing in the pool. Rolando was preparing his shish kebabs marinated in beer, which he had learned to make while he was in the army. Their party was three kids in a pool at an apartment complex, a small radio playing classic rock, while hers, being an Izquierdo, was cumbias on loudspeakers, meat being grilled on a barbecue pit so big it had to be pulled on a trailer, and laughter that could be heard up and down the street, sometimes into the madrugada when everyone in their North McAllen neighborhood was trying to sleep.

"Maybe next weekend we'll see you," Mom had said. "And then we can celebrate Mother's Day together."

Some time later, Victoria set the place of honor for Abuelita at the dining table with the china and silverware from her wedding and handed out white Chinet plates to the rest of the family. She was signaling that it was time to eat, and moments later Lalo brought in the cooked meat in an aluminum pan. She smiled at her family as everyone sniffed at the pan, and watched Lalo set it on the bar. Stacked high were strips of fajita, plump shiny Polish sausages, mollejas, and browned chicken halves, cut Jalisco-style.

Each woman was responsible for serving her own family the sides, while the men chose and cut the meat, which took Marisol and Lalo the longest because they were the ones with the pickiest kids. Victoria spooned rice and beans onto Gonzalo's plate first, avoiding the potato salad because Suzana always used too many pickles and Gonzalo hated that. She went over to the tray, lanced some fajitas with her fork, and grabbed a chicken-half by the leg.

Standing near the sink, Gonzalo leaned over toward Victoria and searched for her eyes, as if to make sure she was okay, and maybe a reassurance that *they* were okay. She set his heavy plate on the counter and he kissed the top of her head, smoothing it with his hands.

"Gracias, Amor," he said.

"You're welcome," she said, and smiled at him, but not with her eyes, which were narrowed, focused on his other hand, which held a bottle of beer. Gonzalo playfully raised his hands in innocence, but lowered them when he saw she was not playing along. The Fourth of July, their fight, how drunk he had been, the accusations he had made about her and Cirilo, how easily those vile words had come from his mouth. All of that was in the space between their bodies, in the way she held herself away from him.

She turned away and went about making plates for herself and Little Gonzalo, which was useless because he wouldn't eat the food, but it gave her ample excuse to remove herself from Gonzalo and what she was feeling, how her thoughts were vacillating between remembering his tenderness when Little Gonzalo was a baby and the despicable things he had called her.

Once Marisol served her youngest, there was a lull as everyone looked to Abuelita.

Braulio said, "Before we eat, I think Abuelita would like to say something."

Everyone except Gonzalo got into a circle around the kitchen, their heads bowed. Maggie and Dina stood on either side of Abuelita. Gonzalo was still standing near the sink, drinking his beer, looking for a strip of fajita small enough to eat in one bite.

Come here, Viejo, Victoria mouthed, hating it that he could not wait for Abuelita to give her prayer or for Braulio to say grace. He nodded no and smiled. *I'm fine here*, he seemed to say.

Victoria sighed at his lack of respect and grabbed Little Gonzalo by the shoulders, trapping him in front of her, so he would not distract everyone by running around or squirming.

"Gracias, gracias," Abuelita said, whispering, "gracias por mis hijos." She was silent for a few seconds, and Victoria wondered if maybe she was waiting for the Spirit to guide her, or if she was about to cry.

Abuelita said, "Padre nuestro que estás en el cielo."

She paused the Our Father, waiting for the rest of them. Victoria looked at her family as they said the words, except for Gonzalo, who stayed silent, his eyes open and down, focused at the floor.

All of them, although they wouldn't admit it, winced at the

thought that Abuelita was about to start crying, something that didn't happen frequently, but pained them whenever it did.

"Padre nuestro, te doy gracias por mi familia," she said in her singing whisper. "Thank you for my beautiful children. Thank you for all the years you have given me with Octavio. I ask that you help our Papa Tavo feel better and give him peace. Gracias, gracias, gracias." When it was obvious she was finished with her prayer, and had made it through without weeping, collectively her children, the tíos and tías, dropped their shoulders, as if they had been holding their breath. Braulio then prayed the grace.

After they'd eaten, and the men had gotten serious about drinking beer, some of them, like Dina and the girls, went home at midnight. The ones who had come early to help decided to stay late after Gonzalo told them that he had hired some maria-chis. Gonzalo had paged the leader of the group to find out how much longer they would be. He had called back from a mobile phone, saying that they had a few more houses to go, and it would probably be about two or three a.m. by the time they arrived at Gonzalo's.

Victoria, Abuelita, and the rest of the family were outside in the garage and driveway listening to the radio when a Selena song came on.

"Bailen," Lalo said. "Let me see my girls dance." The way he said it, one word flowing into another, Victoria realized he was drunk, which was not a problem for Lalo, as the worst thing he did when he got this way was bring his strong arm around his cuñados and tell them how much he loved them.

"Bailen," Lalo said again. "Dance. Show your tíos and your tías how you dance Tejano."

Erika and Michely—who were somehow still awake—

started to shake their hips without rhythm. The older sobrina, Michely, knew the moves, but could not keep time with the music. To help them, everyone started to clap in rhythm.

Victoria clapped too and said, "Qué lindas," thinking maybe she wanted to try for a girl next, that maybe this time things would be different, that her thoughts and emotions would not steal the joy of new life. When another sudden wave of sadness threatened to overtake her as it had in the kitchen earlier when family was first arriving, and the shadow Victoria came forward from the darkness of the street and into the circle of family where the girls were dancing, she tried to keep her at bay by clapping harder and saying, "Dance, dance, hijitas!" Victoria moved her hair over the front of her shoulders, shrouding her glistening eyes from the family.

Gonzalo, who had been standing across from her by the stereo, came to where she was seated and stood next to her, as if to protect Victoria from the fantasma of her past self. He smoothed her hair and squeezed her shoulder and bent over to whisper, "Amor," in her ear.

As Victoria looked down at the floor, she saw a hand in front of her eyes. It was Marisol, who was pulling her to the makeshift dance floor with her daughters. Marisol looked for her eyes and said, "Let's make some washing machine moves to wash away the blues, Comadre. ¡Vamonos a bailar!"

"Okay, niñas," Marisol said, lining up Victoria and the girls, beckoning the other tías to join them, "let's show them how we do it!" And once Maggie got up to join them, all of Victoria's cuñadas and sobrinas were kicking out their feet, twirling around, pushing out their gyrating hips, raising their hands in the air. As Victoria twisted and pivoted, she looked over at Gonzalo and waved him toward her because the men were also joining in, but he stayed where he was, always the observer, content to watch them dance from his position outside the family's orbit.

For the next few hours, after they'd grown tired of dancing, while they waited for the mariachis to come for the serenade and the family's energy and patience began to wane, Gonzalo went in and out of the house to call the band leader and check on their status. He came out with updates for everyone.

"They'll be here soon. Only one more house to go." Though he hid it well from the others, Victoria could see that he was getting frustrated. She saw how he checked his watch when he thought no one else was looking, how he tried to reassure his mother, telling her, "Ahorita vienen, Amá, ahorita vienen." The eve of Mother's Day, Saturday night, was the busiest night of the year for mariachis, and though everyone knew this and they weren't complaining, Gonzalo was close to panicking, because this was the first eve of Mother's Day without Papa Tavo at his mother's side, and he wanted it to be perfect for her, as it always had been when Papa Tavo made the arrangements.

Just as Gonzalo was about to go back into the house to make another call, and Victoria decided to go after him to offer reassurance that the family was fine, Victoria heard trumpets coming from down the street. As the mariachis got closer, Gonzalo rushed to Victoria and put his arm around her. Affectionate, yes, but tentative, as if he feared she might pull away from him and leave him standing there alone. The mariachis walked up the driveway, playing their music while everyone made way and formed a crescent around Abuelita. Victoria laughed. They were bareheaded college kids, young men and women, not much older than her nephew Cirilo. Beautiful as they were—with clean, unwrinkled faces, and dressed up in red and black charro suits with ornate, shiny buttons and chains—she had expected them to look like the mariachis of old, like earthen men pulled from sepia photos of the Revolution, like the men and the soldaderas who had lived what they sang. The one with the guitarrón even had an earring, and hair shaved on the sides, slicked back on top. But they began singing "Las Mañanitas" and she stood blinking at them because they did not sound like children at all.

"Estas son las mañanitas
   que cantaba el Rey David
   a las muchachas bonitas
   se las cantamos aquí

As they sang, Victoria scanned the faces of her family, some joyous, some wistful. Abuelita sat there amid them, looking older than she had just hours ago, the years reflected in the creases on her face, the absence of Papa Tavo there like a shadow in the dark circles around her eyes, her smile interrupted by a quivering in her lips she tried to temper by pursing them.

Despierta mi bien despierta
   mira que ya amaneció
   ya los parajillos cantan
   la Luna ya se metió."

Gonzalo turned his face to Victoria as they stood side by side, long enough to communicate he wanted her to do the same. Despite not wanting to, despite how worried she was that her expression would betray all she had been feeling, how the ghost

Victoria of those past madrugadas alone with her fears and the voices had intruded on the present night, she looked back at him.

"Here goes nothing, Amor. This is for you."

Gonzalo stepped forward and wrapped one arm around the lead vocalist, pointing him in Victoria's direction. Struggling to find the right octave, but with gusto, Gonzalo started singing, trying to do his best Jorge Negrete, the mariachi's voice carrying him through the song. He sang, "*Ya viene amanaciendo. Ya la luz del día nos dió. Levántate de la mañana, mira que ya amaneció.*"

Unbeknownst to Gonzalo, his words brought forth Victoria's remembrance of the first time she had slept for more than four consecutive hours after Little Gonzalo was born. Victoria had shaken herself awake, and noticed that Gonzalo was not beside her, then checked the clock to see how long she'd been asleep. Her first thought was that the baby had stopped breathing and she had slept through it. When Victoria saw the empty crib next to their bed, she bolted upright, stumbled around the house, searching in each room, not even thinking to call out to Gonzalo. And when the blood beating in her ears quieted, Victoria could hear singing somewhere in the house. It was Gonzalo's voice, low and off-pitch, which she followed to the living room, where he stood barefoot on the rug, lit only by the brightening morning sky coming in through their bay window. He carried Little Gonzalo against his bare chest, swaying gently side to side. He sang a Spanish song and the lilting refrain of *rrurrurru*, a mother's traditional dove-like cooing to lull babies to sleep, was the only part she recognized. When nursing was a problem, and Little Gonzalo wouldn't latch onto Victoria's breast, the lactation specialist had told them that skin-to-skin contact was important to soothe and calm the baby even if they switched over to bottle-feeding. Gonzalo had laughed at the idea, but there he was that early morning, shirtless, with their diapered son cradled in his arms, a blanket draped over the baby's shoulders. Victoria watched them from the darkness of the hallway in silence. She never spoke to Gonzalo about this moment she had witnessed, not to spare his pride or self-consciousness, but because she felt using words to describe it would diminish it. Victoria also never searched for a way to tell him that what he had done for her that mañanita— and all those nights after they finally agreed to bottle-feed the baby and Gonzalo took most of the night feedings—had not fixed everything, or ameliorated the postpartum depression she would not name, but had helped her get through it.

The song was over now, and Gonzalo went to her, and she leaned into him.

After a few more songs, the mariachis paused, and when no one asked for more, they picked up their instruments again and started playing "Las Golondrinas," the traditional depar- ture song. They walked out single file as Gonzalo paid the young leader with the guitarrón. One by one, the family gave their des- pedidas, got in their cars, and drove away.

In the quiet of the house, all that was left were dishes in the sink, a trash can full of paper plates and cups, and the ashen mesquite smell that had crept in from the garage. In the kitchen, Victoria turned on the faucet as hot as she could stand it.

Gonzalo said, "Déjalo, Amor. I'll take care of it in the morning."

"I just don't want to wake up to all this." She took off her wed- ding ring, and set it on the windowsill. Her hand dove through the dirty dishes and slimy food to the sink stopper.

"Go to bed, baby. It's Mother's Day already."

"Okay, then, I'll just clean the table," Victoria said, and wrung out the washrag and turned off the faucet.

Gonzalo sat on the love seat next to the stereo in the living room. He leaned over, plugged in the headphones, and turned it on.

"¿Te divertiste?" he said, too loud.

"Yes, it was good to have everyone here."

"Right?"

"Are you going to stay up?"

"For a little while, Amor," he said, pulling one cup off of his ear, his voice tender and not defensive.

Gonzalo would probably stay on the couch all night, and he would wake up sore and crudo from the beer he should not have drunk.

"No to desveles tanto," she said, even though she knew he would sleep in tomorrow because of it and then want to take her to lunch at two or three after all of the Mother's Day rush had died down.

"I'll be in bed soon," Gonzalo said, "I promise."

"Okay," she said without a tone, nothing to indicate that she wanted to talk more about it. Victoria walked down the hall to the bedroom, thinking to say something else, but not sure what, not sure which of her memories, if any, she was ready to share with him.

After her shower, she went into the bedroom and lit the plain white candle encased in glass, the religious type sold in the supermarkets. Victoria did not like the other veladoras, the kind her mother-in-law had, the ones with pictures pasted or painted on them. Suegra believed that the candles were symbols that the

Holy Spirit was there in the house, reminding the evil spirits to keep away, and Victoria wondered if the candles had the same power over memories, over shadow selves that tried to reassert themselves.

She placed the veladora on the dresser.

Much sooner than she thought, Gonzalo came in and sat on the edge of the bed, took off his boots and pants, and unbuttoned his shirt. He slipped under the covers and she knew she would have to change them tomorrow because the ashen smell would stick to them. He leaned over and kissed her cheek, smelling like mesquite, beer, and cigarettes. Gonzalo paused over her lips, said that he loved her, and she knew that if his kiss had been long enough, that if she had woken up and parted her lips at all, he would have turned her to him, hoping to make love in the darkness.

When she gave him none of their signals, he whispered, "Buenas noches, Amor. Feliz día de las madres," in her ear, his lips brushing across her earlobe. Gonzalo rolled over and soon he was breathing beer-heavy, mouth slack, not exactly snoring.

Victoria opened her eyes wide and looked up at the shifting circle of light from the candle, which resembled the Communion host Abuelita stood in line for every Sunday. Though the house was silent, and both of her Gonzalos were asleep, she thought she could still hear the mariachis and the scraping of her family's feet as they danced across the driveway.

As she began to fall asleep, her recollection of the night took form in the circle of the candle's glow on the ceiling. In the host, she saw herself joining the family in the dance. But she pictured herself dancing differently this time, dancing like she did at church when the Spirit was strong among the congregation. Then, as the dream took hold, other brothers and sisters came near—some from church, some from her family—pressing in as they danced. Little Gonzalo, Cirilo, the other cousins, and some of the tíos and tías were up there in that circle of light too. Little Gonzalo, Seferino, and Michely waved purple and gold banners that swam through the air like fish. Papa Tavo and Abuelita glided past her in a slow cumbia trot. She could sense, but not completely see, Gonzalo there, outside of the host, his presence flickering and swaying for a moment, then fading into the shadows. This final image startled her fully awake, making her heart flinch like it had when she thought Little Gonzalo had stopped breathing in the middle of the night. She patted the bed beside her, and felt Gonzalo's body. He was still asleep, facing away from her.

Victoria pressed her body into his and reached her hand up to settle on his shoulder. She felt him relax, the muscles yielding under her fingertips. When Gonzalo did not awaken with her touch, she brought her right hand of blessing up to his head and it alighted there as she uttered her rezos over him not in English or the tongues of angels, but in Spanish. This was the language Gonzalo had learned first and what might make his spirit understand at last. In those dark first weeks of motherhood, when the evil spirit of depression or her shadow self—whichever it was— had threatened to subsume her for the rest of her days and she could not see past it, he had kept vigil during the watches of the night, warding off the maldad with Little Gonzalo in his arms. And for this, and moments like it, she loved him still. Though neither of them deserved heaven, and Victoria could not know if they would always be together, she wanted to see him there in the expanse of light where there is no sun or moon and the light comes only from the glory of God, dancing for eternity with her and the family.

Victoria's eyes went up to the ceiling, and although the circle like the hostia was still there, it was empty now, the dancers obscured by her wakefulness. The air conditioner kicked on, whispered over the candle, and the flame trembled, but did not go out.

Our Story Frays

Emiliano Contreras writhed like a snake before he died. Over pan dulce and coffee, over iced tea at China Palace, over a bonfire and beer, we the grandchildren of Octavio and Valentina Izquierdo, our beloved Papa Tavo and Abuelita, have heard many versions of how his death transpired, and this is the only immutable truth. It is the only thing that comforts us.

A week before Contreras died, God or the devil revealed his imminent death to him in a dream. After his revelation, he confessed to Father Guerra, one of the priests from St. Joseph the Worker Catholic Church. He told the father about the indiscretions and brujería trabajos he had worked on people, especially our family. His only surviving daughter, Lina, came over that Saturday afternoon and told Abuelita that he had completed most of the prescribed penance. She said that all her father needed was Abuelita's forgiveness. Lina begged Abuelita to come and forgive him, gave our grandmother directions to her own house, and left.

Accounts being what they are, like statements after an accident, people must choose sides. Either we believe what Abuelita and tía Victoria told us, or we believe what we know. Why did Contreras feel the need for forgiveness all of a sudden? What had changed in him? And why did Abuelita honor Contreras's request after all he had done to us? This man was responsible for Papa Tavo's illness and ultimately his death.

Some of us agree with Abuelita, that, being the good woman that she is, she wanted only to forgive him. In this version, she called Victoria for a ride because our aunt had the flexibility in her schedule, and because she knew how to pray. If this was completely true, why didn't she call her own sons or daughters? She could have called Braulio, who calls himself a prayer warrior now, or Maggie, who is a prophet, or Dina, who is practically a nun. We ask ourselves why our grandmother, being such a devout Catholic, chose sin vergüenza tía Victoria, who never finishes the Apostle's Creed because it becomes too Catholic after the Trinity part. The truth we do not admit, but are certain of, is that she called Victoria not for her gift of tongues or because she liked her, but because she needed her help to end Contreras. Tía Victoria was supposed to be there. She ushered Contreras into the next world. In other words, Abuelita needed a chingona, and say what we want about Victoria, she was definitely the biggest chingona of all our tías. No one can deny this.

Victoria pulled up to Abuelita's house in her new forest-green Mustang. Although we do not admit thinking of her this way, we picture Victoria as she stood under the garage waiting for Abuelita to lock the burglar bars, her thick black hair over her shoulders, looking good even in her baggy blue nursing scrubs.

They said their saludos and Victoria helped Abuelita into the front seat, which was so low to the ground our grandmother felt as if she were sinking. We see Abuelita in the black-lace widow's velo she now wears in church. We see them as they drive out of the Zavala barrio in that beautiful car with the illegal tints.

Some of us are satisfied that the children of Contreras died early and violent deaths, as if we had been gifted with vengeance before the black magic trabajos even took their toll on us. The oldest son Emilio must have looked instead of ducked, because a 7.62x39 round went through his helmet and took off the top of his head, dappling the jungle leaves of Vietnam with bits of brains and bad Contreras blood. The younger one, Gregorio, was found floating in an irrigation canal in Dennett a few years ago. The cause of death was "undetermined" to the authorities, but not unknown to us. The oldest daughter Iraís got sick from the diabetes she didn't take care of and eventually died because of the botella and her refusal to change. Other than Lina, his youngest, the old brujo's children did not live for the same reason Papa Tavo lost who he was and seldom remembered any of us after the breakdown, only knowing that he wanted a cigarro we could never give him. The results of Brujo Contreras's evil did not end or begin with Papa Tavo's sickness, just like they did not end with either man's death. Our tío Wally is only twenty-six and already he's tried Paxil, Prozac, and Tofranil, and nothing seems to pull him out of the depression that started when he blamed himself for not maintaining the brakes on that school bus where all those kids went over the edge of a water-filled caliche pit and drowned. Oso Negro vodka hasn't worked either. Tía Dina had been cooped up in her house, where she played records, prayed the Rosary all day, and worried Eusebio and the girls. Her daughters, our dear cousins, are headed down the same path, with their talk of visions and saints and following the traditions of the mystics.

All of this sadness in both bloodlines, Contreras and Izquierdo, happened because that demonio Contreras cursed his family by cursing ours, all because of his envidia. He threw bottles of urine into our yard, which we hear is an old curse that is supposed to ruin your enemy's crops and dirty their seed forever. He burned black candles to Satanás, praying that the little fortune from our grandfather's business would abandon us. He severed the cloven hoof of a goat and a rooster's foot and buried them, among other things, under Papa Tavo and Abuelita's bedroom window. Because of this entierro, el Diablo walked around in Papa Tavo's dreams, never giving him peace. The worst maldiciones we know about are the pictures. We know that he found a panoramic portrait of us where we're sitting with our parents and our abuelos on the lawn of St. Joseph the Worker Church and wrapped it in barbed wire, in hopes of imprisoning our souls. The worst part was Contreras pushed a .22 bullet through the chest of our oldest male cousin Cirilo, hoping that he would someday get shot like his own son, which he almost did in a drive-by. The last buried curse we know about was the entierro that Gonzalo and a curandero unearthed and burned last winter. It was a photo of Gonzalo and Abuelo leaning against the new red Ford they had just bought. They lost this truck after Abuelo had the first nervous breakdown, when Gonzalo was a teenager and he supported the family, becoming a man before he should have.

We barely recognize Papa Tavo from copies of this picture. He beams at us, his Stetson tilted to the side like the chingón that he was, his strong dark hands resting on the shiny hood. Those of us that knew him too late only remember his mouth the way it looked from the hospital bed, our tíos and tías wiping the spittle away from his lips. We remember our fear when our mothers asked us to go to Papa Tavo to give him our saludos, knowing he would not recognize us or even respond. As we stand in that room of our minds, we see him fading before us, his skin going gray. All that keeps us from dwelling on this is Gonzalo's hard, immortal stare in the picture.

In his white T-shirt and khakis, his hair piled high with Tres Flores, he seems to say, *Chinga tu madre, güey. Pinche Contreras, I will outlive you. And my wife, a woman, will destroy you. How do you like that, cabrón?*

When Abuelita and tía Victoria got to Lina's house, we imagine both of them prayed for different things.

Here is where our story frays and we the Izquierdos must choose a thread to unravel it, decide for ourselves what we want to believe about what happened that night.

We hear Abuelita in her lispy storytelling Spanish. All the way up to the door she asked God for strength to let it all sink into the sea of forgetfulness, to wash away any drop of unforgiveness in her heart. We wonder if she meant it.

We see Lina's house as they walk inside. It was impressive with the bounce and smell of freshly laid carpet and new white paint. Both of them thought that this was not the house of a brujo's daughter. Where were the black candles, cobwebs, rooster feet, bottles of piss, malas hierbas? No, the house was well lit and clean, maybe a little tacky because of too many brass knickknacks, maybe smelling like this morning's barbacoa. Gilded picture frames of hopeful girls smiling for their own confirmations, quinceañeras, and weddings decorated the walls.

Lina explained that she had been looking for our grandmother, Señora Izquierdo, all day, calling around for her, calling

Braulio at the Izquierdo and Sons number and driving around the block by her old house.

Abuelita explained that our tía Marisol had asked her to come along with her across the border to the boticas in Reynosa to buy medicinas, and that they had stopped at a taquería before they crossed back. She apologized, although she did not need to, although she should not have.

Lina told them that her father was waiting for them in the back bedroom. We picture Contreras in the darkness as he searched the thick shadows for the death angel.

Lina called to her father and said that Señora Izquierdo and her daughter had arrived. *Her daughter?* they both thought, and realized that Lina did not even know who her father had been cursing.

Lina turned on the lamp and Abuelita saw Contreras up close for the first time in years. His spotted head shone from the light. Greasy smears and the lamp glare on his glasses obscured his eyes. Abuelita probably thought, *This is the man that tore down my husband?* He sat up. All he wore were chinos and a worn undershirt. His gut hung over his pants and they could see his saggy old man's breasts through the gray cotton.

Contreras stood and told them, "Pásenle, pásenle. I am so happy you came."

Contreras did not waste time and told them he was sorry for being jealous of them all these years. It wasn't Octavio's fault that the Contreras family had to find work wherever they could while the Izquierdo family got to live in the same place all year-round. He apologized about selling them to the devil, and wept in the pathetic way of the men we had tried to ignore in those nursing homes where Papa Tavo had stayed. If we had been there hearing him say our Papa Tavo's name, we would have dropped him where he stood.

"I would take it back if I could," he blubbered. "All I can do is end this envidia, and pay the blood payment with my own life." He went on to explain that it was revealed to him that the curses on the Izquierdos would die with the sons of Octavio Izquierdo, but there would still have to be a reckoning for the evil that had been cast out into the world.

We agree.

Contreras then said, "I am loved too. I am loved by God just like you."

We do not agree.

He asked Abuelita if she could forgive him. We see her face. Abuelita had creases and dark circles under her eyes from so much lost sleep and unhappiness, but Abuelita's eyes were as strong as they had been on those full-moon nights when she had had to call Gonzalo to help her with Papa Tavo or the night when Gonzalo came over to burn Papa Tavo's chair in the field out past La Balboa.

"I forgive you for everything you have done." Abuelita said this despite looking into Contreras's face and remembering Papa Tavo's, how he had looked catatonic in the front seat while watching them burn the chair, without relief or understanding.

"Thank you, thank you," he said through his stuffed nose. "God bless you, God bless you," he said, as if he needed to tell her she was blessed. He asked her if she would please pray the Rosary with him. We know he requested the Rosary because he did not know the Apostle's Creed or the Order of the Mysteries or the Glory Be to the Father. No one had seen him go to Mass since he sold his soul. Contreras was trying to use her as if she were a Seventeenth Street prostitute.

After raising so many boys, Abuelita knows the needs of men, but not their motives. Or she just did not care. She set a candle she had brought in her purse on the nightstand and lit it. Lina and Victoria stood mute, not certain what to do, but pleased by the candle's warmth. Out of respect, because Abuelita asked with her eyes, Victoria agreed to kneel like the Catholic she may have once been, but only prayed unintelligible words. We are not sure what Lina did. Contreras knelt with them on the floor.

Abuelita prayed the Our Fathers and Hail Marys in her whisper that calms us. Our grandmother was dignified even as she knelt on the Italian tiles. She managed not to shift knees or wince. Contreras wept as she prayed. "Perdóneme, forgive me, Señora Izquierdo."

When they were finished, he did not presume to hug our grandmother, but instead reached for her hand. We do not like to think of those hands that have handled unholy entrails and other dead things touching our grandmother. His eyes red and greasy, he said, "Gracias," and shook her hand, enveloping hers in his. This makes us shudder to think of it.

Abuelita said, "I could do nothing else."

Contreras said that he felt better and was ready for God to take him. The man actually said this with a smile, as if he truly believed that this was a possibility for him.

He hugged his daughter, who was kneeling with him now. Lina said, "It's over, Papi, it's over." She too had lost everyone, was the only sibling left now that Iraís, Emilio, and Gregorio were gone, and she hoped that her father's visions were not true even though she knew she was lying to herself and she would lose him as well. Then the brujo looked at Victoria. She was so lovely and young, with girlish features: a small pushed-up nose, black eyes close together, and that indígena hair like a shadow that must have taken him back to his youth in Mexico. Victoria turned her body to face him, and we see him as he opened his arms to embrace her.

Contreras held Victoria too tightly and it scared her at first, his sour old-man stink and evil at lover's length. We believe that what happened next was a part of Victoria and Abuelita's plans all along. To hasten his demise, Victoria did the unthinkable and leaned into his embrace, reached behind him and stroked his head, her fingers lingering over his ear. We see his sick, bloated face as he enjoyed this. Lina could not believe what she was seeing. Abuelita did not look surprised because she knew what was about to happen and had even planned it. She didn't try to stop what was happening because she knew it was the only way.

Victoria put her mouth close to his ear and whispered something that neither of them could understand, the message she was there to deliver. At first he smiled all quivery, and she laughed a little, but then his spirit knew what she had spoken over him. His body went limp, and the women rushed forward to help.

Victoria said, "Give him room to breathe," and she checked his pulse and his breathing. Lina probably agreed, because Victoria was a nurse with her scrubs and name tag. Victoria held Contreras in her arms, his yellow eyes open to her black, the glasses crooked on his face. Under his clothes, Tía felt his flesh quiver, and she accepted what she had done. Victoria did not let go, and tried to hide from Lina what was roiling in her eyes.

Contreras lay there in silence and surrender until a low hum in his chest grew into a groan. He coughed, and they heard phlegm rattle as he convulsed with the effort. Then he vomited a little, his white tongue stretching out of his heavy face.

As Victoria searched for something to wipe his mouth, his midsection jerked upward like a striking snake and she heard something inside him crack. Abuelita gasped and crossed herself. His body slapped the tiles, and his skin rippled. Victoria held him tight, calmly ignoring the worming of his flesh under her touch.

Contreras looked at them bug-eyed from another realm, and cried, "¡Por favor! ¡Ayúdenme!" They looked on and did nothing but watch his body squirm and shiver.

Lina rushed to him again, but all she did was tug at his pants leg, wailing, "¡Apá! ¡Apá!" Her eyes veiled by her black velo, Abuelita crossed herself, rubbed her rosary beads, and prayed for it not to be too painful. If she had chosen to, we know she could have prayed for it to stop, and it would have.

"¡Perdónenme! ¡Perdónenme!" he cried out as some new pang grew within. "¡Déjenme!"

We imagine Victoria stroked his hair and caressed his cheek, holding him like her own. She said, "Sshh, sshh, sshh. It will pass and then it will be okay."

When she did this, Contreras tried to say something else. He hissed through his teeth, spitting into Victoria's face. She only wiped it off and rubbed it into her pants leg with her fingertips.

There was horror and confusion on his face because he could not speak. He needed to complete his word, perhaps one final curse. Contreras closed his eyes, gulped, and settled. They listened as his breathing subsided and leaked into silence. Victoria leaned down. Her hair brushed and covered his wet face. She turned her ear to his open mouth as if she expected Contreras to utter some final confession or curse.

Abuelita and tía Victoria first told us this story over beers in Abuelita's yard while Gonzalo softly sang corridos and strummed an out-of-tune guitar and the firepit warmed our toes on one of the few cold nights we have had.

Abuelita explained that Contreras had completed Father Guerra's penance and that the writhing before his death was a struggle for his soul. Abuelita had forgiven him on earth and God had forgiven him in heaven, and thus God won and San Pedro let him into the kingdom, she assured us.

Tía Victoria said that although she could not understand the prayer language she spoke to Contreras, and Little Gonzalo was not there to interpret, she thought the Spirit within her rebuked the demons and told Contreras to ask God, and not Abuelita, for forgiveness. According to her, his response, like a hiss, was him trying to say the beginning of the word *saved* or the ending of *Jesús*, words that meant he had asked for forgiveness from the only true source. Our grandmother and tía Victoria agreed they felt a spirit of peace descend in the room after he took his last breath.

To their faces, we agreed with their story of Contreras's redemption, and continue to do so anytime they tell it. We heard their words and we said, *Pues sí, pues sí*, but we did not believe them then and do not believe them now. They maintain the lie, not to deceive us, but so that the burden of what they had to do will not be placed on our backs as well. On their first telling, as they assured us of his salvation, Abuelita and tía Victoria looked at each other and a secret passed between their black eyes glinting in the firelight. But we knew what they were protecting us from, what they did not want to change our lives forever. We saw what they could not hide. We watched the shadows of the women they had to be dancing inside their burning vision and turning and lengthening in the thorny mesquite trees behind them. These dark others seduced Contreras into writing like the serpent he was. They trampled him under their bare, blackened heels and threw him into the fires of Gehenna, wailing and weeping for all we had lost.

Padre Nuestro

EN EL NOMBRE DEL PADRE

On the night of Papa Tavo's passing, Gonzalo was watching the midnight replay of that week's Lucha Libre, Mexican wrestling, the only kind he would watch. Like on so many Saturday nights before this one, Victoria had gone to bed early, because even though the wrestlers were entertaining with their acrobatics, colorful costumes, and wrestling máscaras, it was still wrestling. *At least they don't show women with their nalgas hanging out like they do in the gringo wrestling,* she often said, even though she herself wasn't afraid of showing skin now and then. Victoria was many things: a fearless fighter, a good mother to our cousin, a chocante fisgona who sometimes noticed everyone's flaws except her own, a devoted wife to our tío even after all our family had been through, a protestante in every sense of the word, and backup to our Abuelita Valentina, both spiritual and physical. But on this night, she was about to become so much more, or show us who she had always been.

Little Gonzalo was lying on the floor with his Lucha Libre wrestling dolls scattered around him, under his legs and next to his cheek. Some of the dolls were tangled up in the rubber-band ropes of his toy wrestling ring, the one Gonzalo and Victoria had bought for him on one of their trips across the border to Reynosa, back when it was safe to do that. We remember having these same toys, lying this same way, feeling like we were floating as our fathers picked us up and took us to our beds. We also remember telling our fathers we were just resting our eyes so that they would think we too were chingones who could stay up as late as them.

On this Saturday night, tío Gonzalo sat there, watching the luchadores fly through the air, thinking how much better a job that would be than installing new shingles on roofs with his feet all sticky from the tar that burned through his boot soles like summer asphalt on bare feet. Some of us have never figured out why he chose this work instead of partnering in the family business with our tío Macario and tío Braulio. The rest of us know that you have to live your own life and not do what your father did, that you have to be your own man no matter how hard it is. As he took a sip from his warm beer, the one he had been drinking with an unexplained and uncharacteristic lack of enthusiasm, he knew Papa Tavo needed him. Gonzalo could not explain why or how. All he knew was that he needed to go see Papa Tavo and it did not matter how late it was.

The thing was, Papa Tavo was dying from cirrhosis of the liver. Papa Tavo was not, nor was he ever, an alcohólico. Gonzalo made sure everyone knew this. The cirrhosis was from the depression and anxiety medication he had been taking for decades. We remember those pills as if it had been us taking them. In our memories, we see Abuelita going to the top of the refrigerator and pulling down the Gamesa cookie box full of Papa Tavo's medications. Each time she pulled down that box, we pretended she was giving us Canelitas or those cookies with the bright pink and yellow sugar tops. It should never have been that way. Those boxes should only have been filled with cookies.

It would be easy to say that the cirrhosis that killed Papa Tavo was from the evil unleashed by Emiliano Contreras and his jealousy of our success. It is too much for many of us to accept that our trials are our fault, or that they are just a normal part of life. So they cling to this idea that our tristezas are *only* Contreras's fault and that he died a violent and ugly death because of the curses he heaped on us. Some of us know that this is only part of the truth, though it is only mentioned in whispers after birongas have loosened our tongues and the chisme starts flowing. The truth is that the sangre pesada between Contreras and us Izquierdos started because of Gonzalo and what he did to Emiliano Contreras's daughter Iraís.

Those of us who have accepted that an Izquierdo is to blame also understand how Gonzalo made the offense that caused Emiliano Contreras to hate us. We know how we are with women, how this has gotten us into so much trouble, and this is why we understand the mistake he made. Somos perros. Our mothers and wives and girlfriends can attest to this truth. Our women have also told us about our confidence, what they were thinking the first time they saw us walk into a room. They tell us stories of how they looked into our eyes and thought, *That one, he is the one I will love.* At the party or baile or church where they first saw us, they saw how other women squeezed our arms and

shoulders in conversation, how those women shortened the dis-
tance between themselves and us.

Our women also know our pasts, the things we have done
that we are ashamed of, the things we spend our lives running
from. Even though we do not deserve it, they have forgiven us
our pasts and trusted in us despite the things we are capable of.
And in the same way, we forgive Gonzalo, even though we don't
all want to.

If Iraís had not been the daughter of Emiliano Contreras, the
neighborhood brujo, Gonzalo's night with her would have been
just a regrettable mistake, something Gonzalo never would have
told anyone else. But being who Emiliano was, Gonzalo was setting us up for something he could not have known the future of.

On the night it happened all those years ago, when Gonzalo
was a teenager, he saw Iraís sitting in one of the orange booths
at the Spot Burger, the one on Old 83, with her friends. Gonzalo
was there alone because his brother, and only friend, tío Braulio,
was out with his girlfriend, our tía Ofelia. If only tío Braulio had
been free that night, he and Gonzalo would have done their usual
thing. They would have gone to the Valley Drive In or Cine El
Rey to catch a movie, or bought their quarts and drove around
town, looking for girls or a fight and avoiding the chotas.

As it was, Gonzalo looked at Iraís and saw how the skirt she
was wearing hugged her short legs. Tío Gonzalo had it bad for
petite women. And like us he hated being alone. Iraís had thick
long hair that fell all the way down her back.

Gonzalo knew Iraís's father was an hechizero, a healer gone
bad who got back at people by cursing them with buried objects,
powders, oils, and candles. But still, our uncle walked over to
the table of girls, watched how they got quieter the closer he got.

Gonzalo enjoyed it, how they looked at him, like he was the best-looking Mexican they had ever seen. We wish he had just kept walking, happy knowing he was the chingón that he was, but we know how it is being an Izquierdo man. He could not resist those girls or the way Iraís gave him the eyes.

Gonzalo took Iraís driving in his red Ford truck. It was relatively new and she said how nice it was. Gonzalo had bought the troca with the money he made from Papa Tavo's business, the one he would later abandon. This troca only exists in our memory as a symbol of the way things were before Papa Tavo had his first nervous breakdown and before he started taking the medications that would eventually kill him. When Papa Tavo got sicker, Gonzalo sold this truck to help the family out. He has a new red Ford F-350 with running boards and a chrome grille. In every way it is better than the first one, but we know he always thinks about the one he lost. Así somos, always searching and searching for what we have lost.

"Look in the glove compartment," Gonzalo said.

It was a bottle of Presidente. Iraís, like her father and some of us Izquierdos, was a borracha since she was born. Something changed in her eyes when he offered her the brandy, and Gonzalo knew she was his. It was too easy, even for Gonzalo. Our tío should have seen this as a warning to forget about what he was thinking, to forget her altogether.

They drove and she drank the liquor straight from the bottle, some of it dribbling down the side of her mouth.

They pulled up to the stoplight on Old 83 and Twenty-Third and tío Gonzalo looked at a carload of gringo boys in the lane next to them. He made his eyes big, threw his chin up, and said, *¿Qué pinche onda, bolillos?* He then pointed his chin over to the parking lot of Brownie's Feed and Seed, challenging all of them to a fight.

They acted like they did not see him and drove off, even though there were four of them and only one of him. They knew our tío could have taken all of them. None of us can forget the stories about the gang days when he ran with Los Diggers, stories about our uncle being outnumbered in bars and at dances, how he evened the odds with tire irons and brass knuckles.

Gonzalo's hand moved up and down Iraís's leg, and she did not mind at all. Her skin yielded to his touch like she had been waiting for him her whole life.

Iraís asked him to go to the Bronco Lounge so they could drink a few over there.

Gonzalo told her no. He told her he had another idea. Pobrecita.

He kept driving down Old 83 past McAllen, and they pulled up to the Red Carpet Inn in Pharr.

Iraís giggled and swayed on the bed as Gonzalo undressed her in the yellow lamplight of the motel room.

"Turn off the light," she said.

"No, I want to see you," Gonzalo said. We ourselves have said the very same thing to women. We do not know why it is in us, this need to see.

As he lay next to her, she whispered, "Gonzalo, ever since I was a little girl and I used to watch you play outside with your brothers, I have always loved you." When he heard this, his first thought was to get off of the bed, but it was too late. Though his instincts were finally telling him the right thing to do, he chose not to stop himself.

If he *had* stopped, so many things would not have happened.

Iraís would not have come over to Abuelita and Papa Tavo's house drunk a few nights later. She would not have scratched on Gonzalo's window like a vampire, saying, "Gonzalo, why have you forgotten me? Let me come in to be with you."

Gonzalo would not have said, "Vete, ya. You got no business coming here. I don't ever want to see you again." Things would have been better if he had said something else, even been a better man and let her down gently.

Iraís would not have begun to wail, crying, "Vas a verlo. You're going to regret what you have done to me."

She would not have gone back to her father and asked him to light a candle in the shape of Gonzalo so that he would burn for her. Contreras would never have started making binding curses against Gonzalo, then curses of ruin against Papa Tavo and all the Izquierdos, asking Satan to afflict us with susto and sadness like his own daughter when the candles failed to work.

If Gonzalo had just done the right thing, Iraís Contreras's blood would not have passed through him to our family, and our families would not have been intertwined in ways we do not like to think about. Papa Tavo would not have started having dreams where he saw our tíos and tías and us, his nietos, dying slow, painful deaths due to starvation. He would never have gone outside in the middle of the night to look for buried hechizos. And Gonzalo would not have had to follow his father outside only to see him sob like a scared little boy when he could not find the buried curses. Our tío would have stayed home that Saturday night watching Lucha Libre. He would have picked up Little Gonzalo in his arms when the wrestling was over and gone to bed himself, and slept peacefully knowing that he had a beautiful, faithful wife and a good son. Gonzalo would have visited a healthy Papa Tavo the next day at his house in the Zavala, and not at a nursing home.

It is easy for us to hear this story of Gonzalo's mistake and say all these things about how he could have avoided it, but there is no way our uncle could have known what would happen. Still, we agree that Iraís Contreras did not deserve what she got. All of this is on Gonzalo, and by extension on us, even if we don't want to admit it.

EN EL NOMBRE DEL HIJO

When tío Gonzalo walked into Papa Tavo's room at the San Juan Nursing Home, the orderlies and the night nurse circled his father. He saw their hands moving rapidly to save our grandfather's life. Gonzalo would later tell someone that they, with their white shirts and coats, looked like angels to him.

When tío Gonzalo first told the story of Papa Tavo's death, we wanted more than he gave us. With all of the curses and miracles, dreams and visions in our family, we wanted him to say that he saw, heard, or smelled something unexplainable, some glimpse into the eternal. We wanted to hear him say that for a brief second, just as the nursing home staff stepped away from Papa Tavo, he saw the spirit of our grandfather ascend. We wanted him to say that there was the unmistakable smell of roses in the room, that for an instant the windows of heaven had been opened and Gonzalo had gotten to at least *smell* the paradise that awaited Papa Tavo. We got none of that, however, only the statement that Papa Tavo had died, that he was too far gone to be brought back to us.

Tío Gonzalo did not see the faces of the nursing home staff

as he moved in closer to his father. Gonzalo could not even look at Papa Tavo's face. He only saw his pin-striped hospital shirt, his emaciated arms, the blue veins, the thin yellow skin and liver spots. The smell of a dying man was thick in Gonzalo's nostrils.

"We'll call the doctor so he can come pronounce him," someone said. Another rolled up a towel and placed it under Papa Tavo's chin so his mouth would not be agape and he could look peaceful.

Gonzalo said, "Good, that's good," but he did not know why he said it, because none of this was good. It sounded so funny to him: *pronounce*, as if *pronouncing* Papa Tavo could do some good somehow.

Gonzalo made two calls on the nursing home telephone, one to Abuelita and the other to Victoria. We do not know what was said, or if Abuelita cried or said, *No, no, no,* like many of us figure she did. We imagine that Victoria said she would pick up Abuelita without Gonzalo even having to ask.

Victoria and Little Gonzalo and Abuelita got there together. What they saw, many of us do not believe.

Supposedly, when they walked in, Gonzalo was manic, looking through the closet, drawers, and cabinets, and underneath the bed. He did not hear them come in, could not hear them as their voices grew louder, asking, "Gonzalo, what are you doing?"

Gonzalo kept on looking for Papa Tavo's things, trying to stuff everything into a black garbage bag he had taken off of the custodian's cart. His eyes were wild, and his upper lip was curled back, and it made them both shake inside for fear of what they thought was beginning in him. Pobrecitas.

It has been said that he moved about the room manically just like Papa Tavo used to on those full-moon nights when he was looking for black objects he believed were filling his house with an evil presence, like the night they burned his recliner.

Gonzalo said, "Where is his white guayabera? The white one, I know it was here in the closet. Ladrones, they probably took it. ¿Y sus zapatos? Victoria, help me, why are you just standing there? Amá, por favor, ayúdenme. ¿Mijo?"

Victoria did exactly what Abuelita had done on those nights when Papa Tavo lost it. She did what Gonzalo requested, hoping to calm him, even though she knew how insensible it was. Victoria looked under the mattress and under and inside the nightstand.

"Come on, chiquito, let's help your father find Papa Tavo's things," she said to Little Gonzalo as if it were a game so she would not scare him even more. Our little cousin got under the bed and he looked in the cabinets underneath the sink. Pobre Little Gonzalo, he probably wanted to hide like he used to when there was thunder and lightning outside or when tío Gonzalo and tía Victoria are fighting.

Gonzalo was moving faster and Abuelita started to get scared. She followed him around the room, trying to touch him on the shoulder so that she could calm him down. Abuelita was scared because she was seeing the sickness all over again, watching her strongest boy losing it. Tío Gonzalo had asked *her* for help, had looked into her eyes just like Papa Tavo had.

Not everyone believes Gonzalo was moving about the room in his frantic state. Many say he was just being practical, gathering Papa Tavo's things so the thieving night orderlies would not take them. This is what Gonzalo himself tells everyone. Those who believe him believe because they *have* to. He is our strongest uncle, el mero mero chingón, the one we watched working the punching bag in Abuelita's carport, the whole roof shaking with each hit. The bag was so beat-up it had to be held together with duct tape. In the mirror, all of us would practice tío Gonzalo's gacho-cold look that said, ¿Qué pinche onda, güey? I own you. We boxed our shadows, praying that someday we would be as strong and feared as our tío Gonzalo. If Gonzalo did succumb to the curses and mind sickness, none of us are safe.

We will never know for sure how he reacted. All that is important was that as soon as the doctor got there, he got ahold of himself and started acting like a stable man, like the man that he was.

Dr. Barratachea was nice, buena gente. He was the one who gave us Chupa Chups lollipops whenever we saw him at the nursing home, which was not often.

He came in, put a reassuring hand on everyone's shoulder, and said in Spanish, "I am deeply sorry for your loss, but I am sure he is in heaven. Octavio was a good man."

Abuelita would always remind us of Dr. Barratachea's kindness whenever she told this story, and Victoria would remind us that Papa Tavo had confessed Jesus as Lord and that was really why he was in heaven.

But at the moment, she focused on the word was. When Abuelita heard Dr. Barratachea say it, she started to cry, and so did Little Gonzalo and Victoria. Gonzalo did not cry, just like he did not cry at the funeral.

We had watched him the whole time he sat in the pew at Ceballos Funeral Home. Tío sat there, and his eyes looked tired, yes, but dry. Our other uncles had wet eyes, each of them crying, and some weeping openly, like tío Macario. We boys looked to tío Gonzalo, our oldest uncle, for one drop, something to tell us it was okay for us to cry too. We saw nothing and tried our best to have the same dry faces as tío Gonzalo even if we now know better.

EN EL NOMBRE DEL ESPÍRITU SANTO

The women and Little Gonzalo looked away as the doctor opened Papa Tavo's eyes to check the dilation of his pupils. Dr. Barratachea leaned in close to Papa Tavo's face, but still he could not see. Since Papa Tavo's eyes were so dark brown anyway, there was no way for him to know. He could have turned on the harsh fluorescent light above them, but out of respect he decided to go to the nurses' station to look for a penlight.

Dr. Barratachea said, "Ahorita vengo, espérenme tantito."

Gonzalo held the doctor's arm and said, "No, Doctor, it's fine, here you go." He handed Dr. Barratachea the small black flashlight he always has in his front pocket, the one he uses to look inside peoples' attics at work. This is the same flashlight he uses to check pots of menudo or marisco he makes outside at night. Now, whenever we see this flashlight, we think of what he and the doctor must have seen in its beam that night, the wide dilated blackness of Papa Tavo's eyes that the women and Little Gonzalo could not bear to see.

The doctor pronounced him at 1:46 a.m. Dr. Barratachea again offered his condolences, and said he had to check on a few patients, but that he would make the arrangements. If there were any questions or concerns, he was there for them, day or night. *Buena* gente.

All of them, Abuelita, Victoria, Gonzalo, and our cousin Little Gonzalo, stood around the bed, not sure what to say.

Abuelita closed her eyes tight, and began to pray in a whisper, sniffling back her tears. We do not know what she said, but imagine she was praying to San Pedro to let our Papa Tavo into the Kingdom of God. We know he did.

Gonzalo—who had not been to church since he was a young man living at home, who never showed up on time for the Rosary at Christmas or seemed to care when tío Braulio said grace over the meals we all ate together—said, "Padre nuestro que estás en el cielo, santificado sea tu nombre." He breathed in deep to finish the Our Father.

No one in the room noticed that at first Victoria did not say a word. She looked at each of them, at their closed eyes, each of them with a hand on Papa Tavo. At first she did not pray the words because she never said the Catholic prayers. Gonzalo tried to begin praying again, but he was unable to go on without his voice breaking, which was something he never allowed himself. When Victoria saw he would not be able to continue, and Abuelita was silent as well, she cleared her throat and said, "Santificado sea tu nombre." She led Gonzalo and her suegra and son, praying not a prayer of vain repetition, but one of earnest supplication, a prayer for herself and every family member who wished they could have been there. With Victoria leading them and by extension leading the entire family as she would continue to do thereafter, they were all saying it together: "Perdona nuestras ofensas, como también nosotros perdonamos a los que nos ofenden." Victoria, Gonzalo, Little Gonzalo, and Abuelita made that oración over our beloved Papa Tavo, and the words they spoke came out of that barrio in our Izquierdo hearts where letting go and relief and hope are all the same thing.

Epilogue

Family Unit

I was outside this house at a place called the Pinewood Inn in Cannon Beach, Oregon, on my spring break. Just me and this old dude at his front door, with him blinking fast as if he could not believe what I had just said to him, as if I were speaking Spanish. Even though I didn't want to get all racial about it, that's how I read his expression. It had been hard for me not to throw out the *r*-card since I got off the plane in Portland and it seemed like the only people brown like me were the ones mopping the floors and emptying the trash cans. I mean, I protested with everyone else and was as pissed off as everyone else. And even though I wanted to take a break from that because it was my vacation, after all, out here in Oregon, I found myself leaning toward being Chucky Chicano, Mr. Activist, Mr. Wave My Flag, Mr. Speak Spanish to the Workers Whenever He's Got the Chance. If asked now about the walk-outs, my undocumented brothers and sisters, I would have proudly said that my family didn't cross over the border, but had the border crossed over them. Still, it is tiring always having to be the voice, the educator of all things border-related every time I'm north of the checkpoint.

Anyway, this was not the point of me standing there in Oregon, of all places, even though I was starting to dwell on it. *Fight it, hey, fight it*, I kept telling myself. I stood in this wooden doorway painted white much too long ago because of my beautiful wife Evelyn, because this was where she wanted to spend our spring break.

But, with the way this most-likely owner of the Pinewood Inn stood at the door, blocking me from looking inside, and talking to me condescendingly with, get this, an English accent, of all things, it was hard not to think like that. This wasn't just your average gringo entitlement, this was your from-overseas gringo entitlement, the old kind where gringos not only expected the best for themselves, but also told you what was good for you.

"I *said* I would like Unit Five."

"Tell me your name again, please."

"Seferino Buentello."

The volume of my voice surprised me. My teacher voice only sounded normal when I stood in front of my classroom, pointing my dry-erase marker at my eighth-graders, trying to make a point about how we should always be mindful of our civil liberties and those of others, that this class was based on those principles. Or other times, when I had been reading too many articles during my prep period to see what the latest outrage chisme was and was feeling like Chucky Chicano, I would tell them that if someone had just paid attention in the sixties and made things better, we wouldn't be having any of these problems now. The kids usually just stared back at me and said nothing, and on days like this, I thought that teaching high school would be better for me because maybe they would get it. But out here, in the quiet of late morning, using my teacher voice was out of place, like when my colleague Mr. Arrambide wore his coaching shorts out to lunch on staff development days. I also came off sounding like I thought *he* was the one who didn't understand English. How would he like being an emergent bilingual? It was not the right tone, though, not if I wanted this to go well.

"You mean the one on the end? You know that's a *family unit*, right." Again with the condescending, with the pinche white colonialism. I wanted to say that my people crossed a river, yes, but his ancestors crossed a whole pinche ocean.

I was overreacting, but this guy was killing me. He was really shitting the stick. "Yes, the one out *there*," I said, and pointed across the green, green lawn and past the arbor, where Evelyn was sitting in the rental car waiting for me. I didn't even want to look at her face, as she would probably know that this *was not* going well, and because I had told her that the reservation was a sure thing, that it was in the bag, no hay problema, that it was a done deal. If Evelyn thought she had to get out of the car to give me backup, this trip would be all over. Evelyn would get results like she always did, but it would be good night for me, adiós muchacho. I just waved and gave her the thumbs-up like it was all good. Evelyn just kept looking at me, no smiles and no encouragement. Those ass-kicking brown eyes of hers had to fight themselves from rolling.

The man flipped through this black binder with crinkly pages that had gotten wet too many times. With the sun right on him at this time of the morning, the hoods of his eyelids were purple, actually purple, fluttering with the effort of looking at the bright pages of that binder. I could see the question with each of his movements: Why does this couple want to pay for a family unit when those are more expensive? I heard the rental car door open and shut behind me. He looked past me to the car to make sure it was still just the two of us, as if maybe there were more of us hiding underneath the car or in the trunk, like we were Mexicans trying to sneak into a drive-in movie. Evelyn stood by the front of the car, stretching her legs and cracking her knuckles. Her brow was pushed down and I couldn't tell if it was from the bright morning sun or because she thought she had to put me out of my misery. This was going to be bad if I didn't fix it. I looked at her and she gave me that smile with no teeth showing, the smile teachers give kids who've complained to their parents about them, the one that says, *I am acknowledging your existence, but that is all you get, cabrón.*

"Mister . . ." he said, and paused. Here was another thing. I'd had to pronounce my name *every* time since I'd been out here. It makes you tired.

"Seferino Buentello," I said and let it roll out Chicano brown and proud. I wasn't playing that today, wasn't about to pronounce my double-*ll*'s with a single-*l* sound so it would sound better to his ears. I didn't even tell him that my family all called me Sef.

"Yes, yes. My apologies, I can't seem to find anything, which doesn't necessarily mean that you didn't make the reservation. It just means that I can't find it. I guess these things sometimes happen."

I had to say, "Yes they most certainly do." He was right, and these things did happen. How many times had I lost my grade book or students' assignments underneath all the piles and piles of papers on my desk at Dennett Junior High? How many times had I filled in a grade for one of my social studies students who had supposedly turned something in, which I may have remembered seeing but had no record of? I would tell them, *Yes, I remember seeing your time-line of the Treaty of Guadalupe Hidalgo, but I can't find it now, so I will give you full credit, because as you young people like to say, It was "my bad."* I could always get a laugh out of the kids when I tried to speak like them. Even the students knew that these things did happen, and some huercos even took advantage of this, saying they had turned something in when in fact they hadn't. These wise ones knew that if they spoke with complete conviction about turn-ing in that assignment, and kept at it, I would believe them. Here, standing before this man, was a great example of applied learning.

It was clear he was getting frustrated as the pages started flying and he started to breathe harder through his nose. These sounds did not belong on such a fresh quiet morning where it was cold in the shade, where I did not warm up until I stepped back and felt the sun on the backs of my legs. We could have gone anywhere else for spring break, and I had even priced out the Bahamas and Las Vegas, but Evelyn had insisted on coming here. She had chosen Oregon because they had lived here when she was very little and they were migrants. She wanted Unit 5 because that was where her father had brought them one time to spend the weekend, and she wanted to relive this happy memory. *Why do I want to go somewhere hotter than Texas? Seferino, please.* I had not thanked her for choosing Oregon, for choos-ing this place that could be hot and cold on the same day at the same exact time, that had mountains (other than Mount Hood, she called them all hills) and old trees. Before Evelyn, I never in all of my imaginings would have thought that I would be in Oregon. All I knew of it was what my grandfather had shown us kids on Saturdays when he got his maps out. He would plot out a route to cities across the map, point to places, and narrate landmarks we would stop at, animals we would see on the side of the road, making up places where we would stop and eat. To my knowledge, Oregon is the farthest any Izquierdo has gone. And if we could just get past the micro-aggressions, it would be a lovely place.

I decided to take a different approach with this man, because this was going to get ugly if I did not get that room. "Well, since you can't find it, is it okay if we just stay there tonight? I mean is anyone else going to stay there? I am certain that I made the reservation, but the mistake could have been mine. I do remember speaking to you, but perhaps we didn't solidify things. Tom is your name, right? Perhaps it would be okay if we got that unit, Tom." Okay, maybe throwing *Tom* at the end of that sentence was a little too much, as if we were compadres, bien simpáticos since way back in the day.

"Yes, but I don't remember talking to you, and I have a memory for these things. This is most disconcerting. I don't know if anyone else is going to stay here. It's just that I might get some drop-in that's a family, and I would hate not to have a family unit available for them, as Unit Five is the last one I have. You sure you don't want to stay in one of the other units? They're very spacious for a double and they also have the kitchenette. Surely you see the predicament this puts me in."

Though some men I know would tell him the whole story of what this trip and what that room meant, start crying about all their problems and their reasons, this Tom did not deserve it. He was no compadre at all. Some men I knew, the ones without shame, were out there with things like this. I would like to say that it was a thing only gabachos did, but the one time I'd gone to an ACTS retreat, I'd seen Mexicans darker than me with deep Valley accents (even though their Spanish was broken like mine) cry and talk about all of their struggles, their hardships, their secret sins, the promises they would try their best to keep. They shared these things with men they did not even know like they were on daytime TV or in the confessional booth. These men would blubber and tell this complete stranger Tom that they wanted Unit Five because their wife had requested it, and that they really needed to make their wife happy on this trip, that everything needed to be perfect, that if it was not perfect their remaining days together could be in jeopardy. Then they would tell them why their marriage was in trouble, things they had done and said, the terrible thing that had happened to them. They would be hanging out there with it for everyone to see, even if it was none of their business. How do you tell someone all of this? You don't. At least, you shouldn't if you have any respect for yourself. Instead, you do what I did.

"How about we do this?" I said, and got out my credit card. "How about I pay for Unit Five now with my credit card and give you cash for the deposit?"

"But I can't find the reservation," he said. This Tom, he was all about the rules, all about what could be found in that black binder.

"I know, I know, but it will be all right. The deposit you can keep regardless." It was like I was talking to a kid in the Gifted and Talented Program. Those kids would tell me things like, *But Mr. Buentello, last time you made a rule that you were going to take off ten percent each day the assignment was late. You can't give her full credit now.*

I handed him my credit card wrapped in two hundred-dollar

bills I had ready for something like this, even though I had mostly done it for fun and had not expected to actually use them. My compadre Omar would laugh about this when I got home, about me paying a mordida on this side of the border, all the way in Oregon, even. "You take this and get the receipt ready and I'll get the bags down from our car." I handed the credit card wrapped in the bills like Tom was just another aduana officer I was paying to get through the lines quicker. Tom looked at the money and raised his eyebrows for too long, like the aduana knew not to. He then tried to act like nothing was out of the ordinary, but those purple eyelids could not lie. You could keep any gifted and talented student quiet with an extra-credit opportunity that suited them.

"Oh well, I suppose we'll be fine like you say. Don't anticipate many families today, being the middle of the week and all. I'll just go and get the key." He walked back into the house, where I glimpsed a living room darkened by thick brown curtains covering tall windows. I took two steps closer, and could smell the sweetness of pipe smoke. On the back wall was a full bookshelf as high as the ceiling, a small desk with papers scattered across the top next to it. I took two more steps closer so I could read the titles, but the room was so dark I could not make any of them out. The only title I could read was one sitting on the coffee table in the middle of the room, opened facedown, *Lies My Teacher Told Me*. It was a book I had read for an undergrad class at UTSA, one of the few books I had loved enough to keep.

Tom came back and smiled at how close to the front door I was now, as if I were a mate popping over for a pint. "Excuse the mess," he said, and did not block the doorway like he had earlier.

I smiled at this, kept the title of the book to myself, deciding I would only mention it later if I needed to.

Tom said, "Well, as you know, it's a family unit, so you have your choice of two double beds. You could even use the sofa bed if you were so inclined."

"I think we'll cross that bridge when we get to it," I said, and laughed, despite this being something a Mexican would never say or laugh at. You can make innuendos about women all day as long as it's not about your own wife or mother. That one is a deal-breaker. I threw in a wink too. *If I were so inclined.* I would have to remember that one.

⁓

IN MY WAKING HALF-SLEEP, I told myself that all I was certain of was that this beautiful woman next to me on the bed was asleep. I had no idea who she was or where we were. The walls were paneled with a dark wood, and the failing light filtered through baby-blue gingham curtains. The words *Unit Five* rolled through my mind, though I didn't know what they meant. Our clothes were on and both of us lay on a bed that was still made. The clothes told me nothing, where we had been or where we were going, but the fact that we were on top of the covers told me a few things. First, this was a nap. Second, we had not been sleeping since nighttime, unless we had been partying and had passed out together. Her leg was thrown over mine in a way that a lover's would be. I turned on my side, slid my leg out from beneath hers, and leaned forward. I breathed her in: a citrusy perfume I did not know the name of and the smell of the day in her skin, a sweet mixture of her body's oil, shampoo, and perfume, but no bar smoke or alcohol from the night before. A kiss would bring it all back to me, who I was, who she was, and, most importantly, who we were together.

I leaned in to her face, and just as I was about to kiss her sleeping lips, she said, "What do you think you're doing?"

"I can't remember who I am or you or any of this. I was hoping a kiss from your lips would jar my memory and bring it all back to me."

"Ay, por favor, Seferino, ya with the amnesia game."

"This is no game, woman. I don't know who I am. Why am I here?"

She sucked her teeth and turned away from me. Evelyn was not playing along with our game. Other times past, Evelyn would have told me that I was a spy who had my memory erased by surgery or drugs, or a fugitive from the future. One time she had even told me that my soul had gotten lost between worlds and that the only way I could get it back was to make love to her, to complete some connection. Evelyn's amnesia stories would always result in my sharing some recent memory, some quiet observation about her beauty, followed by an exchange of love. If she had played along now, I would have told her that I remembered leaning over her shoulder, looking out of an airplane window with her as the pilot told us it was a clear day and that we could see Mount Hood on our left. She had said, *I bet I could get one without the espresso and it would still taste great and not upset my stomach.* Evelyn was talking about a coffee drink made with Mexican hot chocolate she had grown fond of when she lived in Oregon as a teenager, a drink I'd once jokingly told her was a cultural appropriation. I wanted to tell her that I remembered her profile at the exact moment when she said this, how the sun made her eyes look lighter, almost yellow, and the tip of her chin was so delicate and small. I wanted to say that I kept alternating my attention between her face and this mountain and the decision about which I preferred to look at was an easy one.

Evelyn was not playing, and I did not ask if she was all right. Too many times recently, she had said that, no, she was not all right. I mean, what do you say to that?

"Baby, are you hungry. And if you're not hungry, could you at least eat something? And if you can't at least eat something, could you sit with me while I eat? And if you can't sit with me while I eat, do you mind if I go pick something up?"

"Ay, Seferino, you're such a baby sometimes." Even though she was turned away, her voice told me she was smiling. Funny how the sound of a voice can do that, describe someone's face in ways that words cannot.

EVELYN HAD A LIST FOR EVERYTHING. On this trip alone, she had made three lists that I knew of. She had a list entitled "Going Away," which detailed all of the things we would need for the trip, things we would need to do before we left. Of course, the things "we" had to do before we left usually meant things *I* had to do. Evelyn's lists were not just for responsibilities. She also had lists for fun. For this trip to Oregon, she had a list of places where she wanted to eat, divided between "Bite to Eat," "Sit-Down Fancy," "Nice," and "Sort of Nice" restaurants. She also had a list of things she wanted to see, like the Astoria Column, Multnomah Falls, Haystack Rock, this American Stonehenge she did not know the official name of, and the Devil's Punch-bowl. All of these things she had seen when she lived here, years back when her parents had moved to the Pacific Northwest for the crops and stayed to work in a nursery for a few years. Her father called Oregon the "Cielito Lindo" he now thought of when he heard the mariachi song of the same title. From the days we had spent driving from the Gorge through the mountain pass to Central Oregon, I saw what my father-in-law had seen all those years back.

"How about that restaurant that has that good soup in a bread bowl? That's close by, isn't it? Or is that by the river?"

"You mean *Hood* River? No, it's here in town. I suppose we could eat at Mo's. That actually sounds really good to me. And it's chowder, not soup."

"Hood River, the coast. Soup, chowder, what's the difference? It's all new to me, Miss Oregonian."

"Soup is soup and chowder is chowder. Chowder's like thick. And you can't even compare the coast to Hood River. They are *way* different and not even close to each other. And if you say Or-e-gone again to get on my nerves, I'll have to punch you in the arm. It's Or-uh-*gun*."

"Okay, mujer, whatever you say. Yes, chowder is a different thing altogether. And the coast and river are two entirely separate experiences. And I won't even say what you don't want me to say. The last time you punched me you left a bruise." I cradled my arm in fake woundedness.

Here, she moved forward quick as if she were about to hit me, but then touched my nose, smiled, and pulled her finger away before I could move forward to kiss it. Something moved in my chest.

This Mo's was more of a diner than a nice sit-down restaurant. It had to be on her "Sort of Nice" list. I kept thinking that this place would not even touch the seafood at Muelle 37 or even

La Pesca, but you don't say this when your wife is excited about something and smiling, which you have not seen in a while.

"Just wait, I know it's not much to look at, but once you taste the chowder, you'll know what I've been talking about. Don't even waste your time looking at the menu. Just get the Cannon-ball." I nodded without saying anything, as if I were considering her words. What I was really thinking was whether they served un principio like they did at all the other marisco restaurants in the Valley, a little cup of seafood broth to quiet your stomach and to get you ready for the feast ahead.

To reinforce her point, she said, "Seferino, you can *eat* the bowl." How could I argue when Evelyn knew me so well? I did anyway.

"I don't know. These fish and chips sound pretty good."

"Seferino, you can get fish and french fries in the Valley. You always get that."

"I know, but that's what I like."

"Ay, terco, just get the Cannon Ball. Get something you've never tried before." She *was* in a good mood. An Evelyn bossing me around was always a good thing.

"But what about this shrimp sandwich? That sounds good. Besides, you can get a cup of the chowder with it on the side. That way I get to taste two new different things."

"Listen, quit being chiflado. You're just messing with me now, and I went for it. Hook, line, and sinker." Evelyn rolled her eyes at her own joke.

I made a sound like a fishing reel and pretended I was reel-ing her in. "Yes, you got it, boss, I am going to get the Cannon Bowl or Cannon Ball, whatever they call it. What man can refuse a bowl you can eat?"

"Ay, Chiflis," she said, her affectionate name for me when she said I was acting like a spoiled little boy who wanted his way.

The whole time through dinner we did not speak, and the chowder *was* excellent, with a pat of butter floating on top and a sprinkle of chili powder. I looked out the window at the ocean and rocks, and at the families sitting around us. Like my Evelyn, the mothers and wives in the room held on to their coffee cups with both hands. Was every woman's hands always cold? My eyes went back to the ocean. It wasn't like I was some Mexican from the rancho whose dry crusty feet had never touched the ocean, but I still could not look away from it. It was not like our gulf at Padre Island at all. It was wild and dangerous.

Evelyn said, "It's way different, huh?"

"The soup?" I knew what she was talking about.

"You know what I mean, Chiflis. The ocean, the beach. It's way different from the Gulf."

꙳

EVELYN WAS RIGHT. It was nothing like standing on South Padre Island or Corpus Christi and looking out over the waters. I had never seen rocks that big and we had not even seen this Haystack Rock up close, but it was out there, and it looked like a mountain to me. Families with little kids, families with dogs, and couples walked along the beach with us. Some of them wore fleece sweaters or vests. I had on a T-shirt and anytime a cloud covered the sun, I got a chill and wished I had listened to Evelyn when she told me to bring a sweatshirt. Who brings a sweatshirt to the beach?

Another item on Evelyn's list of things to do was to put her feet in the ocean and see how long she could bear it. This was something Evelyn had done as a child with her brothers and sisters when they lived here. I guess it was a Chicano thing, because I did something similar with my cousin Gonzalo when we were younger. At parties, we used to put our hands into the ice chests to see who could handle the icy pain longer. But icy ocean water? Because I only knew the Gulf, which was much warmer than this, I had no idea what she meant about the ocean being so cold. As I stood there without my shoes on the wet sand, I wondered how cold the water would be if the sand was this cold, and I started to understand what she was talking about.

I said, "You go first."

"What, are you scared?"

"No, I just want to see you go. Just see how it goes."

"Whatever, big gallina. Just watch and learn." With this, she walked into the water past her ankles and shut her eyes.

The foam washed over her feet and went up to where her pants were rolled on her ankles.

After a minute or so, I said, "Is it cold yet? Can you handle it?"

"No, really, it's not that bad. Just come closer and check it out."

Evelyn's eyes were still closed, and I hesitated. I thought she was going to kick cold water on me.

"Come here, hold my hand and enjoy this with me."

The water washed over my feet and it felt like needles. I didn't know how she had been standing in it for several minutes and was okay. It was killing me. It was worse than standing with Little Gonzalo with our arms up to our elbows in that ice chest water challenging each other to see who could stand it the longest.

I reached out for her hand and she grasped it harder than she had in a while. "My sisters and I used to hold hands when we were trying to see how long we could stand it. We could always bear it longer when we held hands. I don't know if it kept our mind off the pain or what, but it was somehow easier."

I closed my eyes and said, "I know what you mean." It was true; I wasn't thinking about the water anymore. It was Evelyn's hand in mine, the contours of her palm, the tightness of her grip. Then, without wanting to, I thought of when we took the maternity class at the hospital. I remembered Evelyn walking around the room with a handful of ice. This exercise was meant to prepare her mind for the pain of childbirth. It was meant to train her to focus on other things during labor or embrace the pain by telling herself that this was a good pain, that her body was doing it for a reason. I remember feeling helpless during the exercise, not able to hold the ice for her, just walking around the room with her, telling Evelyn to breathe, rubbing her back, looking at the faces of the other partners, each of them as helpless as me.

I opened my eyes to focus on where I was now. Evelyn kept walking and the water was getting deeper. I tried to pull away from her, but she held me tighter.

"Come on," she said.

"That's okay. I think I've had enough of this."

"Fine, then," she said, and pulled away.

"What are you doing?" I didn't like the sound of my voice. It said, *Don't do anything crazy. Please come back.* I wasn't okay with sounding like that.

"Come on, now. Don't be a chicken-livered ninny." When Evelyn was in a good mood, she did this thing where she talked like a cowboy. She would say, *Oh, that's a bunch of hooey,* or *Go on, now,* git! She did this mostly on Friday nights when we were getting ready to go dancing at Hillbilly's in McAllen, which we hadn't done in a while, since way before we took this trip. She'd be putting on her pair of boots, squeezing into those jeans she only wore on a Friday night, and she'd say, *Now I'm all gussied up and rarin' to go.* However, there was something different in her voice now, as if this Evelyn here were making fun of the Evelyn who used to say those things.

Evelyn was past her ankles in the seawater, and she was going deeper. I was wishing she had her boots on, as I was afraid she would step on something sharp. That was all we needed. She had been in such a good mood and something like that could send her down to the place she had been for so long. It could stop her from hoping, from thinking that this vacation could make things better. She dipped in all the way up to her thigh as she got close to the rock. I felt a twinge in my throat. I wanted her to say something, to make a joke and let me know she didn't plan on going any deeper. Evelyn just kept walking into the water, but now she was moving away from the rock, deeper out to the water beyond.

I said, "Evelyn? *Evelyn?*" I knew I sounded afraid for her, but I could not stop myself from sounding like some over-dramatic woman in a telenovela. I tried to think of something funny to say, but came up with nothing.

I smiled at an older woman who had been playing with her grandson nearby, picking up rocks and putting them into a bucket. She gave me a smile, but it was tentative. She could tell something else was going on with us. The grandson beside her wore green rubber boots with frog's eyes on the tips, and a yellow raincoat. The boy's hair was a red I had never seen before, a red I could only describe as cinnamon. I stepped between him and Evelyn to keep him out of sight, but I knew it was too late. They had both seen each other.

Evelyn moved out farther and I made up my mind to go out after her if she did not turn toward the rock. She stopped in the water with her face turned away from me, and I wished I could see her expression. The water was up to her hips. She lowered her head. I felt a hand light on my arm.

"Is everything okay?" the grandmother said. She held the boy in her arms. The old lady had one gray tooth and green eyes that were younger than the rest of her.

"It's all fine," I said. "She's just remembering."

"You go get her out of that water. It's not good for her to be getting that deep without a wet suit. She could catch her death. She can go remember somewhere else."

When I turned back, Evelyn was climbing up the rock. I breathed.

I called to her across the water. I said, "Don't those things hurt your feet? I'm not sure that's such a good idea."

"What things?"

"You know, those sharp things stuck on the rock." The word was there, but I could not think of it just then. All I could think about was Evelyn walking out deeper and under.

"Barnacles, Seferino. Do you mean barnacles?"

"I guess so. Be careful, you're going to cut your feet if you're not careful."

Evelyn seemed to know where to step to avoid the sharp parts, but she knew her limits. She sat down on a lower part of the Haystack and didn't go any higher.

"I didn't bring the camera," I said. "I should get a picture of this. I guess I could use my phone."

"Don't worry, we'll come back tomorrow and take some real pictures."

"I guess I'll just have to take a mental picture."

We were walking back on the sand when I said, "Is it always cold like this? I mean, the sun is out, but it's still cold." I could not think of anything else to say.

"You think it's cold? I've been through colder. One time we came out when there was a winter storm, and you should have felt it then. The cold got up into our clothes and didn't leave until we were sitting by the huge fire our dad had made out of the bundles of wood he had to buy because he had forgotten to pack any in the truck. He blamed us girls because we were always rushing him when we came to the coast because we just couldn't wait."

❧

WE GOT READY FOR BED IN SILENCE, focused on the task at hand as if it were a work night. I knew better than to ask her if she was okay or talk about what had happened in the water. If she was on her way back to being okay, my question would definitely make her take a U-turn back to where I didn't want her to be.

The sheets were cool on my bare legs as I waited for Evelyn to come to bed. I thought of joking with her like I sometimes did about how she was like a little grandma, putting on creams and lotions just to come to bed. The door to the bathroom opened and I imagined the next few seconds. How she entered the bed would tell me everything. If she jumped onto the bed and landed on her knees, we would make desperate love, no kissing or eye contact, just she and I taking everything from each other. If she slid in next to me and put her hand on my chest, we would make slow, wordless love and she would look into my eyes the whole time. Or, as had happened every night the last few months, she would slide in and immediately lie on her side, facing away from me, and tell me to have a good night. The expectation would be for me to leave her alone, let her sleep, kiss her head, pat her shoulder, and fall asleep on my side of the bed.

Evelyn turned off the light in the restroom and stood by the bed. In the available light, I could see that she wore her long-sleeve nightgown, the one she saved for those nights back home when we had a cold front. She lay on the bed and got under the covers next to me. Just as I thought she was about to settle in and turn on her side, she stayed on her back. This was something new, an in-between gesture I did not know how to read. I turned to her and put my hand on her ribs, my hand heavy so I would not tickle her. I made sure to go no higher or lower than this. Evelyn's eyes were on the ceiling and she would not look at me. Her skin warmed to my touch, but she did not hum like she did when she was inviting more.

I said the only thing I could.

"I love you too," she said.

"You tired?" I said, which was our language for, *Do you want me to leave you alone and go to bed now?*

"Yeah, I'm *kind* of tired. It's been a long day for me." This could have meant the decision to make love was up to me, but I didn't want to guess wrong. Even though it had been long enough after the surgery and her body was ready, I wanted her heart to be ready, to want it as much as I did. I wanted us to be sure together.

"Okay, baby. You sleep now." I tried my best to say this without defeat or frustration or resentment, anything that would make her feel guilty, which often made it hard for her to sleep.

I began to pull my hand away and Evelyn gripped it, and

moved it down. Her belly was soft and yielded to my hand as if it were always meant to be there. This was what I had thought the first time I had touched her face, those years ago when we had a day-long date at South Padre Island, that my hand fit her face perfectly, my palm on her chin, my fingers curling up to her cheek. Now I thought of my hand reaching down through her skin to fill that space in her belly that had cradled the baby girl we had lost, but would forever be empty. I thought that if I could do that somehow, fill this space with my love and strength, she could feel better. And if that didn't work, I could always reach under her body and hold Evelyn and our angel baby hijita up for the rest of my days. And then, for some reason, as I started to fall asleep, I went back to when I was a boy at my grandmother's in McAllen, back to the Posada plays at Christmas when I played Joseph. I'd be standing there with my older cousin Dianira, holding the aluminum plate with the ceramic Baby Jesus who lay on a bed of colaciones, those little round and bumpy multicolored candies. Everyone always counted on me to hold up the Baby Jesus on that plate the entire time we said the prayer, and I held and held and though the plate always wavered and some of the colaciones rolled off to the floor, my strength never failed me and I always did my part. And then I thought of how big my family was, my sisters, my tíos and tías, and all my cousins, and how Evelyn and I would have no children of our own blood to add to the generations of Buentellos and Izquierdos. I secretly feared we were a disappointment to them even though my family had never showed us this. They had come around me and Evelyn, calling and texting us, bringing platones of food, each uncle and aunt calling us mijo and mija as they gave us their abrazos, holding us close as if we were their own children. They told us it was okay, but it didn't change our future, Evelyn and I old, no children around us like Abuelita and Papa Tavo. I had to stop myself from going down this other path of grief, lamenting what would never be. I focused on Evelyn beside me and listened to her breathing change, and I knew that she was asleep. I pulled my hand away. At least I had given her a peaceful night of rest.

WHEN I WALKED OUT THE DOOR in the morning, with Evelyn still sleeping, Tom was watering his plants and flowers, the fine mist rainbowing across the lawn.

"Good morning, Tom. Say, do you know where I can find one of those drive-through or walk-up espresso stands?"

He seemed confused by my question. "Just thinking about which one's the best. What are you looking for, Seferino?" He had gotten my name mostly right. At least he was trying.

"I don't know, just a place to pick up coffee. Get one of those Mexican mochas I've heard about."

"Somewhere to sit awhile or to just get it and go?"

"Get it and go," I said, and motioned my head toward our unit.

"You should go where I go, but I don't want to send you too far. It's on the other end of town and by the time you walked back, your coffee would be cold. Don't want you to go to the bakery either. They have great pastries, but their coffee's for shit. Too weak, like drinking tea. You could go to the new one that just opened, the one with the Italian theme, the dark colors and paintings, but you're going to be paying for that ambience, and the coffee's just okay. The baristas aren't hard to look at, though. You should go up to main street, take a right, and just after a women's clothing store turn the corner and there you should get a decent cup."

"Thank you, Tom. I appreciate that. Enjoy the rest of your morning."

"You too, buddy."

"Sounds good, friend. And Tom?"

"Yeah, buddy?"

"We are a family."

"I'm sorry?"

"Evelyn and I. Yesterday you said that Unit Five was for families. We are a family. She is my family and I am hers."

Tom said, "'A nation of two.' That's what Vonnegut called it. I get it, buddy. Enjoy the family unit and stay as long as you'd like."

I nodded at him to say thank you, and walked down the hill. This old güero was all right, and I felt bad about misjudging him.

The dog walkers and joggers were the only ones out on Hemlock. *Why would you do that on vacation?* I thought. Once Mr. Arrambide had asked me if I wanted to start jogging on the track before school started, and I had told him the only time I ran was when I was being chased. Otherwise, it just wasn't worth it.

When I got to the little coffee shop, I was not impressed. This was not a sit-down kind of place unless you wanted to sit on patio furniture and look down at old linoleum. A college-age girl was behind the counter, behind plastic-wrapped muffins and scones and glasses filled with pre-wrapped biscotti and sugar-encrusted pretzel sticks. She must have been at least six feet tall, a basketball player that would have towered over any of the players in my district. She was tall and morena and had dreadlocks, which I had never seen up close.

"How's it going this morning?" she asked. She had big white teeth, a space in between the middle two.

"Oh, it's going," I said, and immediately regretted my tone, as I had told her too much. It was like those Monday mornings with students when you told them too much with your tired, sagging body, with your eyes that would not look at them. If you stood up there like that, you let them know you were not having a good morning or week or life and you were just begging for them to ask you more. Some of them tried to get details because they didn't want to do any work that day, and others asked because they cared, because they were the type who would come to visit you after they had graduated.

"What can I get you?" she said. "What can I get you that would make sure it's going *well* and not just going? I'm up for the job," she said, and rolled up the sleeves of a long-sleeve shirt she wore underneath a puffy green vest. Here was something new, not just a question about why I was not feeling great, but a solution. I wished I had a grown son or daughter or even nephew with me who could talk with her, and take the pressure off of me to say anything.

"I would like two Mexican mochas, both mediums, and one of them without the espresso. I know that sounds crazy, a mocha without the espresso." I thought to explain how Evelyn had talked about these Mexican mochas from Oregon for years, had wanted us to have one together for so long, but could no longer stand the taste or smell of coffee, even now that she was no longer pregnant and never would be. I thought to tell this girl how Evelyn had looked out the plane window at Mount Hood and had mentioned the Mexican mochas, that getting her one was as important to me as getting Unit Five.

When I was sure she wasn't going to respond to my comment, I said, "A mocha without coffee. You must think that's a contradiction, huh?"

"Actually, it's not, I make them all the time," she replied over the steamer, and went about the business of smacking the grinder lever to fill the handle and tamping it down. This was loud and fun to watch, and I started to understand why else this had once been on Evelyn's list, this experience of watching someone in Oregon who wasn't wearing a green and black uniform make coffee for you.

"How hot do you want the Mexican mocha with no espresso?"

"Regular temperature, I guess. Why do you ask?" It was a strange question.

"Because if it's for a kid, I don't steam it for as long. Kids don't like it so hot. Is it for a child?"

My voice could not find itself, weak and lost somewhere between us. Finally, I managed to speak in a voice that sounded like it belonged to someone else, like I was standing nearby listening to the conversation, wanting to hear the words that came next.

"It's *because* of a child," I said. The girl stopped the dance of her hands, turned her head sideways, and looked straight into me, waiting for me to continue. In the breath before speaking, I saw myself going on, for me, for Evelyn, for our angelita—our little nation of three stretched across heaven and earth—and for the Buentellos and Izquierdos who had always enfolded us.

Acknowledgments

When the author sits down to write, they are never alone. They sit with their ancestors, family, and friends enfolding them. I acknowledge and give thanks to the first people who lived and continue to live in what we now call the Río Grande Valley of Texas, the Tejanos who lived here when it was still the country of their birth, and those who came after when it wasn't.

For sustained support, fellowship, and encouragement in the written word, my friends Margie Longoria, René Saldaña, Jr., Irma Nikicicz, Sergio Troncoso, Luís Alberto Urrea, Kali Fajardo-Anstine, Franciso X. Stork, Malín Alegría, Natalia Sylvester, ire'ne lara silva, Jen Hinst-White, and all the others. Your blurbs, calls, letters, texts, and introductions to opportunities and others in the writing community mean more than I can say.

For seeing something good enough in my work, and being in a place to do something about it: my past editor Gregory Wolfe; my current editor Nneoma Amadi-obi, who deftly and gently helped me shape this book into what it is today; my dedicated media rights manager, Katrina Escudero; and my wonderful, powerhouse literary agent, Tamar Rydzinski. Your love for the Izquierdos and belief in what I'm doing propels me forward. Tamar, we did it!

And to the Family Degollado and the Family Garza, my abuelos and abuelas, primos and primas, sobrinos and sobrinas, tíos and tías, you lifted me always, praying for me when I needed it, embracing me, and always reminding me where I come from, these two proud families living together in me. Mom and Dad, Nerio and Jovanna, you are always with me.

To my children, who gave me time to write on Saturday mornings, thank you! And to my biggest supporter and forever first reader, my bride Julie, thank you for your love, your patience, all you do for our nation of five, and for always dreaming with me. I'd be half a person without you.

Finally, Abba, in you I live and move and have my being. I can never repay you, but here is my offering, such as it is. Soli Deo Gloria. Solus Christus.